SUMMER OF '42

HERMAN RAUCHER

DIVERSIONBOOKS

Also by Herman Raucher
A Glimpse of Tiger
Maynard's House
There Should Have Been Castles

Diversion Books
A Division of Diversion Publishing Corp.
443 Park Avenue South, Suite 1008
New York, New York 10016
www.DiversionBooks.com

For more information, email info@diversionbooks.com
For more from Herman Raucher, visit www.hermanraucher.com

First Diversion Books edition May 2015.
Print ISBN: 978-1-62681-889-7
eBook ISBN: 978-1-62681-806-4

To those I love—past and present

1

He had always intended to come back, to see the island again. But the opportunity had never quite presented itself. This time, however, with a break in his schedule and with events moving remarkably in his favor, he had driven far up the New England coast to see if the magic still prevailed. Aboard the old ferry his Mercedes convertible earned the icy nonchalance of a half dozen craggy islanders, for very few new cars ever make that crossing. Cars that come to Packett Island are usually well into the varicose stage of their lives, and as such, they are by time and temperament unconcerned with a return trip to the mainland. "Cars come to this fuckin' island to die." Oscy had said that. Oscy, the big deal philosopher. And it was as true in 1970 as it had been in 1942.

He studied the faces around him, each turned to the wind, taking the breeze full face. It was apparent that none aboard remembered him. But then, he was barely fifteen the last time he forked over the twenty-five-cent fare. And in the intervening years much had changed, including the twenty-five cents, which was now a dollar, and himself, which was now forty-two. How, then, could anyone remember him? The nerve.

The Mercedes moved with disinterest along what purported to be the Packett Island Coastway, for the speed limit was thirty, hardly a challenge for an exhumed LaSalle, let alone a hot Mercedes-Benz. To his left were the familiar dunes, sulking in the grass, incongruously scattered with the uncatalogued refuse and bleached timber that the sea could toss so casually across the road whenever it felt so disposed. And to his right, the sea itself, choppy and gray-green. And large. Very large indeed. One of the largest in the world.

The luxurious car turned the bumps into cotton as he looked through the broad windshield at the odd glaze ahead. It was midmorning, but the sun hadn't been informed, and the fickle mist could be counted on to fritter about for a time or two before giving way to what, in those parts, was referred to as day. Visibility was confined to a struggling halo of brightness that extended no more than fifty yards in every direction. Yet the sea winds were already pushing in, and the mist was grudgingly giving ground, retreating inland in spiteful little gushes. He could see the fog move, herding its lumpy shadow before it, and the heavy-hanging gray curtain showed small signs of perhaps lifting to blue. A silhouette appeared, crouched on a high dune a short distance up the sea side of the road. A house, cedar-shingled and indomitable. A house far off, yet so well-remembered that he could recreate it in his mind nail by nail. Dorothy. I love you, Dorothy.

He stopped the car and stepped out, listening to the affluent sound of a Mercedes slamming its door. He looked down at his Gucci loafers, forty-five dollars. He had come a long way, none of it easy, but all of it worth it. He headed toward the beach-side dunes, leaving the road to walk along the high-rising crests. When his Guccis filled with sand, he removed them, plus the corresponding socks, which he then stuffed into their respective shoes. He had done that before around there, a long time ago. He sank his feet into the good sand, and his toes flexed like cat's paws. He took off his navy blazer and slung it over his shoulder, and in this manner did he walk ahead toward the house on the horizon—and back toward the last painful days of his once-glorious innocence.

The air proceeded to take upon itself a momentary snap of autumn, disregarding all that was August, and the ocean rolled around in oil-painted chunks like seascapes in Boston museums. He had come down to beach level, walking on the hard mud where the surf came up as far as the sandpipers that blithered ahead of it, announcing it. And only a gull or two dared venture the optimism that the sun, still probing for an opening, would soon shove its way through the grim overcast.

The house on the dune was now up and to his left, sitting atop the same twelve pilings, guarded by the same fourteen wooden steps he had once descended in such absurd confusion. And the low and sagging lattice fence still stood benignly impotent, a balsa barrier against the tolerant sea, a magnificent example of man-made self-delusion. And whether the music was actually there or whether it was simply tumbling from his memory drum—it didn't matter. Because he could hear it. Soft and sad and reminiscent and torchy and sentimental and sacred.

> I saw you last night
> And got that old feeling...

And then the voices, calling from almost thirty years away, rising on the wind and cutting through the fog. Boys' voices, imperative, anxious, buzzing the sand, then ending in the squawk of a seabird.

> Hey, Hermie...
> Come on, Hermie, for Chrissakes...

Up ahead on the beach three young boys dashed out of the fog and furtively clambered up the dune to the overhanging house. They advanced as though carrying out a complicated military maneuver, the first man giving a hand signal, the other two following in crisp sequence, plopping alongside their leader, prone bellies to the sand. And whatever they were looking at beyond the boweled rim of the dune, it was not visible to the man who watched from the beach.

The man stood still, looking again at the weatherbeaten house, only the roof of which could he see from his vantage point. And he didn't hear the sandpipers squeaking their preamble to the sneaky tide, nor did he really become aware that the sea was up over his ankles, splashing his trousers to the knees. He just stood there, wanting so badly to be a part of the three boys, as he once had been, how many sweet songs ago...

> Boy, oh, boy, Hermie...
> Knock it off, Oscy...
> Hermie, will you quit staring...

When he was fifteen and his family came to Packett Island for the summer, there weren't nearly as many people or houses. The geography of the island and the singularity of the sea were far more noticeable then. And if a guy wasn't to die of loneliness, his family made certain that other families from his neighborhood contributed other kids to the island. Present with him in the summer of 1942 were his best friend, Oscy, and a close friend but not yet qualified for the "best" designation, Benjie.

Oscy was tousle-haired and strong, not looking like a city kid at all, but more as if he had run away from Iowa country. He featured an indelible smile. Only on rare occasion did it not appear. In pain, sorrow, anguish, despair—the smile was Oscy's flag, and he was never known to strike his colors. He was a month older than Hermie, and he wielded those thirty-one days as a weapon of superiority and supremacy. Oscy carried with him an air of mischief, an unassailable warmth, and a private kind of boyish manliness that presaged a confident and rugged man. Oscy was something.

Benjie was something else. The youngest and scrawniest, owning the physique of a run-down John Carradine, he was more noticeably a child. He obeyed Oscy's directives because he was nobody's fool. And he wore an Ingersoll wristwatch that was more important to him than his penis, which, if you must know, he had yet to discover the true use of.

Hermie was fifteen with unruly sand-colored hair and a couple of teeth that leaned on each other smack in the front of his face. Bigger than Benjie, he was still no match for Oscy, which was why he so deftly convinced himself that it didn't matter who the leader was. At that moment in history Hermie was painfully astride the barbed-wire fence that separated boyhood from manhood. Which way he was to fall might have been screamingly obvious to a psychologist, but to Hermie the issue was very much in doubt. And he would lie awake nights worrying about the responsibilities of approaching age, like lumbago and arthritis, and how to drive a car, and how to put a razor to his cheek, and sinuses and migraines, and should his mother continue to buy his underwear, and when would the pimples come, and how in the world would he be able to screw and when and with whom, and would the police break in. Hermie was a worrier and a sufferer. There never was a greater worrying sufferer. It was beautiful.

They called themselves the Terrible Trio but for no real reason known to man, mostly to just bolster their own egos, to sort of establish themselves on the planet. And they lay there on the dune over which the old house stood, Beau, John, and Digby Geste, Devils of the Desert, steel in their hearts and sand in their Jockey shorts.

The house? The house was *her* house. And nothing, from the first moment Hermie saw her, and no *one* who had happened to him since had ever been as frightening and as confusing or could have done more to make him feel more sure, more insecure, more important, and less significant.

The three boys lay there, pained and paralyzed, listening to the hollow sound of an ax chopping hard at a resisting log. Below their view, in the big bowl of sand between the huge wooden pylons that supported the house, a man's figure was wielding the ax in an exaggerated, incredibly powerful arc, up over his back like Abe Lincoln, then screaming through the air like Zeus. The log below split cleanly in perfect halves, and another soon suffered a similar fate. And another, and another. The boys didn't move and barely breathed. They squinted over the lip of the sand and listened for the crack of God. Somehow it was all of vital interest. That man, that sound, that ax.

Again and again the powerful man sent the big logs to their doom, splitting them asunder, cracking them into oblivion like walnuts. The light changed enough for the man to become more visible. His figure was unbelievably well developed, his muscular definition rivaling that of a Bernini statue. He had the grace of Mercury and the strength of Superman, and the pipe in his mouth marked him as pure English nobility.

Hermie's heart caromed against his rib cage like an imprisoned sparrow when the woman slid out of the deep gray and curled her fair arms about the man. She was slender, yet shapely and with dark

hair that splayed gently about her shoulders. Every movement of
hers was sensual and fluid. Small wonder the man laid aside the
ax. He pulled her to him in a kiss so perfect that it could not be
improved upon. And the three boys watched, somehow sensing
that what they saw was of vital importance, something they would
someday be involved in, a hint of their future, a prelude of things to
come. They eavesdropped with respect and fear and awe. And seeing
the woman kissing and clinging as she was did not make things any
easier for life within the cramped quarters of Hermie's sand-filled
Jockey shorts. He squirmed in silent pain, and his companions did
likewise. They were paying the price of their random voyeurism, and
they were being overcharged.

The kiss ended, and not a moment too soon for the gasping
boys. The woman slid out of the embrace and then proceeded to
load the logs into the man's arms. It was as though he could carry
a mountain. One by one she piled on the logs. Building blocks
for Solomon's Temple. Stones for the Pyramids. Then the lovers
disappeared into the folds of the mist, and somewhere beyond, a
door opened and closed, and for the first time, the boys became
aware of the agitated state they were all three citizens of.

Because Oscy was the leader, he felt obliged to make some
sort of verbal observation, which he did with his usual smiling
countenance. "He's gonna take her right into the bedroom."

"He'd better put the wood down first." That was Benjie's
pragmatic codicil. He loved to say things that were indisputable, like
"Today is Thursday," "The President of our country is Roosevelt,"
"It is exactly two P.M." Anything that Benjie ever said that was the
slightest bit debatable usually earned for him an admonition and a
shove from *Oscy*. That's the way it was. That was the tradition.

Oscy allowed himself to slide down the dune a few feet toward
the beach. Then he stood and turned and walked the rest of the
steep incline, which was impossible. It was even more impossible
for Benjie, who was so gangly that he had no center of gravity. And
so he did what he always did when descending dunes—he fell and
rolled and came to a stop against Oscy's feet, which then kicked

even more sand on him. "Fuck you, Oscy." It was all right for Benjie to address Oscy in so disrespectful a manner once punishment had been inflicted. But to speak in such a manner *before* or without provocation—that would have earned him for his troubles instant death.

Oscy rested one foot on Benjie's chest as if he were claiming it for Spain, and he called up to Hermie, who as yet had not budged. "Hey, Hermie, will you move your ass? *Please?*"

It was difficult not to hear Oscy's voice, for it fell on the human ear like a naval salvo. Hermie slid down the dune as Oscy had done. And when he came to the bottom, he also kicked sand on Benjie since it seemed the thing to do and Hermie was basically a conformist. "Fuck you, Hermie." That came from below, from Benjie who had not yet gotten to his feet. He could say that to Hermie just about any time he pleased because Hermie was not a hitter, he was an ignorer.

Within moments the three boys were running along the beach in a movement that could only be described as "making a braid." They flew at one another with measureless velocity, appearing out of the mist and striking whoever happened to be in the middle at the time. The angles of contact became deadlier and deadlier until Hermie, who valued his life, broke off from the pack like Patty, leaving Maxine and La Verne to carry the melody by themselves. Hermie took one long last look at the house on the dune, studying it, wondering about it. Then he went home a secret way so as to throw off his friends, whom he suddenly no longer cared to be with.

2

Hermie had done all that could humanly be done with the small bedroom in the bungalow that had been allotted for him. One wall, the one with the window, he decorated with autographed photos of Mel Ott, Johnny Rucker, and Hank Danning because he was a Giant fan. All the autographs were forged because the Giants were in New York and Hermie lived in Brooklyn, and to wait till the Giants came to Brooklyn and then have the audacity to be seen asking Giants for autographs—it was much too risky. Another wall featured photographs of the Curtis P-40 Tomahawk, the Douglas Dauntless Dive Bomber, and the Bell Airacobra P-39, none of them autographed because who would he be fooling? A third wall featured Ann Savage, Marguerite Chapman, Karen Verne, and Hermie's own true love, Penny Singleton. He knew that in choosing Penny Singleton he was pretty much going it alone. But Hermie was like that. Let 'em all have their Ginger Rogers and Hedy Lamarrs and Ann Rutherfords; there was too much traffic there, and Hermie preferred a less-traveled road. And with Penny Singleton, when you wrote and asked for an autographed photo, it came back so fast that the ink was still wet and often got smudged up her nose. Hermie had five autographed photographs of Penny Singleton, who was the star of the *Blondie* pictures. Two were with Baby Dumpling and Dagwood, her movie husband. One was with just her and Dagwood. And two others were with just her, *one* in a bathing suit that showed a lot of thigh, and thigh was something you never saw a lot of in a *Blondie* movie so it came as a lovely surprise, the thighs. Hermie liked Penny's bright smile and her piles of blond curls and her winsome ways. He also liked her thighs, which were just two more reasons why he couldn't bear the thought of her bedding down with dumb Dagwood even though he knew it was only a movie. There was a sixth photograph of Penny Singleton in Hermie's possession, but he kept it in a drawer because it had been rather clumsily retouched by Hermie, who was no Norman Rockwell. With a razor blade he had deftly removed Dagwood Bumstead's dumb head and replaced it with his own, aged twelve. It looked stupid enough, but it wasn't helped by Dagwood's idiot bow tie. Dagwood always wore bow ties, which was why Hermie never would. Anyway, Hermie cherished his picture of him and Penny Singleton especially because, in it, one of his hands was about her waist not five inches below a breast and not six inches away from you-know-what. The other hand held her other hand. No hand in Hollywood was ever the object of more or greater sexual fantasies. Anyway—the photograph stayed in the drawer, under his socks and close to his heart.

The fourth wall was mostly a closet plus a door that Hermie kept locked because it not only led out into the rest of the bungalow's second floor, but also led in, and a man's home was supposed to be his castle. On the small piece of wall available for hanging, he had hung a picture of his cousin, aged twenty-two, who was on the island of Kiska, in the Aleutians, just off the coast of Alaska. There wasn't much action up in Kiska except when maybe the Eskimos got attacked by polar bears, but Hermie kept his cousin's picture there anyway because he was the nearest thing in the family to a hero, in spite of the fact that he had asthma and actually faked an attack right in the draft board office but to no avail except that they made him a corporal. If his cousin had been an epileptic, he could've made sergeant. Hermie autographed that picture, too. "To Hermie, bravely, his cousin in combat, Ronald."

His General Electric push-button radio, which his mother got along with a toaster and a lamp, all for twenty-four dollars, was playing Kate Smith singing "God Bless America." There was no escaping Kate Smith singing "God Bless America" those days, so Hermie punched the "off" button with his elbow and got WEAF for a while until he used his index finger and got silence. It was a time for thinking. He did deep thinking two and three times a day because his English teacher told him it was a way in which to develop outlooks on life. Fifteen minutes of deep thinking and Hermie had some headache. He thumbed through his *Aircraft Spotter's Handbook* and felt secure that if a Mitsubishi fighter flew over Maine, he'd be the first to know it.

In this way did Hermie pass much of each day. In musings and deep thinkings and forgery. But he did patriotic things, too. Like saving toothpaste tubes and scrap paper for the war effort. And often when he left the house it was with three squeezed Ipana tubes, which he dropped off at the Civilian Defense Center, and four issues of the New York *Times*, the latest of which his father probably hadn't read, so he left it because, once before, when he took an unread New York *Times* his father barely missed his head with a rolled-up *Journal-American* and the hell with that.

The sun was high and happy when Hermie came out through the screen door on the front porch. And he was pleased to discover that he would not be required to step over the sun-burning body of his sister, which was usually lying faceup on the lawn as if a dog had left it there or it had fallen off of a passing truck. His sister was black on one side and white on the other because they only had the house for eight weeks and, if it meant walking backwards during July and August, he had the sister who could do it. She was one of the greatest and darkest backward walkers of all time. She had a black face and a white ass. It was enough to send shivers up the spine of Boris Karloff.

The Terrible Trio had scheduled a meeting for 2 P.M. on the beach, for music appreciation and general messing around. Hermie was already fifteen minutes late, which meant he'd be the first to arrive. So he slowed down his pace and counted the service stars in the windows. There were nine blues and one gold. The gold was for somebody named Robert T. Kendall, who got killed in the Pacific somewhere, or so he heard his mother say to a neighbor. Hermie never asked too many questions about men in service because he felt like a goddamned slacker not being in it. Anyway, because no one was around, he saluted the gold star and the memory of Robert T. Kendall, and he walked on, yearning to avenge the deceased first chance he got. He stopped to lean on a fence for a while because Oscy and Benjie wouldn't show up for another hour and Oscy had the radio. He hummed some popular tunes until he figured they all three might arrive at the appointed destination on schedule and as planned, late as hell.

3

The three comrades lay flat out on the hot sand, each in last year's bathing suit because bathing suits had to last two years according to the "Mother's Handbook" of how to make your boy walk funny. They never brought towels or blankets to the beach because that was as sissy as carrying an umbrella through a tough neighborhood. As a result, they were covered with wet sand and looked like three freshly slaughtered breaded veal cutlets.

Oscy's portable radio, for which he regularly collected "battery money" from Hermie and Benjie, was playing music. Once, when Benjie gave voice to the suspicion that with the "battery money" Oscy was collecting as tribute, they could run WOR for a year, Oscy didn't bring the radio for two days. He arrived at that decision after first delicately accusing Benjie of being a Jap prick and then following it up with some rapid cuffing about Benjie's face and head. Benjie's only comment on that was an aside to Hermie that both of them together could very likely beat the shit out of Oscy, provided that Fat Willie Melnick sat on him. Hermie failed to see the wisdom of such a suggestion since he had enough brains to realize that, sooner or later, Fat Willie would have to get off, if for no other reason than to go to the crapper, at which time Oscy could be counted on to rise up, track them down, and beat the collective shit out of the pair of them. So it was no deal, and Benjie had to agree that, as usual, Hermie had saved their lives.

Anyway, the Benny Goodman Sextet was playing, and it was one helluvan improvement over Kate Smith and God blessing America. The trombonist took a solo, and Oscy, great musicologist, asked, "Who's on trombone?"

"Tommy Dorsey," said Benjie, mostly because he hadn't said anything in some time and missed the sound of his voice.

Oscy was miffed at Benjie's impertinence. "I asked Hermie. Go look at your watch." Then he turned to Hermie. "Is that Tommy Dorsey, Hermie?"

Hermie delivered the expertise. "Tommy Dorsey doesn't play in the Benny Goodman Sextet. It's Lou McGarity." Then he grew annoyed because they had interrupted one of his moments of deep thinking and he'd be getting a headache for nothing. "Why don't you guys just shut up and listen?"

"I *am* listening," said Benjie.

"Go look at your watch," said Hermie. That was two suggestions for Benjie that he look at his watch. So, ever one for democracy, he looked at his watch.

Peggy Lee's voice was heard, singing the vocal.

> Grab your coat and get your hat,
> Leave your worries on the doorstep...

And Benjie was pleased to observe, "That Helen O'Connell, she's something."

Oscy looked quickly to Hermie, "That Helen O'Connell, Hermie?"

Hermie sighed. He only wanted to listen without interruption. "It's Peggy Lee."

And Oscy gave Benjie a short backhand smash across the chest that set him tumbling. "As usual, Benjie, you're wrong."

Benjie spit sand from his mouth. "How come Hermie's always right?"

"He's not always right," said Oscy, with the wisdom of the ages. "It's just that you're always wrong."

Hermie was able to tune out his two weird friends almost any time he cared to. It was a secret he had learned in the Orient when he had accompanied Lamont Cranston, alias the Shadow, on a tour of the Nanking opium dens. But his gaze was turned up the beach, and soon Oscy and Benjie were gazing likewise.

It was the man and woman, the ones from the house on the dunes. They were wearing bathing suits and were strolling arm in arm in perfect synchronization. And a person would have to be blind to not see how very, very much in love they were. The man wore a soldier's overseas cap, and again his muscles were rippling shamelessly. The woman was so beautiful, so smiling, so green-eyed and long-legged that the boys all had to roll over onto their stomachs lest their extended antennas bring in police calls. The lovers drew closer and passed by not five feet from the Terrible Trio. Hermie never blinked, never once. His eyes were the eyes of a lizard, lidless and frozen open, focused on the smooth legs and flat belly of the beauty in motion. And when he got a whiff of the pipe the man was smoking, he knew that that was the way he wanted to smell.

"I'm gonna be built like that," said Benjie, referring to the man. Oscy only grunted. "I will," said Benjie. "I'm gonna work out. With weights. An hour every day."

"You'll never look like that," said Oscy.

And Benjie knew he was right. "Yeah. Must be an officer."

Hermie's comment came from somewhere out of left field, surprising even himself. "She's built pretty well, too." Oscy and Benjie, like two heads on one neck, swiveled to look at the madman in their midst. Hermie could feel their staring, and he knew that Tweedledum and Tweedledee were nudging each other at his expense. And he knew that soon, at any time, some inane remark would be directed at him, and he'd be damned if he'd wait around for it like Pearl Harbor, so he went on the offensive. "The two of you are morons!" And he got up and walked away without so much as a by-your-leave. And when he had gone far enough, he turned and shouted to Benjie, "It was Peggy Lee! Pay up!"

Benjie was confused. He looked at Oscy. "Pay up? I didn't bet him anything. Did I bet him anything?"

Oscy gave him a shove and a put-down. "You're inhuman. You know how sensitive Hermie is."

"Yeah? Well so am I. The hell." And he shouted back at Hermie, who was already almost too far away to hear. "It was

Helen O'Connell!"

Hermie kept walking. Only when he'd walked far enough upwind did he turn and shout back. "Peggy Lee!" If Benjie ever said anything after that, Hermie never heard it because Benjie, as usual, was downwind and an idiot.

4

If there was one food that Hermie hated it was veal cutlet. The very sound of it was offensive. But all the way back to the Depression he was never allowed to leave the table until he had finished everything his mother had set before him. And there were no exceptions. So he lingered there, poking his fork at the cutlet in hopes of proving that it was still alive and, in so doing, get out of eating it since cannibalism was not his family's strong suit. But if it *was* alive, the veal cutlet was doing a fine job of playing dead. And by the time Hermie finished stabbing it, it had all the appetite appeal of a handball glove.

His mother was inside with the dishes and *Major Bowes' Amateur Hour*. His sister, now that the sun was down, was in her room mooning. God knew what she was mooning about. It was occult, her fascination with celestial objects. By day she sunned and by night she mooned. She was eighteen years old and a complete foreigner to the rest of the family. From the moment she first sprouted breasts she was never normal. And the more her breasts grew, the more remote she became. And more than once Hermie wondered just what good his sister's breasts were doing anyone if she continued to keep them in her room like lamps.

As for his father, he could only make it up to the island every other weekend. Gasoline was hard to come by, and their car didn't have the right priority. Half the time their car didn't even work. The other half it seemed as if it could only go downhill. His father had mastered the art of coasting because it saved gas. Sometimes he could coast half a block to a red light and get there by the time it turned green. At those moments his father was a happy man. His father was a veteran of the First World War and even had a few medals because he did something at Château-Thierry. However, he didn't have enough of them to impress the Army when he tried to enlist for World War II because he was much too old. Forty-four. Still he managed to keep abreast of the news, thanks to Edwin C. Hill and Gabriel Heatter and Walter Winchell and his Aunt Pearl, who was, in reality, the Voice of America.

Anyway, Hermie was alone at the dinner table, unless you wanted to count the veal cutlet, which was a lousy conversationalist no matter how you sliced it. Hermie had offered his mother what he thought was a very fair deal. He would eat the asparagus, stalk and all, if he could leave over half of the cutlet. It was no deal. Trying to reason with his mother while Major Bowes was on the air was like talking into a catcher's mitt.

Hermie and the cutlet stared at each other for another five minutes, after which Hermie decided to make a break for it. Some lunatic on *Major Bowes* was playing a musical saw, and Hermie's fantastic mother was singing along. "There's an old spinning wheel in the parlor..."

With consummate stealth, Hermie got up from the table and walked toward the door. If the cutlet would not give him away, he could make it. The cutlet, dying of its wounds, sighed just a bit but didn't have the strength to rouse the singing mother from her duet with the saw. "...and it brings back sweet memories of you."

When he reached the screen door Hermie could see them. Oscy and Benjie. Oscy was spread-eagled on the grubby lawn, gazing at the sky. Benjie, in another position of endless boredom, was staring at his Ingersoll. He always stared at his Ingersoll. Maybe someday he'd discover radium. Touched by this view of his exciting friends, Hermie considered returning to the cutlet for a little gaiety. But inertia kept spurring him onward, and he opened and closed the screen door so quietly that not even a moose could hear. But a moose was not a mother, and the voice came out of the living room, filtered through the screen door, and landed on his brain like a cannon. "Herman, you're going out."

That had been a direct statement. Not a question, but a

statement of fact. Mother; noun; female: all-seeing, all-knowing. Jesus. Hermie stood on the top step waiting for the rest because that was the way his mother worked. First, the direct statement that could not be argued with. Example: "Herman, you're going out." Next would come the veiled threat. It came. "I certainly hope you finished your cutlet." There would be a third utterance fairly soon. It would be a question. Questions were deadly in that they called for a response. For a direct statement you could be in Poughkeepsie. But for a question you'd better be in the house. Hermie sat down on the top step and waited for the question. From there he could observe Oscy and Benjie acting out the Fall of Rome. He could also determine whether or not there was any life in the two corpses that the two families up the street had dropped on his lawn. There was but not much. Just a little uneven breathing.

Hermie was always neat. His hair was combed. It didn't get combed too often or too well because it had to be shot to get it down. But every once in a while some primordial instinct would jab at Hermie's conscience, like Peter Pain in the Ben-Gay ads, and it would whisper to him, "Comb your hair. You never know."

As for Oscy, he always wore the same idiot sweat shirt. He claimed that he had four of them, all the same flat gray color. But Hermie strongly suspected that there was no way in which any four sweat shirts could share the same identical grease spots, paint marks, tears, nicks, and blood. Oscy, therefore, was lying. Worse, on occasion Oscy could smell pretty gamy, especially on hot humid days and especially indoors, like in a small closet. As for Benjie, Hermie never took notice of what he wore. As long as Benjie had his watch, he was dressed and all was well with the world. "Seventeen minutes to eight," he said. No argument there.

After a long moment of silence better becoming a graveyard, Oscy had a very important question to ask of the sky. He did it haltingly, thoughtfully, for the answer was crucial. "How many sticks of dynamite...do you think it would take...to blow up...this whole fuckin' island?"

After long and considerable thought, Hermie offered the

correct answer. "Twenty-three." Another long silence prevailed as the boys pondered both the asking of such a question and the veracity of such an answer.

Then came the third sound from the mother within. The question. Zow. "Herman, did you finish your cutlet?" Oscy and Benjie cranked their heads around, fixing Hermie in the crossbeam. For depending on Hermie's answer, the world would plan its next turning. Hermie looked back at them, first at one and then at the other. He repeated that process, quickening the pace until it was apparent to all that he was nodding his head in the negative, which was the cue for the three of them to silently get up and quietly walk to town. They had played that scene many times before, on each of their lawns and in front of many houses in Brooklyn, and it was the law: If you didn't finish your dinner, move on. No man had ever worked out a better solution or a more conditioned response.

Even as he left the house behind, Hermie knew that the unanswered question would shortly bring his mother to the fourth and final stage: a personal appearance in which she would stride onto the porch, hands on hips, looking this way and that, and then calling into the vacant air, "Herman, do not come home until you finish your cutlet." That was the kind of logic Hermie had to deal with. It was the stuff of his life.

5

The old wooden water tower stood high against the sky, a tall, buglike structure straddling the earth like the Colossus of Rhodes, providing a refuge for all mothers' sons who could navigate the forty rungs without breaking their asses. Beyond it the sun was checking out in a conspiracy of reds and purples. Below it the small town stretched lethargically, turning on a few spasmodic lights as talismans against the night. And upon it three boys, their legs drawn to their chests, sat shoulder to shoulder on the narrow platform that embraced the bulging water barrel. In the good company of only each other, they were bored shitless.

They passed the one soggy cigarette down the line, puffing it dramatically like combat men enjoying a brief respite from bloody battle. And the silent and unresisting air provided Hermie the proper climate for his incisive observation: "This has been the longest summer of my life."

Neither of his companions cared to contest that point of view, and so the day spun out and the night began to cramp them with sudden soft gushes of cool air from the bay. The tide was shifting, and the wind was changing, and Hermie used such moments for more deep thinking. But all that kept occurring to him was why that one stupid sea gull had singled him out and kept following him. It had flown over him when he walked to town that morning, barely missing him with a bombload of crud it had slung at him like a diving Stuka. And later, as he was tilling his meager Victory garden, it had circled him threateningly before coming in low in a strafing run that caught his cabbage patch unawares. And finally, the goddamned bird had come in behind him at six o'clock high and let loose a quick burst of shit that splattered on the back of his neck not ten minutes after a new haircut. It had all been very strange because Hermie had always liked to believe that he got along well with birds and woodland creatures even though he was a city kid. And so why this one hysterical bird was causing him no end of grief was a true and growing puzzle. Unless, of course, the bird was doing it all as an act of love. Cats did that. Cats would bring their kills, dead mice and such, to their masters. Yet if that were the case, wouldn't the bird just drop a fish on him instead of clobbering him with shit? It was beyond Hermie's ken. And he knew that, until the gull could find somebody else to love, he'd be the recipient of all its high-flying turds, and he'd be walking around with a paralyzed neck from bird watching. Another thought occurred to him. Maybe, like in *Pinocchio*, the gull had been sent to be his Jiminy Cricket, to guide him through life until he became a real boy. But why the shit? Jiminy Cricket never crapped on Pinocchio, at least, not in the movie. That was probably it. The cricket crapped on Pinocchio in the book, but they cleaned it up for the movie. Hermie considered asking Oscy his opinion, but Oscy was very busy coughing and would not be available for counsel until a lung or two had collapsed. As for Benjie, he was studying his watch, seeing if it truly glowed in the dark. "Eight thirty-one," said Benjie as evidence that his watch glowed in the dark. Oscy whacked him, and he lost his place at eight thirty-one and three seconds. "Fuck you, Oscy." Some things never changed.

Hermie sat in front of the candy store, looking intensely at the latest issue of *Jungle Comics*. Benjie sat alongside him, gazing hypnotically at his watch, timing Hermie. But Hermie was unaware of Benjie having a clock on him because he was deep in the lush tropical brush, swinging with Sheena of the Jungle from tree to tree in twelve lascivious full-color panels to the page. And each panel revealed another angle of Sheena's throbbing topography. Lusty thighs and busty cleavage pulsated within her ragged leopard skin. Girded loins and screaming navel assaulted Hermie's eyes and mind, slamming against his retina and shaking his young brain pan. Even the carnivorous quadrupeds in the panels looked up from the zebras they were devouring to contemplate the leaping lady and to consider an immediate change in their eating habits. There was a lion down there, drooling like a faucet. And there was a tiger who looked as horny as a rhinoceros. Hermie was never too sure why these books were called comic books. There was nothing funny about them. Mickey Mouse might have been funny, but Sheena of the Jungle was nothing to be laughed at. Sheena of the Jungle could drive a man mad and only for a dime. Hermie narrowed his X-ray eyes in an effort to see through the leopard skin in panel nine, the one in which Sheena's legs were spread a mile as she swung across a dangerous precipice while screaming in a white balloon…"Yaaaaaa, Sheena!"

The voice belonged to Benjie, the official timekeeper and general all-around moron. "You've been on that page for seven minutes."

"I wish I was *in* it."

"Seven minutes and seven seconds. You're some slow reader."

"Who's reading?"

"Seven minutes and fourteen seconds. What're you doing—memorizing it?"

"Yeah."

"Turn the page."

"It's the last page."

"Then close the book."

"Close your mouth."

Oscy came out of the candy store just as Hermie was about to roll up the *Jungle Comics* and belt Benjie over the head with it. Oscy came out whistling and acting so nonchalant that he had obviously stolen something. Emotionally, Hermie was still in *Jungle Comics*, halfway up Sheena's left thigh, the one the dumb monkey was looking up at and evolving for, when Benjie gave him a short elbow to the ribs. That ended Hermie's reverie just at a point where his X-ray equipment had succeeded in turning Sheena's leopard skin to cellophane. It was a crushing blow, and Hermie immediately turned on Benjie and rolled up the book and swatted Benjie with all fifty-two pages.

Oscy swept by and was already a short distance down the street by the time Hermie finished flogging Benjie, who took it all on the right forearm, thereby protecting his wristwatch which was on his left wrist, which was in his pocket, which was like a foxhole. Benjie then jumped up, called Hermie something obscene, and took off after Oscy. Hermie stood and straightened up as best he could, which wasn't exactly the letter *i*. Remorsefully, but realistically, he returned the *Jungle Comics* to the newsstand, where it would eventually wither and die. For no one ever bought a comic book. Comic books were placed on newsstands to be read free, as a public service, only don't get caught doing it because Old Man Prowdy could hit a kid and not leave a mark. And so it was farewell until next month to Sheena of the Jungle and her sparkling navel, and onward to Oscy and Benjie and the insanity of life.

Oscy led them to a discreet place where no outsider could observe his criminal machinations. Then he withdrew from his pocket a shiny chrome object, which he displayed to his companions as though it were an idol's eye; only it was a harmonica. Benjie was immediately displeased. "What the hell you steal a harmonica for?"

Oscy shrugged and smiled. "It was an impulse." And he tucked the harmonica into his pocket and walked away.

Benjie followed him, a skinny gnat flailing at solid air. "You were supposed to steal a kite!"

"I can't play a kite."

"You can't play a harmonica either."

"I can learn."

"Jesus, Oscy—we can't fly a harmonica!"

Oscy only flicked at the gnat and then paid him no never mind. As for Hermie, he was dragging a few yards behind, wishing he had Sheena on his secret X-ray table where he could freely conduct his evil experiments upon her anatomy, accompanied only by his faithful manservant, Komo, whose job it was to keep his mother out.

Hermie walked along the main street, a good distance behind his two friends. Sheena was so fresh in his mind and groin that he just didn't care to listen to his bickering buddies. Up ahead he could see Oscy neatly riffling the shiny harmonica between his lips, catching his upper lip in a C# and causing Benjie to collapse with glee. Except, when Oscy finally freed his lip and started swatting Benjie with the harmonica, that's when Benjie became immediately and diplomatically sympathetic.

Hermie was dropping off the pace like a miler no longer in the race. He knew that it was as they said, let an athlete waste time on thoughts of sex, and vap, there goes his wind. As soon as a boxer got married, he was through. The day a football player got laid for the first time, he could hang up his cleats. It was a sports truism. You didn't have to hear it from Bill Stern on the radio, you just knew it. Every man jack knew it. The interesting thing was why so many athletes persisted in doing it when they had to know it was ruining their wind. Hermie suspected there was more to it than Bill Stern was letting on. Hermie's head snapped "eyes right," impaled on the polka dot torso in the store window. For a short moment his eyes were just two more polka dots, whirring about, searching for an opening. But when the smoke cleared and when the eyes had refocused, he could see the two-piece bathing suit on the armless, legless, headless female form. Only the good parts were there, painted a very neat and even tan, kind of cocoa and exciting. Hermie's eyes fluttered with painful realization. Was he forever to be an observer and not a participant? Was he truly doomed to be a sexual time bomb, ticking in limbo until one day when he could tick no more, at which time he'd simply explode, a glob of Herm and sperm on some reformatory wall? And who would make the identification of his remains if his mother was too embarrassed because her son was a saint and that couldn't be his penis squashed through the window bars, reaching for the sun? He made a conscious decision, then and there, no more avoiding the issue. He would do it, and it would happen. He would stand there, in front of that store window, and he would stare the torso right in the eyes. And by sheer will, the bathing suit would drop off and a naked lady would appear. And she would step through the glass like Cosmo Topper, wrapped in invisible ectoplasm, and there he'd be, Hermie in Wonderland, and Komo would stand guard and— Yaaaaaa, Sheena!

"Hermie? Hey, Hermie."

That was Oscy's voice, but Hermie figured that Komo could handle it. Ignore it, naked lady. Your mine, all mine. Yaaaaaa, Sheena.

"He's in suspended animation again."

That was Benjie. Komo, can't you see I'm busy? Get rid of him. Excuse me, naked lady, where were we?

"Hey! Rip Van Hermie! Hey, Hermie?"

Oscy again, loud and interruptive and unavoidable. And so it was farewell to the naked lady, who jumped back onto the torso as a polka-dot bathing suit. Shiiiiiit, Sheena. Komo, you're fired.

Hermie turned to see Oscy and Benjie, who had walked back to rescue him from his most recent trance. He knew it would be senseless to chastize them. They'd never understand. How could they? Not even *he* understood. Oscy cocked his head to one side and smiled at Hermie. "You coming, Hermie?"

"Yeah. Where you going?"

"Ethiopia."

"Okay." Why not? What was left for him?

They meandered down the street and finally ended up sitting on the ferry pier supported by the green moss-covered pilings that didn't look as though they could do their job another day. They were getting very good at sitting on the pier, and Hermie yearned for a tidal wave or a typhoon that would just wash them away. He hoped it would drown his friends while tossing *him* safely onto some island somewhere with two gorgeous girls and his manservant, Bokoto. But it was impossible for Hermie to transport himself anywhere with Oscy sitting nearby, coaxing some truly weird music out of his harmonica. The Gas Pain Symphony. Benjie was looking over the notices tacked upon the town bulletin board, checking them against his wristwatch, timing them. Jesus.

Hermie hid behind his usual expression of utter stupidity, watching, yet not really watching, the people boarding the 2:20 to the mainland. People, children, dogs, carriages, wagons, the last train out of Poland. And them, the man and the woman. Again his blood rushed dizzily at the very sight of her, at the very thought of her name, whatever it was.

The man was in an Army uniform and had a duffel bag hoisted on his shoulder. He wore all sorts of battle ribbons, fruit salad galore. The woman, aaaah, she wore faded jeans and a loose blouse, and her suntan and her hair, and her sweet green eyes all misty, and Hermie's heart was considering stopping altogether because what better way to go out than with an eyeful of ravishing beauty? She was clinging to the man, trying to become a part of him. He was leaving. She knew he had to go. She didn't know when she'd see him again. It was an old familiar story, but it seemed newly strange for Hermie to see it so expertly acted out somewhere else other than in the RKO Kenmore. The lovers stood in the very exact geographical middle of the crowd, like Kansas, and people moved by them, hustling to get aboard the sputtering ferry. Good-bye was in the air, and she was smiling in the face of it, fooling no one.

It was all so weird. The pair of them should have been lost in the crowd, but they weren't. It was as though they were standing atop some high pedestal for Hermie's benefit, so that he could see their anguish and learn from it. The pedestal was turning, ever so slowly, rotating even as the other ferry boarders slid by the good-bye lovers. Slowly, slowly the lovers turned, their eyes forever fixed on each other. The man removed his cap and placed his free arm about her and pulled her close in a long, long kiss, kiss, kiss. Impossibly long. How could they hold it that long and not go further? What control. What manner of man. What an athlete.

Eventually all the passengers were aboard. All but the lovers. And as the ferry began to push out, and as the hawsers flew and the gangplanks drew back and the dogs barked, Hermie knew that he should warn them, say something to them. Behind him, Oscy was tooting his lousy harmonica, but it couldn't alter the tragic beauty of the moment.

Finally the kiss ended, and the lovers separated. The man became aware that the ferry was pulling away. But without being the tiniest bit ruffled, he tossed his duffel bag toward the departing boat. It floated on the air like a hydrogen-filled balloon, taking a half hour to reach the ferry. And during that expanse of time the man turned to the woman, taking her dear face in his two huge hands and bestowing a final kiss upon her forehead, just as the duffel bag reached the ferry and plunked silently onto the stern deck. The lovers broke, their hands playing unseen pianos. Then the man took a few steps and launched himself over the twenty yards that separated the ferry from the pier. And over the water he fairly flew, vaulting the ferry's protective railing and landing on brilliant tiptoe, a modern-day Doug Fairbanks, smiling, waving, magnificent.

Hermie turned back to look at the woman, and she had changed. Standing alone on the pier, she was waving a fair arm to the sea, the wind softly pushing her lovely hair. She was Anna Karenina, Helen of Troy, the Lady of the Lake. And under it all, the lovely tones of a harmonica. Virtuoso. Larry Adler at a Bundles for Britain Rally. Borreh Minevitch doing likewise for Russia. Oscy, the ugly duckling, was playing like a swan.

Hermie turned again to glimpse the fast-fading ferry as it coursed the bay. It was so far away that the man no longer had an identity. He was just another passenger, another dot on the 2:20.

Hermie glanced back at the woman. The last wave still lay lightly on her fingertips, the last wan smile etched unconvincingly upon her sorrow-filled face. Standing there as she was, with the tears forming in her superb eyes, she was the saddest creature in the saddest of worlds. Her hair was strewn with multicolored flowers and she was Ophelia. Warm poison on her lips and she was Juliet. A frog in her throat and she was June Allyson. Greta Garbo, Lana Turner, Linda Darnell. Penny Singleton were Paradise enow. The harmonica theme was stretching hauntingly to the heavens whence it had surely come and her diaphanous gown slowly disappeared before the power of Hermie's X-ray eyes, clearly exposing her ivory breasts so deliciously capped with individual maraschino cherries. And then her dress became undone, and a breeze came up, and the slight garment slid away, gliding…

"Hey, Hermie? Hey, dream boy?"

Shit, it was Oscy.

"Yoo-hoo, oh, Hermie?"

Shit, it was Benjie. Shit, shit, shit.

Hermie turned to see Oscy and Benjie smiling idiotically at him. Side by side they stood, and the stupid smile seemed to begin at Oscy's right ear and extend all the way across both their faces to Benjie's left, leaving nothing between but teeth and most of that sheer orthodenture.

Hermie wheeled quickly again, to see the woman, once more, a last vision, a photo for his memory book, a place on the wall of his heart. But she was gone, and all he saw of her was one small white sneaker turning a sharp quick corner. She was just another lady in faded jeans, no more. And the harmonica was once again excruciatingly horrible because Oscy couldn't play, and that was definitely that.

Hermie bellied up angrily to his two so-called chums, the annoyance spilling out of him, causing Oscy to put aside his harmonica and step back in a moment of smiling muddlement. "You guys!" Hermie ranted. "You never shut up! Why don't you shut up every once in a while? Why don't you shut up occasionally and just think? Or read? Jesus, you never read! Nothing!"

"I read, Hermie," Oscy said, and then he pointed with his thumb at Benjie. "And Benjie, he looks at the pictures."

"The two of you make me sick! You really do! The both of you! You make me so sick I wanna puke!" Hermie was really building up to a full head of anger.

Benjie stepped back in feigned fear. "Please, sir, don't puke on me. I'm only a kid."

Hermie was about to beat Benjie's mouth into oatmeal, but Oscy stepped in, remarkably tolerant. "Hermie, your whole problem is you're a dreamer."

"So I dream! So what?"

Oscy put his arm around Hermie's shoulder and began to walk him up the street. "You see, Hermie—you're supposed to dream when you're *asleep*. If you dream when you're *awake*, people'll think you're buggy." He sought corroboration from Benjie, who was tagging along. "That right, Benjie?"

Benjie's eyes were closed, his arms outstretched like a sleepwalker. "Don't wake me, I'm dreaming."

Hermie's exasperation was beyond containment. He shoved Oscy's arm from his shoulder and stopped walking because it's tough to express anger when you're walking. To express anger you have to stand still, clench your fists, and raise some blood in your eye, all of which Hermie did just prior to giving voice to his displeasure through teeth that let no air in. "Okay, you guys. I'm through hanging around with you, okay? You're beneath me, okay? So far beneath me that I can't believe how far. You're stupid and dumb. You have no idea of current events. No idea at all, none so fuckin' whatever."

The *non sequitur* threw Benjie. "Current events?"

Hermie turned on him. "What's your IQ?"

Benjie turned to Oscy. "What the hell is current events?"

Oscy smiled to Hermie. "Tell him."

And Hermie told Benjie, "You have an IQ of four!"

And Oscy said, "Right."

Hermie broke off and his two friends knew not to follow. If Hermie was going into another period of dark strangeness, they'd just as soon he went it alone. It wasn't even worth yelling at him as he left, even though they knew how much it rankled Hermie to be yelled after in the street. No, they figured, let him go in peace. It would be better for everyone all the way around.

All the way home Hermie kept trying to apply some organization to his chaotic mind. But all he could come up with was Ernie Lombardi's batting average divided by Lucille Ball's bust measurement. That was the equation of his life. And all it added up to was total confusion multiplied by frantic helplessness and then conjugated by three times loneliness. The circling sea gull was not included in the calculations, though it did cause Hermie to accelerate the walk to his house because a bird on the wing was more threatening than two in the bush. Whatever was to show up on the dinner table would have to be an improvement over what was there the night before. One great thing about his mother, she'd never hit a guy with a veal cutlet two times running.

6

The sun was a blooming corker, hot and high, as befitted July. And the waves broke gently over the supine forms of the Terrible Trio as they lay half in and half out of the water like so many beached tuna fish. Benjie had his left arm periscoped into the air to protect his precious Ingersoll from the spraying surf. Oscy, to prove he wasn't dead, pulled his bathing trunks a few inches from his stomach so that the ocean could waltz through and tickle his unit. "I wish," said Oscy, once more imploring the heavens, "I wish that someone would invade this dopey island. I'm going mad. Mad, do you hear? Mad!" To demonstrate the statement, he laughed madly and received a mouthful of salt water for his troubles, plus a tiny sand crab that slid into his trunks and caused a small havoc before going out with the receding surf.

Benjie glanced up at his arm and offered a great profundity: "Eleven minutes to three." No one picked up on his brilliant observation, but it was no loss to the world.

Oscy recovered. "My dumb brother, he's a dentist in the Army. I can't believe it. He was such a tough kid. A dentist. Jesus, he makes me ashamed."

Benjie spoke. "My brother is a cook in the Navy. Says he's getting a Purple Heart for roast beef." Benjie laughed.

Hermie spoke. "My sister's in high school." He wondered why he said that. It could only get him into trouble. It did.

Benjie, the barracuda, moved in. "How come you got no brother, Hermie?"

"My sister's got a brother. It works out." If that was the end of it, Hermie figured he was getting out cheap. It wasn't the end of it.

"I think your sister's got a *sister.*" Coming from Benjie, that was so clever that Hermie was off-balance for a moment.

By the time he understood the depth of the insult Oscy had joined the conversation. "I'm going into the Marines when I go. I like their uniforms."

Benjie had a preference, too. "I'm gonna be a Ranger."

Oscy decided to bait Benjie. It was so easy to bait Benjie that sometimes it just wasn't worth it. But things were dull, so—"It's still the Army, same uniform. You've been conned into thinking the Rangers are their own organization. They're not. Wrong, Benjie. Wrong and stupid. But very typical."

Benjie bristled. "Screw. You wear a thing on your arm that distinctly says 'Ranger.'"

Oscy countered. "From far away it still looks like you're in the Army."

"Screw. When a guy comes up close, he sees that you're a Ranger."

"Double screw. By the time someone comes up to read your arm you could be dead."

"Triple screw to you, Oscy. Long before that guy ever—"

"There must be some girls on this God-forsaken island." It was Hermie again, reporting in from left field, where a ball hadn't been hit in months.

Oscy rolled over in the surf, much preferring to carry on a dialogue with Hermie because Benjie was such a simpleton. "What branch *you* going in, Hermie?"

"My father says the war'll be over before I'm old enough. So I'm not going."

Oscy didn't like the sound of that answer. It was too quick, too good an advertisement that Hermie wasn't of a mind to be drawn into a debate, and he was going to get a rise out of Hermie or die. "What does your father know? He's a salesman."

"He reads *Time* magazine. And cut it out, Oscy, because I know what you're doing and you can't."

On that note of absurdity Oscy rolled over in the water, and the baton was thus silently passed to Benjie, who nobly took the anchor leg. "You know what your trouble is, Hermie?"

"Yeah. You."

"Your trouble is you got a sister in high school."

He didn't intend it to happen, but the lunacy of Benjie's remark got Hermie so peeved that he was sucked in. "And what the hell is *that* supposed to mean?"

"It means if you had a brother in danger, your father wouldn't be so smart."

"I got a *cousin* in danger. My cousin Ronald. He's a major in the Aleutian Islands. In *Kiska*, for your information."

"A cousin's not a brother."

"To his brother he's a brother."

"How do I know he has a brother?"

"He has a brother."

"Yeah. I only have your word on that, Hermie."

Hermie rolled over. There was no dealing with nincompoops and he hated himself for having tried. And so he withdrew from all further discussion. "I don't know why I talk to you idiots. You're idiots."

Oscy was back in the competition, speaking soft but carrying a big stick. "Hermie, you gotta stop insulting us. There's a war on, you know."

"Jesus," Hermie mumbled. For it was precisely that kind of remark that made him prefer the company of cutlets and sea gulls to that of his nearest and dearest friends.

Oscy was standing. Standing and smiling. Hermie looked up as the shadow crossed his face. When Oscy stood and smiled, something was afoot. "Now, Hermie…because I don't want to belt you out, for your punishment I'm gonna take your stupid shirt." Which he did. "I will return it to you when you've learned patriotism."

Oscy walked away, holding Hermie's shirt by one sleeve and dragging the rest of it through the crud that lined the beach where the water washed in all things smelly. Benjie got up and followed Oscy, faithful Igor, the bumpkin. Hermie didn't move, he just watched. It was a time to rationalize his not going to rescue his shirt from Oscy Hitler. First, Hermie figured, he didn't much care for that shirt, which was why he always wore it to the beach and nowhere else. Second, if he never got the shirt back, it would be a relatively easy thing to leak the news to his mother, the Crimson Avenger, who would then take it up with Oscy's mother, the Cat Woman, and after that, not only would the shirt be returned, but Oscy would be in solitary for a week on saltines and water. But all that was mere speculation. The real question was: Was a green-and-yellow checked, short-sleeved, un-Sanforized shirt worth going to war over merely because Hermie's pride of ownership had been impugned? The answer was quick and simple. For a McGregor shirt, you fight. But for Fruit of the Loom, which was the case, the hell with it. Fuck you, Oscy. Choke on it.

Less than fifteen yards up the beach, Oscy reversed gears and returned, not choking. Benjie, the pilot fish, returned with his master. Oscy stood over Hermie and let the shirt drop like a parachute onto Hermie, who didn't budge and didn't even appear to show any interest. "And let that be a lesson to you."

Though Hermie's head was almost completely covered by the Fruit of the Loom abomination, his vision was not quite obliterated. One eye could still see from the shirt's armpit, and it was looking down the beach very keenly. And the eye told the brain what it was looking at. And the brain told the heart, and the heart spread the news to the penis, which began burrowing into the wet sand like a Lilliputian steam shovel.

She was there. A lithe figure striding toward the ocean. The woman. She walked to a place on the beach and claimed it for all time by spreading her beach towel upon it. It fluttered in the breeze, a banner of love, a semaphore of passion.

Oscy's voice. "What's he looking at?"

Benjie's voice. "It's that lady again."

Lady Again then lay upon her back to take the sun. Her bathing suit glistened, for it was made of ten thousand true diamonds, each one cut to perfection by a different Belgian gemcutter, who then died happily. Her legs were long and smooth and pretty, the both of them, the one with the knee up, as well as the one with the knee flat. The legs were glorious and identical; you could take your pick. Her lips were moist and parted, and all the white teeth a woman could ask for sparkled beyond like thirty-two handpicked Chiclets. Her hair was loose and inviting, and even though there was nary a breeze, it seemed to waft within the gentle caresses of a zephyr from the east. Long lashes curtained the emerald eyes that lay within the gossamer lids, recharging their green batteries. And all this lovely landscape Hermie could see with one eye, from ground level, thirty yards away. Ted Williams never had better vision.

Oscy's voice. "Jesus, Hermie, you gonna go into another deathlike trance?"

Benjie's voice. "Hey, Deathlike."

Hermie didn't bother with either remark. Very likely he hadn't heard anything beyond the sounds of angels. He pushed his shirt aside so that the other eye could come into play and tell him if it was really true, really her. For a moment, as the second eye focused, there were three of her. Then four. Then a dozen, spinning kaleidoscopically. But when the spinning ceased, there was only one of her but in perfect focus. Tears came to Hermie's eyes. It was hard for him to figure. Just looking at her caused him to cry. What could that possibly mean? Who cries upon observing beauty? What emotional depth had been plumbed by the very sight of her?

Oscy's voice. "I swear, Hermie, I don't know what's come over you. That's a very old person. I don't see the attraction."

Benjie's voice. "Hey, Deathlike."

Hermie knew, because of having a sister, that if the woman was over twenty-three years of age, it wasn't by more than a couple of minutes. He watched her as the knee that was up came down and as the one that was vice went versa. And there was a thunder going on in his heart, so you can imagine what was going on in his privates.

Benjie's voice. "Maybe it's her mind. Maybe their minds meet and say hello."

Hermie's image of love reclining was jostled because someone, probably Oscy, was nudging him in the small of the back with a sandy foot that featured an ugly hangnail. "Go say hello to her mind, Hermie. Say hello."

Hermie looked up at Oscy, who had a blinding sun at his back. "Cut it out, Oscy."

"No." Oscy pulled Hermie roughly to his feet. "If she's the love of your life, go say hello."

Hermie looked into Oscy's face and hated every bit of it. He wanted to haul off and plaster him one in the chops, but he didn't want to get killed. He tried to take the measure of Oscy's inscrutable grin. From past experience he knew that if Oscy's grin curled left, Oscy was benign. But if it curled right—condition red. In this particular case, Oscy's grin was curled up at the end of both directions. The barking dog was wagging its tail. Go figure it.

Oscy placed both paws on Hermie's shoulders. Then he turned him, hard, pointing him in the proper direction, as in Pin the Tail on the Donkey, and gently but firmly, he pushed Hermie toward the woman. "We wanna see you go say hello because maybe you're some kind of a hotshot lover we don't know about so"—he pushed him very hard, and Hermie flew about three feet down the beach toward the woman—"go say hello, Hermie. Go and say hello."

Hermie followed his feet. He hated himself for his cowardice but praised himself for his intelligence. For he who is afraid of Oscy and runs away lives to run away from Oscy another day. Besides, in his heart, Hermie knew that even if Oscy and Benjie were not on the scene, he'd still find an excuse to kind of amble up to the woman to just kind of see what would kind of come of it. Wrong. Liar. Coward. But an intelligent, lying coward. And a lot of bullshit.

Hermie walked as well as he could, which wasn't bad if you accepted the fact that he was half out of his mind with desire and the other half with fear. Closer and closer he drew to her, closing the interminable gap between them, soon realizing that her bathing suit was not made of diamonds after all. Rather, it was constructed of something sheer and Grecian and breathlessly close to transparent. Or was it his X-ray eyes pumping their beams at her? Time would tell. Onward.

The magical harmonica was once again evoked by the gods, and it sent exotic sonatas spiraling into the sky for the pleasure of the tenants of Mount Olympus. Lord, if that was Oscy playing, Hermie didn't dare turn to look because Oscy simply couldn't play. Which meant that it had to be Benjie, which was even more unacceptable. Before him she lay, haloed in the sun, and wonder of wonders, she was not sweating. No signs of sweat. She didn't sweat. How glorious because who could really desire a woman who sweated? An ape maybe.

And what dreams of Hermie inhabited her mind? What mystical instinct told her how close he was? Errol Flynn on the prowl; Tyrone Power come from Eden; Gary Cooper coming to bat with the bases loaded while Teresa Wright wrung her hanky in the dugout. Hermie circled her like a wolf pack. Silent, stealthy. She was the center of the universe and Hermie its panting perimeter. And because of his circling, again it was as though she were on a slow turntable, served up and presented from every angle for Hermie's delight. The toes were tiny trinkets. The thighs, alabaster carvings. The fingers, tendrils of passion. The elbows and shoulders— connected to the neck bone. Egyptian gold adorned her ears, which were seashells. The hair, pure silk. The lashes, velvet webs. The voices, Oscy and Benjie.

"Hey, lady in the blue suit! That's Jack the Ripper!"

"It's Herman the German, Nazi spy!"

"It's a sex fiend!"

"Hermie the rape artist!"

Hermie froze as the princess stirred, her delicate lashes flickering their awareness, her royal rest disturbed by the raucous sounds of those crude mortals. Hermie's circle became a straight line—away. He took only one last look at the goddess reclined, who, with graceful majesty, was raising herself on both elbows while lightly the curtains lifted from o'er her lustrous twin shamrocks. If Lucky Strike Green had gone to war, it was AWOL in her eyes. And Hermie knew that if she ever trained those emeralds on him, it would be the end of him. Away he went. Hi-ho, Hermie, away. A crow never took so straight a course. A coward never deserted so definitively. Hermie had always known that he was fast—he didn't run high school track for nothing—but there, on that beach, under those circumstances, the four-minute mile, which had eluded man since time immemorial, was being crashed and broken for all time. If only the coach could see. His stride was perfection, his arms pumping well, his breath firing in proper bursts. The crowd was cheering him on, his father's cigar going up into the air with a shout: "Go, Hermie!" He was out there alone, lapping the runner from James Madison, now shooting past the befuddled contestant from Manual Training. Midwood fell. Fort Hamilton quit. New Utrecht never knew what happened. They came at him swiftly, like birds of prey, Jap silent, Jap quick. Oscy hit him low with a fine rolling body block. Benjie would have hit him high were it not for the fact that Oscy had already cut him down. As a result, Hermie looked up from where he lay on the sand to see Benjie flying over him like a bag of shit, striking full force at empty sky, then landing with a scream, right on his stupid nose just as it was inhaling. There'd be sand in his mucus right through October.

Hermie sprang to his feet, and there was blood on the moon. He made no sound, just clenched his fists and advanced on Oscy, who was just getting to his feet and laughing. Oscy turned, bewildered at the sight of Hermie advancing. Then he smiled, neither left nor right, which meant he didn't know what to make of things.

Benjie was back on his feet, snorting sand from his nose like a dragon, then launching a sneak attack on Hermie's back. But the sun was behind him, and Hermie saw the swift shadow and sidestepped like Harmon. Benjie went shooting by, the Brighton express gone out of its mind, smashing once again into total nothingness and refilling his irritated nostrils with another two loads of sand. The scream that followed was unearthly and absolutely unheard by Hermie, who was squaring off, face-to-face, with the architect of the duplicity, Oscy the Fuck.

Oscy the Fuck knew there'd be no avoiding the confrontation, no backing off. Benjie the Jerk was staggering to his feet, steaming like a bull and cursing like a major. Without looking at him, Oscy waved Benjie off. "Leave him, Benjie. Leave him." The implication being that Oscy would take great pleasure in handling matters himself. And so, Benjie, Faithful Beast, obeyed by quickly backing off and immediately assuming the role of sadistic spectator because, as was common knowledge, Oscy could make mincemeat of Hermie.

Oscy was bigger, stronger, tougher, and more experienced, But he was also, at heart, a pretty decent citizen. He didn't want to hurt Hermie because Hermie was everything Oscy wasn't, yet always yearned to be: a scholar, a poet, and a prince. But the little son of a bitch was moving in like Barney Ross, so what could Oscy do? He danced about Hermie, flicking tormenting left jabs at the face, pulling punches as best he could, trying only to demonstrate to Hermie that fighting was not in his best interests. But Hermie kept coming, taking each jab lightly on the schnoz, pulling his head back at precisely the right moment so that very little contact was made. Still, his face reddened, and Oscy grew concerned because his sensitive adversary had yet to back off. "Had enough, Hermie?"

Hermie said nothing, just kept moving, searching, watching Oscy's eyes, waiting for that one opening his father always said was bound to be there if a fella held his ground and protected his chin. Hermie even threw a few punches to let Oscy know his contempt. The punches never landed, but they were psychological. Again he heard his father's voice: "You send out a couple and you send 'em out timid. You let him think that's all he has to concern himself with. You watch his eyes and the points of his shoulders, and you let him know you're not scared." His father had had a few professional fights, but Hermie didn't know whether he won them or lost them. What if he lost them? Jesus, what was he doing following the advice of a loser? For all his thinking and his strategy, Hermie had to sustain a continuous barrage of torturous lefts from Oscy's hummingbird fist.

Oscy grew more and more troubled as blood began to trickle from one of Hermie's two noble eyebrows. "Had enough, Hermie? Tell me when you've had enough?"

Hermie kept coming, still swinging some nebulous punches, only a bit more pragmatically. He was a track man, and Oscy was not. The longer he could remain on his feet, the greater the chances of Oscy pooping out first. He felt the tomato juice slithering into his left eye, and he blinked a few times to push it out. His wind was good, no heavy breathing. His arms were not tired. And his heart was pumping enough adrenaline to keep him going for a year.

On the sidelines Benjie got scared at the sight of blood on Hermie's face. "Cut it out, Oscy. He's crazy."

"I'll stop whenever you say, Hermie," said Oscy, still flitting about gingerly, showing no signs of withering with time.

Hermie kept coming. A few more quick lefts from Oscy and his face was beet red. Soon it would be warm vegetable soup, but he felt no pain even as he thought he heard the seams on his face splitting into midget fissures. He had no thought in his mind other than to kill Oscy. He kept wading in, aware of the fact that the circles they were making were growing smaller and smaller.

Oscy looked at Hermie's squishy face and decided that it wasn't necessary for his adversary to verbalize his defeat. With respect for Hermie's pride and admiration for his staying power, Oscy magnanimously announced, "Okay, Hermie. That's enough." He also dropped his hands. A mistake.

Hermie came into the sky like a Grumman Wildcat launched by a carrier's catapult. His whole body was balled up into his right fist. It buzzed through the air faster than sound and struck solidly on Oscy's unsuspecting nose, sending Oscy staggering backward in a dandy series of drunken steps. His equilibrium thus shattered, Oscy's knees sagged, and he sat down on his ass unceremoniously, looking up at Hermie in smiling incredulousness. In two seconds the blood came gushing from his nose as if the dam had burst. Oscy tried to put it back in, first by inhaling, then by covering his nose with his hands. But the blood came seeping through his fingers, and he looked at Hermie with painful disbelief. "Jesus, Hermie. I mean—you're something."

Hermie was not interested in any pleasant chitchat. His body came at Oscy, knees first. And each knee struck a shoulder so that Oscy plunked flat down on his back. Hermie was astride him like Tom Mix on Tony, pounding away with flailing fists and spiky spurs, lefts and rights and knees and thighs.

His advantage was short-lived. Oscy reared up, spun, and sent Hermie flying over him in a somersault so huge that Hermie landed flat on his back. For one split second in time, they lay head to head on the sand like the hands of Benjie's Ingersoll at six o'clock. They didn't stay that way too long. Hermie's head was ringing, and as he was considering answering the phone, Oscy took that time to spring on top of him. And so it was Oscy on top, holding Hermie down, where just a moment before it had been the other way around. Oscy had him pinned good. His hands held Hermie's wrists so hard that the pulse would be cut completely in another few seconds. Hermie tried shooting his body up at Oscy, hoping to unhorse him; but Oscy was too experienced for that, and every time Hermie tried it, Oscy gave him an emphatic knee in the groin, a strategy that would discourage even a Brahma bull. Hermie could do nothing but lie still and wait for his hands to fall off. Hovering directly above Hermie as he was, Oscy, perversely, allowed the blood from his dripping nose to splat down onto Hermie's face. Hermie kept turning his head from side to side in order to avoid the droplets because he had enough of his own blood on his face, thank you. But Oscy managed to keep his blood plopping right on target so that, in a very short time, Hermie's face looked as though it had been swabbed with red paint. He no longer had even the smallest initiative. He was at Oscy's mercy, but he'd shit in Macy's window before he'd say uncle.

Oscy could read Hermie, but just the same, he was mad enough to entertain Hermie's lack of enthusiasm for quitting by simply pummeling him into a poetic pulp. The smile on his red face had definitely hooked to the right. It was condition red, and Hermie knew it. But like the hostage in the Nazi movies, he manufactured the spit in his mouth and blew it straight up at Oscy. Call it bad luck. Call it a change in wind direction, but it never reached Oscy. It returned to Hermie like a boomerang, right between his eyes. Oscy had to laugh, and the tension eased. "Okay, Hermie. I'm gonna let you up because enough is enough. But don't try anything funny, okay?"

Hermie said nothing. He just looked up at Oscy through the blood and the spit and the sand and the hurt and the whole fucking misery of it all. Slowly, guardedly, Oscy climbed off of him.

The punch hit Oscy so squarely on the chin that it raised him half a foot before shooting him ass over heels onto his back again, a more and more familiar position to him. Quickly he scrambled to one knee only to find Hermie already on one of his own. The roundhouse right came hissing like a scythe, and had he not put up his forearm in the path of it, Oscy would have surely been beheaded. On their knees the two sandy gladiators continued their combat, the blood and sand flying in droplets as far back as Benjie.

Ultimately, having found the opening, Oscy put all his considerable strength into a cruelly well-timed uppercut. Hermie's head snapped back like a Coke bottle just opened, and as he went over and down, he could see the blue sky and his own hair flapping. He saw nothing more for what easily could have been three days.

Oscy got to his feet and looked down at Hermie, who was spread against the sand as though he'd fallen there from the top of the Empire State Building. He was flattened into a two-dimensional form like a fresco in the Egyptian exhibition at the Museum of Natural History. He looked like a cave painting, a poster decrying drunken driving. He looked dead, and he stayed that way for approximately ten seconds.

Benjie came up alongside Oscy, very shaken at the sight of Hermie lying all out of shape like a rag doll. Together they looked down at Hermie, knowing that he was very much out to lunch. But at the eleven-second mark, Hermie's whiplike arm came cracklingly to life, and at the end of it was a hand filled with sand. The sand was meant for Oscy, but instead it caught Benjie in both eyes, and he screamed blindly, "Dirty Jap! Dirty goddamned Jap!"

Oscy, of course, fell down laughing as blind Benjie groped for Hermie's throat, his skinny fists clenched so hard that the fingernails were cutting into the palms. Oscy grabbed Benjie and restrained him. Hermie was lying very still on the sand. He was conscious, but he'd had it. The sand had been his last shot. It was meant for Oscy, but it had misfired. And so he lay there doing and thinking nothing. Bataan had fallen. The Death March would be next. He'd rather have a rifle bullet pumped through his brain. Put a gold star in the window, Mother; Hermie's bought it.

Oscy led Benjie farther and farther away, never letting go of him, until the pair of them were all but out of sight. But Hermie could still hear Benjie, cursing as he rubbed the coarse grains of sand deeper and deeper into his eyes. Oscy turned and called back to Hermie. "We'll see you later, Hermie! Okay?"

Hermie neither answered nor moved. He just turned his head enough so that he could see Oscy, with a firm grip on Benjie, who was screaming curse words that didn't even exist. The pair of them disappeared over the horizon, looking like Abbott and Costello, only a lot funnier.

When they were out of sight, Hermie rolled over and pulled himself to his feet. It must have taken an hour. He was a mess. His shirt was unsalvageable, but he figured he'd keep it as a souvenir until his mother found it and turned it into an inglorious cleaning rag. On a pair of wobblies, he crazily zigzagged into the ocean, the tin taste of his own blood souring his mouth. And when he was in the water up to his knees, he plopped the rest of the way like a felled redwood. His head went under the water, and the lights went out all over the world.

The coldness was refreshing and recuperative, but the salt burned like hell in his gaping wounds. The combination was just enough to keep him from drowning out of sheer exhaustion. He knew that if he had been getting laid regularly, he couldn't have lived through a fight like that. Score ten points for celibacy. If priests ever had a mind to become prizefighters, they'd take every crown, no doubt about it. Anyway, up he popped like a porpoise, filling his lungs with air and paddling back to the shore. Tired legs dragged him the last few steps, and he dropped to his stomach on the wet sand, causing the sandpipers to go bibble-bibble and move farther up the beach than they had intended. Resting his head on his forearm, the salt still wincing his cuts, Hermie scanned the horizon. Hitler and Mussolini were gone, but so was the woman. Could she know the battle he fought on her behalf? Had she any idea that he'd just taken on Basil Rathbone and Bela Lugosi in mortal combat? Well, he'd tell her about it later. He got to his feet and headed home, and for some reason he'd never understand, he felt better than he'd ever felt in his whole entire life.

7

Hermie spent the remainder of the day in his room in highest meditation. He didn't hate Oscy; he understood him. Oscy was just a big kid, a frisky colt, that's all. Oscy was just more interested in hitting a Spalding three sewers than he was in the finer things in life. Oscy was simply more concerned about safeguarding the fucking football against the concrete of the street they played Two-Hand Touch on, which was why the football had two pounds of crisscrossed adhesive tape stuck onto each end so that, when you threw it, it was like throwing a broken leg. Oscy just wasn't interested in sex yet. Still, hadn't Hermie come upon Oscy in the basement of 81 Ocean Parkway only to find his dearest friend masturbating over a photograph of Claire Trevor even though Edward G. Robinson was in the picture beside her? And even though Oscy denied the whole incident as being only an accident, wasn't it fairly obvious, from the size of things, that Oscy was no stranger to sex? As for Benjie, he was a stranger to the entire human race and a blot on the lineup card of the OPACS (Ocean Parkway Athletic Club & Social). Benjie played right field because the OPACS had only nine members, which made Benjie varsity and right fielder because how many lefty pull hitters were there? When a left-handed pull hitter *did* come up, Benjie was roused from his coma and moved to left field, where he could continue reading his comic book without interruption. But mostly, Benjie played right field with all the enthusiasm of a mortician. He even played right field in the football season when the OPACS merged with the Kermit Place Eagles so that they could field a fuller team of lousy players. Benjie was destined to play right field his entire life. He was born to it, a natural fuck-up. He had two left feet and had both of them perpetually in his mouth. One ounce less of intelligence and he'd be under a bell jar at NYU.

> Once you try it, you'll say buy it;
> Tom Mix says it's swell to eat.
> Jane and Jimmy, too, say it's best for you—
> Ralston Cereal can't be beat.

So ended another episode of *Tom Mix* and good riddance. Hermie wondered why he listened to that crap. Probably just out of nostalgia because he'd been listening since he was a kid. He always kept the radio on when he was doing deep thinking because he liked to guess at what the next line of dialogue would be. If he was right, it helped him do his deep thinking with greater confidence. If he was wrong, he'd be right on most of the following programs. After *Tom Mix* came *Don Winslow*, who was still trying to outwit Ivan Shark, as well as the Jap Navy. Then there was *Little Orphan Annie*, who had no eyeballs in the comic strip but who could talk all right on the radio in spite of the fact that she used to have long conversations with her idiot dog, who could only go "Arf." And then there was dinner during which he pretended to be a deaf mute, though it was hardly noticed since his sister was doing a whole speech complaining that there were no men on the island. At the tail end of her speech she left the table crying and ran to her room, where her breasts continued to rot on the vine. After dinner his mother sat around and read *Liberty* magazine, while his father, on the island for a couple of weeks' vacation, went over the bills and grumbled over the ration coupons his mother was screwing up on. Like the chicken they had for dinner: 23 points and stringy. They ate so much chicken in his family that Hermie was fully convinced he'd one morning look into the toilet bowl and discover that he'd laid an egg. It was excruciating and it was also raining, so Hermie spent the rest of the evening cutting out Kay Francis and Jinx Falkenburg and trying to find a place for them on his wall even if it meant shooting down a couple of his own planes. He found Kay and Jinx in his sister's latest *Photoplay* and hoped she wouldn't mind because—who was she kidding?—she had already cut out Joel McCrea and Don Ameche, not to mention Smiley Burnette. It was difficult finding new photographs of Penny Singleton because she was simply not in demand. His radio was offering the world *Fibber McGee and Molly* and then *Bob Hope*, who was up in Alaska freezing his nuts off for the soldiers. Maybe his cousin in combat, Ronald, was part of the audience. It was a thrilling thought. When he switched the radio off, Hermie lay in his bed thinking about the woman and the love that was building in his heart for her. He fell asleep with her fantastic face on the pillow beside him. Then the pillow became the woman, and he gave it to the pillow pretty good. It was a miracle there were no feathers flying around. It wouldn't have mattered if there were because he had reached the point of no return, choosing to finish off his dream in the bathroom, where it was easier to deal with. And all the while, his sister was rapping at the door, unaware of her brother's self-induced ecstasies. It wasn't the first time. Nor would it be the last. The important thing was, he was developing concentration.

8

The alarm clock screamed at him, and he ignored it, letting it run down by itself, maybe teaching it some kind of lesson. He carefully examined the face in the mirror and concluded that there were no bruises to speak of. He brushed his teeth but didn't bother to comb his hair, knowing that to get into any kind of presentable shape would take hours, and he didn't have that much time to squander in spite of the fact that he had no plans for the rest of the day. He tiptoed into the kitchen and had a bowl of shit because it went snap-crackle-pop and he had no one else to talk to. He was essentially so goddamned bored with life that, unthinkingly, he let the screen door slam behind him. He waited for what he knew would follow. A button had been pressed in his mother's mouth, and her voice came out like an air raid warning. "Herman, where are you going?"

He paused on the top step. "To the Planet Mongo."

"It's not even eight o'clock."

"I can't do anything about that."

"Did you take something to eat?"

"An elephant."

"Bring back a newspaper."

"Certainly."

"And a *Time* magazine for your father."

"Jesus." Hermie walked along the narrow sidewalk that had been split and repaired maybe a million times since the Spanish-American War. He felt nothing but emptiness. He passed a few houses and a few kids on rusty tricycles and a few dogs that looked better than the chicken he ate last night. And he looked up to see if his sea gull was around, but it wasn't. Probably filling up on dead fish for a late-afternoon bombing run on his head.

Not many of the summer people were up as yet. But the freight boat was in, and that was good for a half hour of watching before you fell asleep.

Along the main drag he was once again stopped by the polka-dot bathing suit, which all of a sudden was laughing at him. A laughing bathing suit would stop any man, but soon the source of the laughter came through the store's door in the form of two fat ladies laughing so hard that they were coughing. And the fat on their arms went jiggly-wiggly, and Hermie knew that never again would he feel the same way about that particular bathing suit.

He came out of Killerman's Bakery with a bag of sugar-covered jelly doughnuts, freshly made and smelling of tastiness. And when he bit into the first of them, the jelly broke across his face making him look as though he'd been shot in the mouth with a dumdum bullet, which would have been illegal. The sugar, undoubtedly ersatz, cut a swath of white from ear to ear, and he continued his walk putting doughnut after doughnut deliciously away.

He paused to look into the barbershop, where a kid his age, but unknown to him, was getting a crew cut. It made him look like a hairy handball. Worse than that, the kid knew it. Hermie stood there, staring at the kid, because the whole thing looked like a freak show. That was the really worst thing about a barbershop; they always stuck you in the seat nearest the front window as if you were their advertisement. Then they covered you with a crummy sheet full of somebody else's hair which made it look as if you were inside an anthill. And then they charged you a half a buck, and if you had the gall to not tip, they'd curse at you in a foreign language, probably Italian, and the next time you came in you could figure on a few little slices behind your ears because a barber never forgets, especially if he's one of the two barbers on the island and the other barber is his fucking brother. The kid in the chair lowered his eyes and made believe he wasn't there. That's how much he couldn't stand Hermie staring at him. Then, when the barber spun the guy around and flashed a razor which he stropped about an eighth of an inch from the kid's nose, Hermie left the scene. It was all too medieval.

He bought a *Time* magazine that had a picture of Jimmy Doolittle on the cover because it seemed Jimmy Doolittle had just bombed Tokyo. Hermie knew that that was pretty significant because, up till that time, the Yanks didn't really know whether they were coming or going. It was like a home run that tied the score in the fifth inning. When you could come from behind like that, you were in good shape. Good man, Jimmy Doolittle. America is proud of you. Hermie bought a newspaper, too, and proceeded along the street trying to juggle the doughnuts, the newspaper and the *Time* magazine. Then he saw her, and his stomach dropped from behind his belt and filled up both his sneakers.

She was radiant. It was the only word. Radiant. With her long legs and flowing hair and green eyes, soft and limpid green eyes, how in my dreams you haunt me—but look. She was in distress. She had more bundles than she could handle. The damsel was sure as shit going to drop them. It was a job for Super Hermie. For extra strength he bit into the last jelly doughnut and immediately felt all 129 pounds of him harden, really harden.

One of her bundles tottered and began to slip, but she somehow managed to ease it to the ground before it could break open. But then, when she bent down to get a proper grip on it, another bundle began to teeter. It was a losing fight, and finally, all the bundles slipped out of her arms, and she stood there all forlorn indeed. Sadness in a pleated skirt. Helplessness in a gray cardigan.

Super Hermie took a deep breath, wiped the jelly from his mouth, tossed the empty doughnut bag to the winds, stuffed Jimmy Doolittle into one back pocket and the New York *Times* into the other, and faster than a speeding locomotive, he sallied forth to assist the damsel, pray tell. But when he arrived at her side and opened his mouth to speak, he addressed her in so arch a manner as to sound immediately stupid even to himself: "May I offer some assistance?"

He grimaced and she had to have seen it, but she was so gracious. "You may," she said, and gads, she even curtsied. What manner of nobility had he stumbled on?

She wasn't really taller. Actually they were about the same height. It was her stateliness that made her seem so far above him. He dropped to one knee, half expecting to be knighted or given one of her garters or granted a boon. But what he really wanted to do was pick up the fucking bundles, of which there were quite a few. She filled the gap with a sunny voice. Sunny was a good way to describe her. She was a sunny person. "I hadn't planned on buying this much. I should have brought my wagon."

"You should have brought your wagon." Was that him? Jesus.

"Yes." It must have been him because she was agreeing.

Hermie had the fallen bags in tow, but the New York *Times* kept slipping out of his pocket. Thank God it wasn't the Sunday edition. He kept trying to reach around and keep it shoved in. It certainly wasn't easy being a good Samaritan. The woman made a gesture as if to help, "Nay," he said. "It's okay."

"But I can take *one*."

"It's okay." He dropped the "nay." Smart. Still in a feudal position, his arms encircled the bundles until his hands met and clasped like Stanley and Livingstone. Something ripped. It wasn't a bag. Either he had just gotten himself a hernia or his shorts had given way. "What you really need is a wagon." He said that immediately, to cover the sound of the ripping. It was all that occurred to him.

"I think you're right," said the sunny voice. And then she was kneeling alongside him. Hermie was mortified, but she spoke kindly, not at all patronizing. "If *you* carry some and *I* carry some, I think we can manage. And I'll be glad to pay you."

"I wouldn't think of it." That sounded better, more secure. They were both standing, the green eyes planted on his. The ice had finally been broken.

"I'm afraid my house is a pretty long walk." She smiled.

"I know where it is." That was a slip.

"You do?"

He regained his composure. "Yeah. It's that way." He pointed in the direction where *all* the houses were. The woman smiled and shook her head so that the brunette hair would not cover her face.

And her perfume shot out at him, and it went up his nose right into his memory. Then they were walking.

Hermie could think of nothing to say, but she filled the void. "You live on the island?"

"In the summer."

"With your family?"

"Yes, but they don't bother me. I pretty much go my own way." He felt it important that he establish his independence.

"What do you do?"

"Oh—interesting things." Like what? Cutting out pictures? Listening to *Tom Mix?* Eating chicken? Humping pillows?

They continued the walk with Hermie trying not to reveal the difficulty he was having hanging onto the bundles. By then he had figured that the rip he heard was in his shorts and not in his groin. But the bags were getting heavier and gravity wasn't helping, and the next rip would be his testicles exploding under the pressure.

Over the rim of the highest bag Hermie saw the two morons. Oscy and Benjie were coming toward him. They were the last lunatics in the world he wanted to bump into. He pulled his head in like a turtle and walked by following his toes. Soon his two sneakers passed the four sneakers of his friends. The question then was: Had they seen him? Not likely, though stranger things had happened. He kept walking. The bags were like lead. He glanced at the woman, who smiled, so he smiled back, trying not to talk because talking used up energy.

"Hey, Hermie!" The voice was Benjie's. But it stopped quickly, as though Oscy must have delivered unto it a good elbow to the labonz. Good old Oscy. Somehow he knew that Hermie was involved in something important. Good old, mature Oscy. A guy doesn't jerk off over Claire Trevor for nothing.

"Did somebody call you?" she asked.

"Not me."

"Your name Hermie?"

"Yes."

"Somebody back there called you."

"Not me."

"He called 'Hermie.'"

"It's a pretty common name."

The woman smiled and did not pursue the subject further. They walked on. It seemed as if they were walking to Chicago and just wait till they had to cross the Appalachians. Where the hell was her house? Periodically, Hermie would let a bundle slide onto an upraised knee, thus allowing himself a furtive moment to renew his grip. And on occasion he called upon self-hypnosis in an effort to convince himself that the bags were filled with inflated balloons and that his arms were not stretching out like thin rubber bands and that she was not making him carry home four bundles of bricks. Maybe she was a carpenter. Maybe she was going to ask him to build a wall, maybe all the way around China. Or how about something more simple, like a tank barrier or a submarine pen? Or how about a tree house, a thousand feet up? He could carry the bricks up one at a time and finish by the time he was a hundred. Hermie knew that if they didn't get to her house soon...

"This is it," she said.

"I can go further." That ranked with some of the more idiotic things he'd ever said.

And it puzzled her. "But...there's really no need." She pointed to her house, as if maybe he couldn't see it.

"Okay."

Entering the house from the road side, he found there were no stairs to deal with, and thank God for that. He followed her, able to see only the top of her head. "Can you bring them in, please?"

"My pleasure."

They entered the house, and music came up because everything was so special even though it was pretty much like every house on the island. He followed the dancing hair across the porch and through the tidy living room all suddenly bright with color because she was passing by. As he passed the mantel, Hermie saw a framed photograph of the man. It was just a quick look because Hermie had no time to linger looking at pictures; still, he'd remember it forever. The man was so handsome that Hermie knew he shouldn't be in the same room with him. The smile was rich and masculine. And he was in uniform and had a pipe clenched between teeth that were blinding white. Hermie despaired. Everybody in the world had straight teeth except him. His teeth more nearly came in like a mako shark's. There was some handwriting on the photograph. An autograph. "All my love, forever, Pete." Pete. So that was his name. Hermie knew he was much closer to something or other.

"In here. In the kitchen."

Hermie went into the kitchen, which was alive with flowers that she had in about a dozen vases. She certainly liked flowers. Lucky for Hermie he wasn't allergic. "Would you just put them on the table?" she said.

Hermie had intended to set the bundles gently upon the table. But as it turned out, all the muscles, tendons, and ligaments in his arms quit at the same time. The bags slammed to the table like Jimmy Doolittle hitting Tokyo. Also, Hermie's shorts tore a little more, and he knew that they were hanging in his pants like two separate hankies. He felt stupid and angry. "They should make these bags stronger." He tried to gather up the items that were trying to escape or roll around just to be nasty.

"Please let me give you some money." She had her purse open, and she was fishing around inside. If it were his mother's purse, it'd take her a year and the quarter she'd pull out would be a Roosevelt/Wallace button.

"I wouldn't think of it." Shit, was he ever gallant!

She smiled at him. "But how can I repay you?"

"I don't know." Maybe she had something in mind. Something else. Naaaaaaaah.

She put her purse aside and turned her attention to the bundles. "I bought these marvelous jelly doughnuts." Hermie gagged as she pulled out the bag that said *Killerman's Bakery*. And he like unto shit when she took from the bag the very same jelly doughnuts he couldn't eat again if his life depended on it. She put them on a plate, and when her back was away from him he coughed in an effort not to throw up rudely. "I've got some coffee," she said. "It's from this morning, but, well, we've all got to make things go further." She turned on the burner under the coffeepot, and then she turned to Hermie. "You *do* drink coffee."

"Before the war I drank a couple cups a day." Before the war he was on Pablum.

She was still unsure. "I mean, I *have* milk."

He misunderstood her by a mile. "I take it black." Then he suddenly understood and felt stupid again. Whatever had become of the natural poise Oscy so often told him he possessed?

"Please sit down," she said. And Hermie sat at the little kitchen table. He sat right on Jimmy Doolittle and the New York *Times*, a very lumpy thing for a man to do. So he got up, pulled both items from his back pockets, and then smoothed them out on the table. They looked as though Jumbo had sat on them for a year.

"Oh," she said, looking over her shoulder from the stove where the coffee was returning to suffering life, "*Time* magazine."

"I read it regularly. It's informative." He wouldn't read *Time* magazine if they gave him a medal for it.

She put some fresh flowers into clean water, and the colors reflected in her eyes. "Are you in high school?"

"Yes. Erasmus Hall. In Brooklyn. You can't miss it. I'm a sophomore."

"Ah, a sophomore."

"Yes."

"Ummmmmmmmm."

"I was a freshman last year."

"I thought you were older."

"And next year I'll be a junior and so on."

"Well, don't be in too big a hurry. You'll be in the Army before you know it."

"It'll be finished by then."

"By when?"

"By then."

"I see." But Hermie knew she didn't. The feminine mind had

trouble grasping certain things. Feminine minds were good at coffee. Except *that* coffee looked as if it didn't care to try it again. It huffed and waddled and steamed and even complained. "Well," she said, "I hope you're right."

"But if it *isn't* over, I'm prepared to go. I'm taking preflight courses in high school, and I expect I'll fly a plane pretty soon."

"That ought to be very exciting." She was watching the coffee, wondering if it hadn't been used too much, hoping it wouldn't come out white.

"Maybe I'll team up with my brother. He's a paratrooper. Maybe I can drop him out." Out of what, his mind? His imagination? The nearest thing he ever had to a brother was his sister before her boobs bloomed.

"Ah, your brother's a paratrooper."

"Well, mostly I have a sister in high school." Confession was good for the soul. Especially if he ever brought her home to meet his family.

"Coffee's ready." She brought the pot to the table, and she poured two cups. Like the fool he really was, Hermie picked up his cup, and acting as though it were something he had been doing all his life, he immediately boiled his tongue. How he lived through it without screaming was a testimonial to the poise Oscy had so often referred to. But his eyes began to run, and his tongue kind of fell out of his mouth and hung down on his chest like a necktie. The woman gasped. "Oh! I should have told you! It's very hot! Are you all right?"

"Yeth. Thertainly." He could feel the steam from his tongue moving right up his nose. Maybe it was good for his sinuses. A lot of people steamed their noses.

She was very rattled, feeling very much at fault, and she was hovering all about him—like a mother, which he already had one of. "Would you like some ice? I can get you some ice. Why don't I get you some ice? I'll get you some ice. Ice. Ice." She was scurrying around at the refrigerator. Maybe she was a Red Cross nurse. Maybe he'd have to lie on her bed and have his tongue bandaged.

She returned and plunked a few ice cubes into his cup so

quickly that for a moment Hermie thought that maybe they were red-hot. He looked at the ice cubes shriveling away in his cup. He didn't have much time. They'd be gone in a trice. So when her back was turned, because she was trying to chip out more ice cubes, he leaned over and rested his tongue on the expiring cubes in his coffee cup. It provided immediate relief. Jesus, she made the hottest coffee in town. Wheweeeeee.

He wasn't quite sure how long she had been talking or just what it was she was saying. He was more involved in tickling the ice cubes with his tongue. When the cubes finally disappeared like explorers in quicksand, leaving the temperature of the coffee a mere nine hundred degrees, he looked up to see where she was and what she was doing. She was sitting opposite him and was eating one of the—ugh—jelly doughnuts. She was also talking, and he tuned her in in the middle of a sentence. "Such an old stove I can never quite regulate it. And as far as getting it repaired, there's just no one on the island who knows what to do with a 1934 stove." She became aware that he was staring at her, and she figured she should stop babbling. So she smiled and switched the subject back to him. "Do you have many friends on the island? Hermie? Hermie?"

He had never seen a woman speak more beautifully. "Two," he said. "I have two. But very immature." His tongue was coming around, recuperating nicely.

"Well—what do you do? To keep busy, I mean."

"I lean toward basketball but I think there's a lot to be said for baseball. At least, in baseball, you don't get round-shouldered from dribbling."

"Oh."

"I also run track."

"You're very athletic."

"Yes. A lot of people are. The trick is to be good at it."

"Do you…like music?"

"Yes. I'm quite musical." He could feel the conversation really flowing. He was in control. Life was good.

"Do you play an instrument?"

"Yes. I sing."

"Oh," she said, and she laughed.

Hermie hadn't intended that as a joke. He'd have to straighten her out. "I think a voice is like an instrument."

"Oh, I do, too." She was being nice. What the hell did *she* know about music? All she was was the most beautiful woman on earth. What the hell did she *have* to know about music?

"Anyway—for a change, you can whistle. Gives a man a lot of range." That he had intended as a joke.

But that she missed. And she only shook her beautiful head in serious agreement. "That certainly is true."

"I play around with things poetic, on occasion." He was surprised that he said that. He had never told that to anyone, not even Oscy. Nor did he ever leave any of his verses around where someone might come across them. Everything he ever wrote he burned. It was better that way. He could always keep the dream that way. If he was never read, no one could say he was lousy.

"Well, you certainly have many interests."

Hermie stood up. He had read somewhere that the experienced man knows when it's time to go. "Well, I guess I'll be moseying along. Next thing I know, you'll be making me lunch."

She stood, too. "Must you go?" She seemed sincere. She really wanted him to stay longer, to tarry awhile, to linger on.

"Yes. I've got some bacon grease to bring in. Three weeks' worth. They use it for making ammunition. Do you have any old stockings? They use it to make powder bags for naval guns."

"I don't wear stockings in the summer."

"That's very patriotic."

"I don't know how patriotic it is, but it's certainly a lot cooler." She was smiling. That was some kind of joke.

He smiled and even attempted an adult chuckle. She wasn't too funny, but then, how many women were Red Skelton?

"I wish you"—she was putting some doughnuts back into the Killerman Bakery bag—"would take some of these delicious jelly doughnuts. Seems the least I can do." She thrust the bag into his arms. The doughnuts were his for all time.

"Thank you very much. I'll eat them as soon as I can."

"Oh, I thank *you*, Hermie."

"Then you're welcome. It was a privilege." He was backing toward the door with the uneasy feeling that he was knocking things over, which was precisely what he was doing. A chair. A lamp. A magazine rack.

She smiled and didn't seem to notice as she walked with him. "Next time I'll be sure to bring my wagon when I go shopping."

"I think you should. You could get a hernia." Why he said that he would never know.

She shook it off, thinking perhaps that she had just heard it wrong. "Perhaps I'll see you again."

"It would be a privilege." He was running out of things to say. He'd better beat it before he'd be saying hello again. He was at the door.

"Good-bye," she said.

"Good-bye," he said and the screen door closed behind him. He kind of slipped out of the house and waved to her, wanting desperately to say, "I shall return," but suppressing the urge. He walked down the road toward town, carrying the bag of doughnuts as if it were a dead and putrefying corpse. He was very annoyed with himself for his unfortunate turn of a phrase, for his oral ineptitude, and he pounded his fist repeatedly against his thigh, again and again, as he said to himself, "A hernial Jesus!"

Oscy and Benjie seemed to form out of nowhere. One minute there was nothing, and the next they were squarely in his path. A pair of binoculars dangled about Oscy's neck, and was he ever smiling. "Hi, Hermie."

Hermie executed a neat semicircle around them. "Hi," he said as he went loftily by, hoping they'd disappear in a puff of green smoke, but they didn't. He couldn't hear their Apache feet, but he could feel them trailing him. But he was too intent on letting the sea breezes cool his tongue to talk with fools. He continued on, his tongue hanging out of his mouth like Lassie's.

Oscy shortly closed the gap and was soon walking alongside. "As it so happens, Hermie, you were under our surveillance. We were watching you from a range of thirty yards."

"No shit."

"You were in there a long time, Hermie. You could've brought those bundles in and been out in ten seconds. What happened?"

Hermie considered not answering, but that would be like ignoring a bee up your ass. Next he considered lying. But lying was not really his style. It was too out of character in spite of the lies he had told the woman a moment ago. Finally he decided to tell the truth but in a manner that would dazzle. "We had drinks."

Oscy's eyes lit up. "You're kidding."

"Okay, I'm kidding." And he quickened his pace.

Oscy knew he wasn't kidding and caught up, turning to Benjie, who was tagging along the required ten steps back. "They had drinks."

"Big deal."

Oscy, really interested, leaned confidentially in on Hermie even as they walked. "Hey—she let you get funny?"

"You had the field glasses. What'd you see?"

"They don't work around corners. Come on, Hermie. Did she let you get cute?"

Hermie wanted very much to stay above the crudity of it all. "You're a dope."

Oscy might have been a dope, but he was also relentless. "An older woman like that—what's a little feel to her? Hey, Hermie, baby—she let you have a feel?"

"She gave me some doughnuts." Hermie chose not to lie about his escapade. He was too tired and worn-out and was too worried about a hernia to make his chance meeting with the woman into a romantic saga. Without looking, he tossed the bag of doughnuts over his shoulder to where Benjie could catch it.

Benjie saw it coming, a soft pop fly to right field. He moved his hands to catch it, but owing to his unearthly lack of coordination, the bag hit him smack in the middle of the forehead. "Cut it out,

Hermie," he said. And then he kicked the bag as hard and as far as he could—three feet.

Oscy kept after Hermie. "Hermie, what the hell'd you do in there all that time?"

"I wasn't aware of the time. It flew quickly." The memory of her caused him to wax rhapsodic, and his tongue was feeling so much better that he sucked it back into his mouth like a large piece of macaroni.

Oscy was going crazy with his own imagination. "Boy, I tell you, I think *I'd* like to give her a good feel."

"I thought you were mature, Oscy." Hermie noticed that the sky had never been bluer. Nor had the breeze ever been more pleasant. Nor had he given himself a hernia. Things could never seem so lovely to a man with a hernia.

"It's very mature to feel girls. My brother does it all the time."

"Then how come he's a dentist?" That remark was on behalf of his sister. Better a big-busted sister than a brother who was a dentist.

Miffed, Oscy placed himself directly in Hermie's way. "Don't be such a big shot all of a sudden. And don't try to tell us that something happened in there with that lady!"

Hermie tried to sidestep Oscy without displaying fear, a totally impossible maneuver. "I'm not trying to tell you *anything*."

Oscy kept the way blocked, Horatius at the Gate. "Which is exactly like telling us that a *lot* went on in there. A lot!"

Hermie found himself getting angry, not because Oscy was acting like a moron—Oscy *always* acted like a moron. It was just that he was acting like a moron so *soon* and was ruining Hermie's memory of his precious rendezvous before it had even had a chance to solidify. "Screw you, Oscy!" ("Screw" was somehow gentler than "fuck." Maybe he wouldn't get a rap in the kisser for saying "screw." Saying "fuck" so close up to Oscy was a guaranteed mash in the mush.) Hermie continued, "I'm not gonna tell you something happened if nothing happened! Nothing happened! And if that makes you believe that something happened, then I'm sorry for you—because nothing happened! Jesus, I don't even know her name!" And that realization really upset Hermie, and unthinkingly, he shoved Oscy out of the way.

A man seldom made first contact with Oscy and got away with it without some memento in the eye. But Oscy saw how disturbed Hermie was, and so he decided to withhold punishment, at least for the nonce. Instead, he fell in step again and resumed the shouting match. "You expect us to believe that!"

"Well—I don't give a hot crap *what* you believe. I'm going home. My father's waiting for his newspaper and his *Time* maga—" He pulled them both from his back pockets. They looked like hell. "Jesus!" What could he tell his father? That they arrived on the ferry that way? That a steamroller ran over them? He looked at the cover of *Time* magazine. Jimmy Doolittle had a few wrinkles there that would take a normal man seventy years to acquire. He looked as if he had tried to escape from Shangri-La, which was exactly the place President Roosevelt said the planes were launched from. Wasn't that a coinci—

"You going home?" Oscy kept after him.

"Yeah. I'm going home. I have things to think over. I'm going home."

"What're you gonna do later?" Oscy was being very nice.

"I'm gonna kill myself!"

"*After* that—"

"I don't know. Oscy, I don't know!" He left his friends there and headed home, still smacking his fist against his thigh. Still berating himself. "Hernia. Oooooooooooh!"

9

The rest of the day had very little purpose and went nowhere at all. Most of the time Hermie lay on his bed, his hands locked behind his head, very deep in thought. His thoughts were mostly random, hard to nail, tough to catalogue, and they rattled around in his mind with great and rapid disorder. Foremost, of course, was the woman, so lovely and intelligent and patriotic. But then there was the man, Pete. Hermie knew that if things went well for the United States, Pete would one day return and would have to be dealt with, and Hermie had scruples about servicemen. An appreciation of his own lunacy kept whipping about in Hermie's mind, washing over his brain, and leaving him with the stark reality he could not truly suppress. He was a young boy infatuated with an older woman, Andy Hardy on the half shell, Henry Aldrich running for class president. Once before it had happened to Hermie. In freshman math, Miss Randall, Josephine Ruth. But he got immediately over it the afternoon he hung around the classroom to ask a question he already knew the answer to, and he caught her removing an upper plate that was studded with false teeth. That ended Josephine Ruth for him right then and there, and later, whenever she came to mind, it was as an old hag cackling as she dropped her dentures into a glass of Polident for the night and then poisoning a dozen apples for the Snow White kid. Still, his latest heartthrob was different. Her teeth were real. They had to be. God couldn't be that cruel two times in a row. And her legs were real. Long and tan and crazy. You can't fake false legs nohow. Her hair, that was no wig. There had been at least three separate gusts of wind that would have surely blown a wig to kingdom come, and her hair had stayed on in the face of it.

Her breasts, well—they might have been a little on the spare side, but if the truth were known, Hermie leaned toward small-breasted women, like Margaret Sullavan. Besides, all the classical beauties of history were small-breasted. Diana, Juliet, the White Rock girl.

Hermie thumbed through *Popular Mechanics* for a while and read about a man in Joplin, Missouri, who built his own airplane out of old automobile parts, three unicycles, and a glider wing. Thrilling.

Dinner was novel. Meatballs and fruit salad, on separate plates. Junket, otherwise known as the Pink Plague. And cookies baked by his sister during a moment when she wasn't examining her boobs. The cookies were flat; the sister wasn't.

After dinner his father expressed some dismay at the condition of his *Time* magazine. Hermie explained that he had been attacked on the way home by a lost Italian paratroop brigade and was lucky to have escaped with his life. His father dropped the subject because his son was talking nutty again, better call the doctor.

His sister was reading Jane Austen again when Hermie left the bungalow that evening. And his mother was washing the dishes while humming along with the radio. This was incredible because the news was on. The leading RAF ace, Paddy Finucane, had been shot down, and the last words he said were: "This is it, chaps." That his mother could hum along to that kind of news was a fantastic thing, fantastic. When Hermie stepped out onto the porch, his father, whose head was lying under a bamboo fan, mumbled something about all four Roosevelt boys being deep in the war. Hermie agreed and let the screen door shut behind him.

And there they were, resplendent on his lawn. Oscy and Benjie, the Happiness Boys. Oscy had a beginners' book for harmonica players and was forcing out a melody that approximated "Jingle Bells," a brilliant musical selection for a midsummer night. As for Benjie, he was playing a Hi-Li, counting each time he hit the rubber ball that was attached to the wooden paddle via a red rubber band. Benjie was up to one hundred and forty-three. That meant that he had cheated about seventy-five times because, with his spastic coordination, there was no way in which he could ever hit the ball more than three times in a row, unless, of course, he'd lay the ball on the ground and stand over it and swat it with the paddle. Oscy and Benjie saw Hermie, but no mention was made of any prior problems they might have had earlier that day. That was the code. Dinner washed out the day. Whatever happened before dinner was over the bridge. Whatever came after was dull.

So it was "Jingle Bells" and Hi-Li at ten paces for the next fifteen minutes. Because he had eaten his meatballs and Junket, there was no voice berating Hermie from within. He could pick up and leave any time he pleased. No one would stop him. He could go to town with his chums and get ice cream. It was up to him. So they went to town, and Hermie had strawberry with chocolate sprinkles because Mr. Sanders, the druggist, really laid on the sprinkles. Oscy had chocolate mint, which Hermie despised. And Benjie had bubble gum, which he couldn't work very well and which ended up on his nose as it always did. They watched the last ferry go out, and then they went home, each to his own house. Another exciting evening on Packett Island had gone into history.

Hermie sneaked into his room without saying goodnight. Usually that angered his mother because she was such a stickler for saying good-night. But because she was involved in a heated discussion with his sister, his mother overlooked Hermie's transgression. Lying on his bed, Hermie could hear them. His sister didn't want to write to a certain guy because he was a jerk. But his mother said that even jerks like to receive mail when they're in the Army because they were risking death for their country. His sister asked how the jerk could be risking death if he was stationed on Governors Island. His mother countered by asking about the size of the mosquitoes on Governors Island in the summer. His sister ran to her room screaming and slammed the door. His mother stood outside and shouted about patriotism. His father came by and shouted about the shouting. Then the incident was over, and everyone went to sleep.

Hermie lay in bed and wondered why life was so swiftly passing him by. He switched on the radio and learned that Rommel was loose in Africa and seemed able to go anywhere he pleased. Hermie wished that Rommel would get to Packett Island before the summer ended. Surely there was something of military value on the island that was of interest to the Germans. Why else would there be a Coast Guard station there? Hermie then reflected on just what it was that the Coast Guard did beyond guarding coasts, which seemed the height of stupidity since Packett Island was *all* coast and had no inland to speak of at all. He then decided that an even dumber branch of service was the Merchant Marine because he didn't even know what was meant by Merchant Marine. He had an uncle in a leather goods store who called himself a merchant. Could it be that a certain part of the Marine Corps was made up of leather goods merchants? Was that where the word "leatherneck" came from? Hermie fell asleep with the woman's face floating through his dreams. He wished there was some way in which he could save her life.

10

On the beach the next day the sun worshipers clustered tightly together on an infinitely narrow strip of sand, despite the fact that there were broad expanses of beach available both left and right. It was the herding instinct or something, and as he stepped over and across the seemingly disembodied arms and legs of the sunbathers, the smell of Skol and Noxzema danced up his nose. It was a very unsexy smell, and it subverted the very reason that he and Oscy and Benjie had chosen to walk through the collection of partially nude bodies. They had come to get a look at the girls since that was the place where girls in risky bathing suits hung out. As for the men, what few there were, they were mostly under draft age and not much older than the Terrible Trio, though they were a little larger and undoubtedly a little wiser. Hermie, Oscy, and Benjie picked their way through the suntanned humans as though walking through a minefield. Portable radios blared out a symphony of popular songs of the day, the lyrics of one riding over the lyrics of another as the stroll progressed.

> There'll be blue birds over
> The white cliffs of Dover
> Tomorrow, just you wait and see...
> He's One-A in the Army and he's
> A-One in my heart,
> He's gone to help the country
> That helped him to get his start...
> I'll walk alone,
> Because to tell you the truth

I'll be lonely…
Fillaga-doosha, Shinna-maroosha…
Johnny got a Zero, He got another Zero…
Along the Santa Fe Trail…

Oscy peered lasciviously at the sprawled girls, pretending he was looking for someone he knew, hoping perhaps to recognize her by the familiarity of her crotch. Hermie followed a few bodies behind. And Benjie was way back, clumsily managing to trip over a few knees and ankles in his effort to keep up with his friends.

Eventually, having covered the field and proved nothing, they regrouped on sand less populated, leaving the music and the high sexuality behind them. Oscy was insistent. "Boy, I'd like to feel every one of those girls. I should've tripped right on top of a couple of them, like that nutty redheaded broad, did you see her? She'd never of known I was getting a feel. Goddammit!"

Hermie felt very mature, too mature even to have come along on that walk in the sun. "That's not the way to do it."

Oscy spun him around. "So what's the way to do it?"

Hermie shrugged him off. "You have to *say* things."

"I'll say excuse me."

"You know what I mean. You just don't go up to a girl and fall on her. It isn't done."

"We did it with Gladys Potter."

"She was twelve years old. What'd *she* know?"

Oscy smiled reminiscently. "I don't know, but she didn't seem to mind."

"She was surprised."

"So was I. She had nothing to feel." He turned to Benjie, who was having trouble standing on the hot sand. "Come on, Benjie. What the hell you doing, dancing?"

"Shut up," said Benjie as he plopped down on his ass and studied the fried soles of his feet.

Oscy confided to Hermie: "I don't know what's going to become of him. He has no emotions."

"He's just confused." Hermie sat down on a wormy log.

"Tell you the truth, so am I." Oscy sat down and waved the flies away while snuffing out the lives of a dozen little bugs. He grew very pensive. "I been waking up in the middle of the night a lot."

"That's okay," said Hermie. "So do I."

"But I wake up feeling crazy and thinking about Vera Miller."

"So what?"

"So I *hate* Vera Miller!"

"So stop thinking about her."

It must have occurred to Oscy, the topsy-turvy emotionality of love. "Jesus, do you think I'm in love with her?"

"I don't know."

"I *hope* I'm not in love with her because I *hate* her."

"What kind of thoughts do you have about her?"

Oscy became evasive. "I forget."

"Then how can I help you?"

"Who the hell's *asking* you to help me?" He shoved Hermie roughly, and Hermie flipped off the log and landed on his back, face to the sun. Somehow he didn't mind. It was more comfortable and gave him a view of his toes he hadn't had since he was six months old. Oscy smacked the undersides of Hermie's feet. "Sometimes you act too supreme, Hermie. So watch yourself."

Hermie lay there and gave his line a Jack Benny reading. "I'll watch myself, I'll watch myself."

Benjie moved into the scene. "What're you guys talking about?"

Oscy waved him off. "Nothing you'd understand."

"Fuck you, Oscy."

Oscy became malevolently tolerant. "That's your whole problem, Benjie. You're only interested in fucking me. How about fucking a *girl?*"

"Okay."

Oscy laughed down to Hermie. "Okay, he says. Boy, that's something." And turning back to Benjie: "You wouldn't know the first thing to do."

"I would so."

"What's the first thing to do?"

"You *feel* 'em."

"Wrong. You *kiss* 'em."

Benjie looked puzzled. "We didn't kiss Gladys Potter."

"We weren't in *love* with Gladys Potter. If you're in love with a girl, you're supposed to kiss her." He punched Hermie's foot. "Right, Hermie?"

Hermie gazed up and took a moment to frame his answer. "Well, it's polite." Sky is blue, clouds are white; the stupid gull is nowhere in sight. Poem. "Looking at Sky," by Hermie.

Benjie was agitated. "Polite, shit. It's not required."

Oscy got up and walked over to Benjie. "It's required, you dumb ninny." And he gave Benjie a jarring shove.

Benjie backed up, of course. But he didn't back off his point in the discussion. On that he was still adamant. And he put his hands on his hips and stood there toughly and said, "It is not required."

Oscy was curious about why the stubbornness. "How the hell do *you* know?"

"I know."

"How?"

"I found a book."

Oscy just looked at him, not even breathing. Hermie rolled over and stared at Benjie likewise. Then Oscy looked at Hermie, and Hermie looked at Oscy. Then they both looked at Benjie again. There was a great deal of looking going on. Because, Benjie, of all people, had brought fire to mankind.

11

The abandoned chicken coop was perfect. It smelled a bit of days gone by and of former occupants, and its tilting walls were so caked with chicken drippings that very few people found it to be an inviting tourist attraction. The late-afternoon sun was sluicing through the overhead slats, and the three boys were revealed, together with their huge eugenics book. Hermie and Oscy were deeply into the text while Benjie paced about through the crusted chicken turds, keeping an eye on his former friends. Benjie also kept a peeled eye on the three-foot high entranceway to the coop, just in case his mother happened to be in the neighborhood. The neighborhood being an overgrown field covered with falling-down structures. No mother would be caught dead there.

"If my mother knew I took that book—" Benjie was a low moaner. "It doesn't belong to me. It doesn't even belong to my mother. It belongs to the *house!*"

There was no response from Oscy and Hermie, who simultaneously had turned both deaf and studious. Hermie hadn't really cared for the selection of the chicken coop because of his antipathy for chickens. But it had to be better than a cutlet coop so he went along with the choice. He wet his index finger, preparatory to turning the page. Oscy's grubby hand shot across the page. "Hold it."

Hermie withheld turning the page. He waited until enough time had passed for even a moron to read the page. Then he got annoyed. "Oscy…"

"Kill me, I don't read as fast as you do." Oscy took a few more precious moments to read to himself. "Mmmmm. Mmmmmmmm.

Mmmmmmmmm. Okay, turn." Hermie turned the page and they both leaned in anew in their diligent thirst for knowledge.

Benjie was a sullen sentinel and an evil prophet. "You guys get your fingerprints on those pages it's your funeral."

Oscy and Hermie kept studying, saying nothing, giving the book their undivided and enraptured attention. Full-color bits and pieces of the female anatomy floated every which way in the form of acetate overlays. It knocked Oscy out as he flipped them about. "Jesus, you can build your own girl!" He then built his own girl, leaving out the intestines. He shuffled about some more overlays and built a girl without a vagina. Then he built one with *just* a vagina. He laughed insanely, and when he got tired of the many combinations, he turned the page to a full-color photograph of a nude female capriciously spread-eagled to the camera. The caption read: "The Human Female External Genitalia." And there were slogans all over. Clitoral shaft. Clitoral hood. Clitoral glans. Labium majus. Labium minus. Urethral meatus. Vaginal outlet. Perineum. It was a whole new world, a whole universe of sex. And it was all there for them to see and get crazy over. Oscy prodded Hermie with joyful disbelief. "Hermie, you believe all this stuff?"

"It's a medical journal," said Hermie. "Why would they lie?"

Oscy's eyes remained riveted to the nude. "Who do you suppose she is?"

"I don't know. Could be anyone." Hermie was pretty riveted, too.

"I wonder what her name is."

"I don't know."

"I think she looks like a Barbara."

"Yeah. Could be a Barbara."

"Maybe Alice."

"Yeah. Maybe."

"How do they take *pictures* like this?"

"They have special cameras. High speed."

"I think I love her."

"You can't even see the face."

"You don't fuck the face, Hermie."

"You're getting carried away."

"What drugstores would develop pictures like that? If we brought in pictures like that to be developed, we'd be in reform school."

"I guess they develop 'em themselves." Hermie leaned in closer. "Yeah. I guess that's what they do."

Benjie was hovering over them. "Lemmee see."

"Bullshit, Benjie." Oscy covered the page as if Benjie were trying to copy his answers in a test. "You probably looked at this book a thousand times."

"I didn't." Then Benjie added hesitantly, "I started to—but I was made very nervous."

Oscy taunted him. "How could you be nervous? This is what it's all about."

"I know," said Benjie. "I think I should see it. Besides, it's my book."

"The hell," said Oscy. "It belongs to your house. Boy, I wonder who owns that house." He jabbed Hermie. "Maybe Barbara, eh?" Benjie was pressing in, and Oscy pushed him back. "Go away, kid. You'll foam at the mouth."

Hermie, otherwise known as King Solomon, intervened. "Let him look."

"Okay," said Oscy feeling ornery, "I'll let him look. But let's let him look at something in full bloom." Oscy thumbed ahead a few pages to a photograph of a man and woman in the act of copulation. He then shoved the book to Benjie. "Here you are, Sporty."

Benjie studied the photograph for a hundred and fifty years, not moving, not breathing, not even hearing Oscy say, "That's Barbara and her boyfriend. His name is Big Dick."

Finally, years and years later, Benjie spoke, but in a very small voice. "I don't believe it."

Oscy laughed. "They're doing it, Benjie. That's it. Full bloom. They're fuckin' to beat the band."

Again the small voice. "I don't believe it."

Oscy grew suddenly rattled. The intensity and the excitement were getting to him, reaching him where it hurt, in the pants. "Well, you'd *better* believe it, Benjie, because one day *your* time is gonna come and you better know what you're doing!" He was beginning to perspire, and there was a limit to how much his sweat shirt could absorb.

"I don't believe it," Benjie said. "It's…impossible."

Oscy was ranting. "*Why* is it impossible?"

"Because…people don't bend that way."

"People bend that way when they *have* to!"

Benjie was formulating quiet evaluations. "Especially fat people. Fat people can't do that."

"Fat people do it more than anybody!" Oscy didn't know what he was saying, but then, he didn't even know he was screaming.

"Well, I'll tell you"—Benjie was oddly calm—"my mother and father never did this." He tapped his knowledgeable finger upon the photographed page.

Oscy was ready to punch him out. "Why not?"

"Because it's stupid."

"How do you think they got *you*, Benjie—in a box of crackerjacks?"

Hermie had been silent throughout the exchange. So when he finally spoke, it was with the air of a great sage. "I hate to break the news to you, Benjie, but that's the way it's done. And fat has nothing to do with it. As a matter of fact, it might even make it easier. Who knows?"

Benjie flared up, and his eyes glowed red. Confusion reigned in his mind. "You guys better stop teasing me because—it could be dangerous. It really could."

Hermie made it a point to remain calm. In heated discussions it was important that at least one party remain calm. "You see, Benjie, if you just look at this picture, well—I guess it *does* look dumb, but if two people are in love, it's all supposed to be very…pleasant."

Benjie turned his anguish on Hermie. "How do *you* know? You've never done it!"

Hermie was magnificent in his Biblical patience. "You

see, Benjie—"

"Fuck you with that you see!"

Hermie didn't let Benjie's little outburst deter him. "You see, Benjie, it's all here in this book. In black and white." He glanced at the vivid overlays and added, "And in color. That's why people *kiss* first. It gives them a chance to get to know each other. Then, once they get to know each other, they fall in love. And once they're in love—"

Oscy grabbed the book and screamed insanely. "Foreplay! It's called foreplay! Everybody takes off their clothes, and they play foreplay! Then he does this!" He was thumbing wildly past various photographs. "And she does this! And he does this! And before you know it, they're fucking!" He slammed the book closed so hard it sounded like a trench mortar. "Now what could be simpler than *that!*" Oscy was really going. Benjie was frightened. Hermie was surprised. But Oscy was out of his fucking mind. He paced about the low-roofed chicken coop like Groucho Marx in heat. "Now then, before I saw these photos, *I* didn't think it was possible *either*. But these are photos, Benjie. Pho-to-graphs! These are not drawings! I have *seen* drawings. These are pho-to-graphs! And goddammit, we're gonna get in on it!" The tears rose in Benjie's eyes. Something else rose in Hermie's jeans. Oscy, their leader, would not fail them. Today foreplay, tomorrow the world.

12

The lights in town were kept modified in accordance with the wartime regulations on dimouts. There were two blackout drills on Packett Island that summer, but for the most part, the inhabitants needed only to concern themselves with partial blackouts. Or dimouts. Or, in some places, brownouts. Therefore, the electric sign that served as the marquee of the movie house had bare bulbs, the upper halves of which were painted black. It gave everything a kind of weird look, like walking down the street with a baseball cap over your eyes. Other than that, it was just another thing to get used to. The posters outside told the world that the feature film for the week was *Now Voyager*, starring Bette Davis and Paul Henreid and featuring Gladys Cooper and John Loder, the last of whom, rumor had it, was going hot and heavy with Hedy Lamarr. The people mingled about in front of the movie house in quiet anticipation of the eight o'clock showing. Most of the adults were women. And most of them towered above Oscy, Hermie, and Benjie, who were ogling.

Oscy was shamelessly cruising girls. Hermie seemed rather indifferent, choosing to hang back with a wait-and-see attitude. Benjie merely wished he was somewhere else, like Burma. The three of them seemed comparatively small as they pressed in and out of overhanging adults. They seemed even smaller because of the ice-cream cones they carefully juggled so as not to strike the arms, rears, and stomachs of the people up above. Three pinballs on the table of life, that's what they were. And in their own inimitable way, they were looking for a score.

Aha, Oscy had found a proper target! He nudged Hermie, who immediately experienced that same sick flicker in his stomach that he always felt when the chips were down. Oscy was pointing through a separation in the crowd at three girls who were chatting and giggling their stupid secrets to one another.

With a gesture that smacked of military significance, Oscy indicated to his cohorts that they were to wait there for him while he went out to reconnoiter. They nodded their comprehension, and Oscy moved out.

As it just so happened, the three girls were slightly taller than Oscy. They were also undoubtedly a shade older, as well as a hair more mature. But none of that bothered Oscy, and Hermie marveled at the manner in which Oscy sailed into combat. Oscy picked out the one blonde, who was also the biggest-breasted, and politely tipping his cone, he said, "Good evening."

The girls looked at one another, thinking: *The nerve of this little squirt.* But Oscy was not easily dissuaded. He concentrated his mature dialogue on the big-boobed blonde, whose name, he'd shortly learn, was Miriam. "A fine night for an evening of movies." It was apparent to Hermie that Oscy's girl would be Miriam. The other two were for him and Benjie. One was halfway pretty, with the smile of the Pietà. The other was a complete mess. Hermie silently decided on the former. Benjie knew he was destined for the latter.

Miriam, nobody's fool, was going to test the little man who stood before her. She straightened her shoulders, and as a result, her breasts almost broke Oscy's nose. "You old enough to stay up this late?" The girl who was the mess giggled goonily, revealing a set of steel braces that would have rivaled the Brooklyn Bridge. Benjie's heart jumped, over the side. The other girl, Hermie's, kept smiling prettily. She was either deaf or stupid.

Oscy, spurred on by the heroic quality of Miriam's breasts, ignored her insulting question and kept the witty conversation flowing. "I have with me two charming friends." Miriam pulled out a handkerchief and wiped Oscy's face. "You also have ice cream all over your face." Her friends tittered.

Oscy immediately reached up and grabbed her hand, pressing the handkerchief to his dilating nostrils. He inhaled deeply and feigned a swoon. "Ah, that perfume. I grow dizzy." Miriam, taken aback, pulled her hand free, and was pleased to discover that she was somehow on the defensive. Oscy sensed his advantage. "My friends and I would like you three ladies to join us of a movie."

"Dutch treat, I suppose," said Miriam, still testing him.

"Yes. But *we* will spring for the refreshments."

Miriam huddled with her two friends. Jibber-jabber, flibber-flabber. Then she scanned the crowd while addressing Oscy. "Where are they?"

Oscy's finger swung around and came to rest in the direction of Hermie and Benjie. It was like being caught by the prisonyard searchlight just as you were going over the wall. The next thing would be the machine gun. Hermie managed to force out a phony smile while giving Benjie another of the five million nudges he was to receive that summer. "Smile," said Hermie. "Look older."

Benjie smiled in an attempt to look older and more dashing, talking sideways to Hermie through his ludicrous grin... "They're walking this way."

"Don't panic."

"I'm sweating."

"Don't sweat."

Oscy and the three girls arrived. All the boys were smaller. Especially Benjie, who was digging a hole for himself in the concrete with his Keds. Oscy made the introductions like Grover Whalen. Shit, was he ever grand! "This is Hermie, and this is Benjie. And this is Miriam."

Then Miriam introduced her friends. "This is Aggie." She was the half-pretty, stupid, deaf one. "And this is Gloria." She was the Wreck of the Hesperus.

Oscy, very much in control, announced the pairings. "Hermie, you're with Aggie because you're both intellectual. Benjie, you're with Gloria because."

"I have to go home." It was Benjie using his small voice. And before anyone knew it, he had disappeared into the crowd. Gloria was destroyed at Benjie's bugging out. She buried her face in her hands. A bucket of sand would have been better.

Miriam immediately transformed herself into Louisa May Alcott. She was not pleased with Benjie's behavior. She huffed up, and Oscy unconsciously stood on his toes as her breasts puffed out like twin zeppelins. "If Gloria doesn't go, then neither do we." She neglected to say "so there."

Oscy was not going to let Benjie blow it. Suavely he screamed through the crowd. "Benjeeeeeeeee!!!!!" People turned with surprise because it could have been "Ban-zaiiiiii." One man in particular was more than slightly annoyed because it was in his armpit that Oscy had delivered his scream. But Benjie was gone, sucked up by the night, finished for the evening. Sent home by the sight of his date. *Sic gloria transit.*

Gloria, seeing that Miriam was doing *Little Women*, then decided to play *Tale of Two Cities*—Sidney Carton, to be specific. And the words came out lispingly from between her wet braces. For every syllable there was an ounce of spray. "Ith not important that I go."

Miriam, the noble fool, would not hear of it. "Don't be silly."

"I'm not being thilly. I don't want to go, I thweah."

"Well then," said proud Miriam, "*we* won't go."

Oscy gently pulled Miriam aside. He leaned in and addressed her, *sotto voce*, like Mephisto. "Go without her."

"She's our friend. We stick together." Miriam was adamant.

Gloria again bespoke her lisping unselfishness. "Really, Miriam, ith not nethethary that I thee thith movie."

Oscy had become an eerie echo. "She don't want to go."

Miriam, steadfast. "Then *we* don't want to go."

Gloria, again. "Go withouth me."

Oscy, nudging Miriam. "She wants you to go without her."

"She doesn't."

"She does."

"She does not."

"She left."

Miriam spun around and sure enough, Gloria was gone, vanished within the same cloak of night that had claimed Benjie.

Aggie remained, unsure of anything, her smile beginning to falter, starting to go out like a candle in the wind. She was afraid to look to see if Hermie had run off like Benjie. Hermie was looking into the sky, waiting for Buck Rogers.

Oscy had thoroughly secured the initiative, and he didn't care to lose it. He hooked his arm through Miriam's. "Let's get in line. The night is young, and I don't want to miss the cartoon."

Miriam looked at Aggie, hopeful of getting some hint of her opinion on the issue. Aggie shrugged. She had no suggestions. Only smiles. Miles of smiles. Miriam faced up to Oscy, determined to not sell herself cheaply. "We'll each want a fifteen-cent candy." She said that from between her twin medicine balls.

Oscy looked at Hermie, wanting no argument from him. Hermie understood the rules, so he nodded his agreement. The deal was set, and the four of them got on the line that was slowly beginning to form. Miriam and Aggie were ahead, Oscy and Hermie right behind.

Oscy muttered to Hermie. "That's the last time I ever do anything for Benjie. The absolute last time."

"He's too young. It's beyond him."

"Son of a bitch almost screwed up the whole operation. That Gloria wasn't too bad." Oscy didn't need Hermie to tell him he was wrong. "She's merely the ugliest dog in the world." Then he kind of whispered into the night so that only Hermie could hear, "Run, Benjie. Run. Don't look back." Oscy damned near broke himself up with that one.

"Oscy, I got bad news." It was Hermie reporting in from halfway between forlorn and not giving a crap.

"What?"

"You'll have to lend me a dime."

Oscy slipped Hermie a surreptitious dime, but his thoughts were elsewhere. "Catch the boobs on Miriam?"

"*You* catch 'em."

"She throws 'em, I'm gonna catch 'em. I will be ready." Oscy was ranting like that when Hermie saw something that quickly unsettled him. "Yes, sir," said Oscy, "when those boobs come flying at me, I will be there to catch 'em. When they come at me from out of the wild blue yonder, I will be there—"

Oscy suffered a lightning elbow to the liver, a very obvious danger signal. He stiffened, wondering what the hell it was that was making Hermie so nutsy. Hermie was pointing with a very nervous finger.

It was the woman. She was with a group of adults, all apparently waiting to see the movie. Her lovely hair fluttered, and her eyes caught Hermie. She squinted at him, perhaps receiving the radio transmissions from his throbbing brain. Then she smiled. That smile of smiles. And she came over to him. "Hi, Hermie."

"Hi, there." He kind of waved his palm in a semicircular motion, like a hepcat, and he immediately made a point of remembering never to do that again because it was just too damned unnatural and beneath him.

"Going to the movies?" she asked. Not a particularly clever question because why else would he be hanging around the movie house, waiting on line, with his money ready?

He countered with a sophisticated "Yeah."

And she ended it all with an esoteric "That's nice" and turned away, aiming her bright charm once again at her companions.

Oscy was knocked out. "Hermie! She really knows you!"

"Jesus, it's so embarrassing." Hermie was unhappy.

"What?"

"Her. Seeing me with…*that*." He was pointing his thumb over his shoulder at dumb Aggie, who was smiling hysterically at the night and the world. Maybe her mouth was frozen that way. Maybe she found something secretly funny. Maybe she had a snake up her ass.

Somehow the woman was there again, right next to Hermie and smiling. "Excuse me, Hermie? I was wondering. Could you come by my house Thursday afternoon?" Hermie could feel Oscy sag beside him, the idiot practically fainting. The woman continued. "I'm afraid I have some heavy things to move and"—she smiled and shrugged helplessly—"no man."

Oscy had undoubtedly been winged in the neck by a curare-dipped dart. He grew rigid, then limp; he was collapsing against Hermie at a forty-five-degree angle. Hermie had to lean back at him at another forty-five-degree angle to hold him up. They looked like a tent. "Sure," said Hermie to the woman. "Okay."

"Oh, good," she said, and then added, "Actually, I think the morning might be better. We'd have more time. Is ten o'clock all right?"

"Sure. We'll have coffee." Oscy was dead. He had died right there, leaning against the body of his dear friend, Hermie, who was saying something like, "Sure. We'll have coffee."

"You like it black, right?"

"Right."

"See you Thursday," said the sunny voice. And she was back again with her friends.

Hermie held onto Oscy, who was a zombie, one of the living dead, but still with the power of speech, and it spoke unto Hermie in a flat monotone. "You…are…in."

"Shut up, Oscy. You're dumber than Benjie." Hermie didn't want anyone to see Oscy going out of his mind like that. He held him by the arms and shook him back to life. "Come on. Snap out of it."

Oscy came around and soon the huge smile split his face into north and south. "You're in, Hermie. I can't believe it. She's mad about you. Coffee at ten. Shit!"

"Will you shut up?"

"No. I can't shut up. I'm all a-dither. Where is that Miriam? I'm gonna squeeze the crap outa her! Soon as the lights go out, I'm gonna grab onto those boobs and swing on 'em like Tarzan!" He pounded his chest and was about to emit the wild call of the ape man.

But Hermie clamped his hand over Oscy's face. "You're something. Can't you even wait until after the cartoon?"

Oscy pulled his mouth free, and again his brilliant smile escaped. "I can't wait! I can't wait!" Oscy had finally revealed his true identity.

He was the Werewolf of London, and no one was safe.

About forty paid spectators took their seats in the old wooden theater that had been erected in 1845 by Mexican prisoners of war. Oscy had carefully steered his entourage into the last row back on the left-hand side. Between the people who came to see the film and Oscy and his quartet, there were some twenty unoccupied rows. That was no-man's-land. It separated the logical-thinking people of the island from the two fledgling sex fiends and their intended quarries.

The newsreel showed Harold Ickes complaining that people were hoarding rubber. Also, Sevastopol had fallen somewhere in Russia. Also, girls were knitting argyle socks for their boyfriends who were having a hard time not flashing them around in the Army. Liberty ships were plopping into the water all over America. Frank Sinatra was causing girls to swoon in their pants. And Lew Lehr kept contending that monkeys were the cwaziest people.

Then came the cartoon in which a cat chased a mouse, which then killed the cat about a dozen times, only the cat kept coming back for more, and so the mouse accommodated it. The mouse, in sequence, hit the cat with an anvil, a boulder, a building, and an aircraft carrier. It shot the cat with an arrow, a rocket, a torpedo, and an elephant gun. It also gassed the cat, stabbed it, drowned it, and set fire to it, all to the music of the Loony Tune National Symphonic Orchestra. That was one helluva game cat.

Oscy laughed like hell all through the cartoon because he always rooted for the mouse. Hermie, on the other hand, couldn't quite sympathize with the cat because it was always the one who started the trouble. Still, he felt a certain compassion for the oafish feline because, like himself, it was only trying to make its way in an uncomprehending world.

The seating arrangement had Miriam on the extreme left. Then Oscy. Then Aggie. Then Hermie. Behind them, the back wall. To the left and right and front of them, air. All throughout the newsreel, but not during the cartoon, Oscy kept sneaking sidelong glances at Miriam's breasts which leaned forward like the Rockies turned on their side. Miriam was well aware of Oscy's covetous leer but pretended not to notice. Experience had taught her that all hands were not called on deck until somewhere well into the feature film. So she concentrated on her fifteen-cent bag of popcorn, feeling very safe, at least for the moment. An old pro was Miriam. Those boobs of hers had never missed a cartoon or a newsreel.

As for Aggie and Hermie, one might assume that they hadn't come in together. Hermie intently watched whatever was on the screen, either afraid or unwilling to take notice of the girl beside him in the sweet fluffy peasant blouse. Everything above Aggie's breasts was bare, including the upper part of both arms. Everything below the breasts was covered with a mass of gay ruffles and half sleeves. The sleeves, it should be noted, ran from above the elbow to six inches below the points of her bare shoulders. She looked like the Countess of Monte Cristo with her dress pulled down to near off so that she could be properly flogged across the back. Yet she incongruously sat munching her own popcorn, and whatever thoughts went on behind her soft gray eyes, no man was privy to.

Finally, the feature film came on, and everyone in Oscy's quartet tensed up. It was post time, and in the evening's competition were two fine fillies, one full-blooded stallion, and Hermie, who was somewhere between a scared colt and an out-and-out gelding. The horses were in the gate.

Bette Davis was put through her usual rigors. And Paul Henreid, the dummy, had gotten himself too involved with her and should have known better because he was a married man. John Loder hung around, taking up the slack. Hermie liked John Loder because he was so RAF and gentlemanly and good-mannered. But it was a lead-pipe cinch that John Loder was going to end up with nothing but the air because he was so busy behaving in a lovely manner when what he should have been doing was throwing Bette Davis onto the couch and giving her a real nice screw. Hermie knew that he had a lot of John Loder in him, probably from an uncle on his mother's side who was born in London and may well have been nobility except that he ran a grocery in the Bensonhurst section of Brooklyn for which he could have been rightfully stripped of all claims to the throne. That was some uncle. His thumb weighed twenty pounds. Hermie's mind was zigzagging. He knew it was because of the pressure. He could feel the heat of Aggie's body next to him, and from time to time he could get a whiff of her cologne, which dazed him. She was so hot that he could have slipped a raw egg into her cleavage and it would have come out of her pants poached. Something was moving off to the right. Beyond Aggie. It was Oscy.

The crazy son of a bitch was like an octopus, reaching, encircling. But Miriam had been there before and had at least as many arms as Oscy. For a moment it looked as though they both were swimming. The important thing to report was that Oscy was getting nowhere.

Hermie stayed with the film as it spun on. Bette Davis' mother died sitting in a chair, and Bette Davis, who already had enough trouble in life, decided to feel guilty. Claude Rains, a doctor or something, told her to cut it out, but if she didn't feel guilty, there'd be no movie. So she went on feeling guilty for at least another ten minutes, during which time Oscy abandoned the Australian crawl and switched over to a new approach. Stealth. Slowly he moved his left hand with which he reached across his lap and touched Miriam's left knee. Simultaneously his right arm went behind her chair and her back and over her right shoulder, thinking it hadn't been noticed. Again Miriam was equal to the occasion. The hand on the knee was flicked off. The hand over the shoulder was smartly smacked, and it withdrew. Attack repulsed.

There was no change in the Hermie/Aggie theater of operations. Hermie continued to watch the film listlessly, upset at the fool John Loder was being forced to play. More time passed. Aggie was eating a lot of popcorn. After a while Hermie tried looking over at Oscy/ Miriam but without moving his head. It would have been easier if his eyes had been in his right ear.

Oscy had Miriam's left thigh in a death grip imposed by Oscy's determined right hand. Miriam countered by employing a death grip of her own via her right hand clamped upon Oscy's forearm. Oscy's hand could move no farther up Miriam's thigh. Rommel versus

Montgomery. A standoff.

A moment later Oscy retaliated. His free hand soon applied a death grip upon the wrist of the arm that had a death grip on his forearm. But with her last free hand, her left, Miriam locked a death grip on the arm that was death-gripping her death-gripped arm. An awful lot of blood had stopped flowing what with all that death-gripping. The pair of them sat there like four crossed wires.

In the Hermie/Aggie sector Aggie, touched by the drama on the screen, moved closer to Hermie, not so much out of desire as out of compassion for all human beings in distress. Hermie noticed the imperceptible move because a current of air wiggled and her tiny shifting measured a loud 193 on his seismograph. Dizzily encouraged by Aggie's brazen demonstration of lustful desire, Hermie decided to make his move because it was do or die. The film was spinning out whether Bette Davis liked it or not, and there wasn't much time left in which Hermie could grab a squeeze. Up in the air his right arm went in its intended journey behind Aggie's back. But in the process he miscalculated the distances involved, and thus his hand smacked Aggie in the nose.

"Ooooh," she said, as if it were her fault. And she smiled imbecilically and said, "I'm sorry." Hermie smiled back, because one fights fire with fire. What the hell she was apologizing for was beyond him. But whatever madness motivated the smiling girl, the physical contact Hermie had made, the hand to the nose, had set his blood racing every which way in his confused arteries. And so he counted to thirty, an arbitrary count to be sure, and attempted the arm behind the chair bit once again, but with a little more care. Deftly his arm managed the difficult move without a hitch and came to rest on the back of her chair. Aggie made no move either to protest or to stop. Good news, Hitler. The Netherlands would not resist.

Hermie's fingers curled and moved like a tarantula. Slowly they crept up the back of the chair, coming lightly to rest on Aggie's warm shoulder where they seemed to solidify and die. And still Aggie didn't move. Norway would not resist. Hermie took a deep breath of cigarette-smoky air and coughed. After he finished coughing, he let his hand stay where it was, letting it plan its next move.

On the western front all was quiet. But new strategies were festering. The blood had stopped flowing in both of Oscy's arms, and gangrene was considering entering the scene. Faced with no other choice, Oscy gradually lessened the pressure on Miriam's thigh. Miriam then relaxed her grip on his arm. He then freed her other arm. She freed his other arm. Thus unlocked from one another, they rubbed their respective limbs and got all their blood to flowing again.

Oscy then sat back, disappointed and angry. She had proved too much for him. He'd had it. Miriam went back to watching the movie. Quickly Oscy reached across her lap with a villainous and unannounced hand, causing Miriam to damn near lurch straight out of her chair and right up to the roof. But Oscy smiled wickedly at her, merely dipping his claw into her popcorn bag where, legally, he had certain eating privileges. He also stuck his tongue out at her. Fortunately, Miriam didn't see that. Had she seen it she would have realized that she was with a nine-year-old and the combat would have ended then and there and for all time.

Thus defeated, Oscy turned to see how his ally was doing. The first thing he saw in the dim light the movie allowed, was Hermie's hand lying dead on Aggie's shoulder like a giant omelet. Fascinated, Oscy continued to watch, wondering what great strategy Hermie was employing.

Inexorably Hermie's fingers came to quivering life and groped farther, reaching down like fingers playing a slow-motion piano. Down they moved, over the sweet hot shoulder. But Aggie had entered the movie house carrying a light sweater as ammunition against the cold night air she might have to walk home through. And, unbeknown to Hermie, Aggie had let the sweater lie in her arms during the movie so that much of it lay across her bosom. So when Hermie's fingers came over the top and encountered soft cashmere, they became understandably confused. And they began to pull the sweater slowly toward their palm, bunching it up into a large and crawling woolen ball. Aggie looked down and saw her sweater leaving. She was afraid to stop for fear that she would also be stopping Hermie's timid hand and she didn't want the hand to stop. She wanted the hand to go on and on and on. Anyway, the sweater soon found itself scooped up and shoveled into Oscy's lap, which was immediately adjacent to all the hot action. Oscy accepted it without protest, figuring he'd do his bit to aid the war effort. Besides, one sleeve of the sweater was still kind of caught around Hermie's wrist, another reason why the crazy fingers were so thoroughly floundering every which way in search of flesh. And then, finally, the fingers broke free of the sweater and *were* touching flesh. *Real* flesh. Warm. Firm. Wow.

Hermie's eyes widened. He began to perspire. He fully expected to be stopped right there. Maybe even be admonished. Maybe loud enough for every head in the movie house to turn and call the cops. But no protest was forthcoming from Aggie. Denmark would not resist.

Aggie grew soft and moved a shade closer to Hermie, practically laying her head against his shoulder. And Oscy watched the whole thing, not sure what to believe.

Hermie's hand continually caressed the flesh. It stroked. It squeezed and released. Squeeze, release. Squeeze, release. Aggie's fair breast was pliant and smooth and warmly inviting. But Oscy's bemusement was based on a sad truth that Hermie's fingers had yet to learn. The flesh that they were clutching was Aggie's arm halfway between the elbow and the shoulder. In the traffic and the confusion of cashmere sweater and fluffy peasant blouse, the fingers had gotten sidetracked and had ended up a good six inches off target. Had Aggie been a 34 instead of a 22, Hermie might have realized his mistake. As it was, he had no idea he was doing a Wrong-Way Corrigan and just continued squeezing the arm.

Like the good friend he was, Oscy first gently made sure that the sweater was completely out of the way. Then he decided to correct the hand's erroneous impression of Aggie's geography. He reached over and gently took Hermie's hand, trying to redirect it onto its desired course.

But Hermie felt Oscy's paw on his hand and thought, at first, that it was Aggie telling him to cut out the grabbing. Only, when Hermie glanced down at Aggie's lap, he saw that both her hands were there, holding the popcorn bag. Therefore, it had to be somebody else's hand. But whose? Hermie leaned back and looked behind Aggie's chair at Oscy, who was mouthing something silently, trying to tell Hermie something. Trying to tell him of his latitudinal error. But Hermie grimaced at Oscy as if to say, "Cut it out or I'll kill you! Go feel Miriam!"

No friend could do more. Oscy had tried to correct the situation more in Hermie's favor, but there were none so blind as those who could not see, so Oscy just settled back and became a disbelieving observer, watching Hermie's hand as though it belonged to a great surgeon who was operating on the brain of Albert Einstein.

As for Aggie, she had been on the brink for a half hour, waiting for Hermie's hand to strike gold. She wanted it to. Hadn't she made that clear? Her small heart beat so loudly in her ears that when Bette Davis spoke it was Gene Krupa drumming.

Hermie's hand was half-crazed with passion. Squeeze, release. Squeeze, release. It was convinced that it was stroking Aggie's breast and it deigned to go even further. It slipped its way under the elastic of the sleeve like a wetback sneaking under the barbed wire into Texas. And there it began to search around in hopes of a nipple.

Oscy sat back and enjoyed the whole scene, smiling his big smile and nudging Miriam to get her attention. He got it. Miriam turned to see what new and infantile mischief Oscy was up to. He merely pointed to Hermie's hand, up to its wrist in Aggie's half sleeve, burrowing like a mole under a lawn.

Miriam got the message immediately, and her fist flew to her mouth so as to stifle the laugh that must surely escape. In that small moment, with her defenses down, Oscy sensed a chink in Miriam's considerable armor. So, with both hands opened like falcon claws, he swooped his arms about her and came up with each hand filled with a good portion of breast of Miriam. She struggled for a moment, as befit a nice middle-class girl. But then she relaxed with a deep exhalation, and Oscy fully expected to look and find that it was her boobs deflating in a protective move that nature had granted her when under attack from wolves. But her boobs remained the same size, and Oscy took his pleasure with both hands, massaging her well, his ten mercurial fingers playing a melody of love on her breastworks. Miriam emitted a few squeals of protesting delight as Oscy, a true two-fisted performer, left no breast unturned. In the process of being sexually aroused, Oscy inadvertently knocked his knee, the one next to Aggie, against Aggie's knee, the one next to him.

It caused Aggie to turn to see what was going on over there. Plenty was going on over there. From Aggie's point of view Miriam's breasts looked like two indoor baseballs trying to escape. It bothered Aggie to see so much blatant sex going on so close to her own stagnating situation. She looked down at Hermie's moronic hand, which seemed utterly content to pinch her arm purple. She was at a loss. What to do?

Hermie was in a period of extreme bafflement. His hand had groped all about but…Aggie had no nipple. He knew that nipples came in various shapes and sizes, but how could Aggie's be so small as to escape detection? He went over the area, again and again, like a boat looking for survivors, but still no nipple. He wondered if Aggie wasn't deformed. And the thought of that possibility turned him icy stiff.

Aggie could feel the hand in her sleeve freeze up. And she came to a decision. With her free hand she untied the little lace in her blouse so that her panting breasts could be more readily arrived at, even by a nincompoop, which she was beginning to suspect was what she was dealing with. Then she took that same hand, and reaching across her pulsating bosom, she placed it gently upon Hermie's errant hand. Her objective was to guide Hermie's crosseyed fingers to their true target—and be done with it.

Hermie jolted at her touch. It brought him out of ecstasy and back to reality. Thinking that Aggie was signaling that that was it for tonight, folks, he quickly pulled his hand out of her sleeve, causing the elastic therein to snap so loudly that Bette Davis' kiss sounded like a suction pump. No wonder Paul Henreid wouldn't marry her. Quickly Hermie pulled his hand all the way around Aggie's back and deposited it, still throbbing with passion, into his lap. He looked sheepishly at Aggie and smiled his apology. "Please excuse me. I was carried away."

Aggie could only smile dumbly because what else was left to her? What manner of man was this who would lavish so much attention on her arm? Was there something about arms that she had yet to discover? Were arms "erogenous zones"? They had never been so described in the hygienic sex books she had managed to sneak looks at. She turned back to the movie which made little more sense than her life. She would have some searing questions for her older sister.

Hermie, too, turned his attention back to the screen, but he felt pretty damned exalted about things. He'd had a big, long feel of a nice, warm breast. He was on his way. So what if he missed up on the nipple? There were other nipples. There was a whole world of nipples out there, if not Aggie's, then somebody else's. He smiled to himself because, even two seats away, he could see Oscy making Miriam jump. Dumb Oscy, so crass. Really crass. The trick was to be subtle and gentle. You don't treat a girl like a greased pig. You stroke her sweetly, with feeling. Dumb, stupid, crass Oscy. Hermie watched the film draw to a close, and he was very touched by the last few words. "Why ask for the moon? We already have the stars." That was great stuff. Great moviemaking. Bravo, Warner Brothers. The houselights came up. They pulled themselves together.

Outside the movie house the audience was breaking up into the small dribs and drabs they had arrived as, heading home, or for coffee, or whatever. Oscy, Hermie, Miriam, and Aggie were in their own little group, and Oscy was ready for more action. "What say we go down to the beach and watch the surf roll in?"

Miriam's boobs were as tired as Miriam was. Only they didn't yawn as Miriam did; they just hung there, still advertising. "It's very late. We have to go home."

"Oh, please," said Oscy, weirdly dramatic, "tell me that you're only teasing."

Miriam nodded no. "Maybe we'll see you on the beach tomorrow. Will you be on the beach tomorrow?"

"Well, I ain't gonna be on a *mountain*." Nobody knew what that meant. Nor did anybody really care.

"Then we'll see you. G'night. Thanks for the popcorn." With that, Miriam hooked her arm through Aggie's, and the two girls disappeared like everyone else.

Oscy and Hermie started walking home, with Oscy studying Hermie carefully in the dark. He could not fail to see the triumphant smirk on Hermie's face. But he knew something that Hermie didn't. The trick was to be very careful with such information. "How'd you make out, Hermie?"

"Pretty good."

"Yeah? What'd you do?" Oscy was magnificent.

"Held her breast."

"You *didn't!*"

"Yep."

"Jesus…whew…held her breast. Wow."

"For almost eleven minutes." Hermie was a vision of controlled delirium.

"Fantastic." Oscy was on his way to an Academy Award.

"Yeah. Eleven full minutes."

"You *timed* it. Wow."

"Yeah. Longest I ever got was eight minutes with Lila Harrison. And that was with hands on top. This was with hands underneath."

"Bare boob."

"Right."

"And you broke your record."

"By three minutes."

"What'd it feel like?"

That kind of stopped Hermie. "Whaddya mean what'd it feel like? It felt like a boob."

"Didn't feel like an *arm?*"

"An arm?"

"Yeah. You know—an arm."

"No. It felt like a boob."

"I'll bet it felt like an arm."

"Why the hell should it feel like an arm?"

"Because it was an arm." Oscy tossed it off casually and kept walking as if he had nothing on his mind.

But Hermie stopped. "What's the matter with you, Oscy? Jesus!"

Oscy stopped and faced him. He spoke as softly as he could. No sense in getting excited over a little misunderstanding. "You were feeling an arm, Hermie. I was looking. That's what I was trying to tell you. You were squeezing an arm for eleven minutes." And he added, "You schmuck."

"Listen, Oscy—" He was getting sore.

Oscy was going to finish his thought, which he did, from behind the biggest smile he ever had. "Therefore, officially, the eight-minute record with Lila Harrison still stands."

Hermie was beginning to get a message he didn't care for. "Oscy, I know you a long time and—"

"I wouldn't lie about an arm." He was certainly having a good time.

The truth was beginning to sink in cruelly. Winter was coming with it. The trees turned bare for Hermie. Life was ending, and in a whimper. "An arm. Jesus—no wonder that—I was passing out and…it was an arm."

"Yes. A very lovely arm." Lord, was Oscy enjoying himself!

"No wonder she had no nipple."

"What?"

"I couldn't find her nipple."

"You're lucky you didn't find her elbow."

Hermie grew suddenly furious. "You son of a bitch!"

"What?"

"Why didn't you just let me go on thinking it was a *boob?*"

"Shit. I thought you should know the truth. I thought you

should know so that you wouldn't make a mistake like that again."

"You just wanted to ruin my memory of it, you son of a bitch bastard!"

Oscy wasn't going to stand for that kind of language. "Fuck you! What do *I* care if you spend your whole stupid *life* squeezing arms! I just thought you oughta face reality! Especially if you're puttin' a *clock* on it and goin' for *records!*"

Hermie's attitude softened. The truth, unpleasant, unbearable, had to be faced. In his jeans he felt his penis shrivel up and fall off. It dropped to the ground. If he ever found it again, he'd discover that it had been dragged off by an ant. "God...how can I ever face her again?"

"Make sure she's wearing long sleeves." That was Oscy's idea of hilarity.

The two boys looked at each other for the longest of moments. Then they simultaneously went into their laughing banshee act. And they whacked each other hard in masculine good fellowship, with maybe Hermie whacking Oscy a little harder than he should have and Oscy allowing it because he understood human behavior.

They resumed the long journey home, laughing and whacking and generally screaming into the night such observations as: "It was an arm!" "An eleven-minute arm!" "Lila Harrison, your record is safe!" Their voices trailed in and out of opened windows, and some of the people beyond them didn't even know who Lila Harrison was.

Hermie lay in bed that night torturing himself with worry, wondering if he'd ever get things right. He told himself that all men went through adolescence and came out the better for it. But he questioned just how long *his* would last. At the rate he was going, twenty years was a fair guess. Adolescence. It had never really concerned him before, mostly because his face had never been ravaged by pimples like other guys. He figured that that was because his pimples were on his brain. He convinced himself that he didn't have to feel like a jerk on

Aggie's account because he had no intentions of ever even bumping into her accidentally again. And good riddance to her and her two elusive tits. Then he thought how lucky indeed he had been not to reach her elbow. A nipple with a funny bone in it could set a guy back quite a few years. He fell asleep with his radio on, but the magic mother must have come in and turned it off without waking him. He liked his mother in spite of the cutlet shit. He liked his father, too, and wished he could spend more time with him and get a few sex questions out of the way. He knew not to ask any sex questions of his sister because she was forever in the throes of her own woes and had a few pimples on her face that not even Max Factor could hide. No, when it came to sex, a guy was on his own, Columbus without a road map, Jack Armstrong lost in the Hall of Mirrors, Hermie in thin air, riding the wind on his own inflated scrotum, being careful lest the needle-nosed nutcracker puncture all his dreams, looking out for the full-of-shit sea gull. Here a shit. There a shit. Everywhere a shit-shit. He fell asleep eighty-three times that night. The last time in the arms of the wonderful woman whose face had been sifting in and out of all his thoughts, a lighthouse beam coming around, coming around, coming around...

13

Thursday finally came, but it had taken its own sweet time. Don't ask Hermie what happened in the time between *Now Voyager* and Thursday morning. It was a blank, a big zero. Voluntary amnesia. Or was it involuntary? Or did it matter? Who cared? He stood in the bathroom in front of the medicine chest mirror, combing his hair. In moments of stress he would think about Penny Singleton because somehow she was a trusted friend as well as a phantom lover. She was no stranger to his desires, for he had confided in her often. And many wet kisses had he bestowed on her photographic countenance, stealing the shine from more than one autographed eight-by-ten glossy. He kept making new parts in his hair, never quite satisfied that it looked correct and flattering, always wondering why nature hadn't given him the kind of hair he'd always wanted, kind of Richard Denning with a touch of William Lundigan and a smidgeon of Gilbert Roland. He had lavished so much water on his hair that he figured he might just as well take another shower, which he did because he had succeeded in getting himself all sweated up in anticipation. In the shower and out he sang "As Time Goes By" as only he could.

> You must remember this, a kiss is still a kiss;
> A guy is just a guy.
> The fundamental things apply
> As time flies by.

> Play it again, Sam.

> And when two lovers, woo, they still say I love you,
> A guy is just a guy.

The world will always welcome lovers,
As time flies by.

Sing it again, Rick.

Moonlight and love songs, jealousy and hate,
Hearts full of passion, lovers need a mate;

His sister was knocking at the door. Fuck her. Big finish.

Woman needs man and man must have a date...
On that you can rely.

The part in his hair was the best he was able to do under the circumstances, because his sister was still knocking on the door and the bathroom was so steamed up that by the time he'd wipe the mirror and put a new part in his hair, the steam would return and he couldn't see what he'd done. He stuck a finger into his sister's jar of Mum and rubbed the goo under both his arms. Then he washed his hands of the stuff, which was close to impossible, and he massaged his face with a few drops of his father's Lilac Vegetal, probably French and a good thing to have around. He opened the window to let the steam out and then wiped the mirror so he could see himself in total splendor. He stepped back and rehearsed a few poetic sayings he'd worked out for the morning. "Good morning, there, and is the coffee perking?" "And where are these heavy objects?" "Ah, no, no, no. I couldn't take any money." "Ah, laughter becomes you." That last line he knew he'd have to work hard to fit into the conversation smoothly. But it was so typically him, so much in keeping with the image he knew she had of him— He tried it again. "Laughter becomes you." As he said it, he quickly tossed his head sideways in an effort to catch a view of his profile before it knew he was looking. He failed. He'd probably go through life not knowing what he looked like from the side. He left the bathroom before his sister began screaming for help from her mother to get him out. Before leaving, he had to make certain he wouldn't have to go back for three hours, because that's how long his sister would be in there. Sometimes that could be hard on his bladder. Once even, he had to take a pee in the kitchen sink, but no one was the wiser.

He dressed but not in his best clothes because that would be too obvious. Still, they were clean clothes, and logically, he selected a brown checked shirt in case he spilled the coffee again. He wore sneakers rather than go barefoot as most of the islanders did. It seemed more mature. Besides, who needed a splinter on the road to love? He wore short pants for mobility and dexterity. They were clean and freshly ironed by his mother, who ironed everything she found lying around the house. Once she ironed his oilcloth raincoat and that was the end of that. But he figured there was a method to her stupidity. He had that raincoat for six years, and it was too small, but his father said there was no budget for a new raincoat. By ironing his raincoat, she did away with it very neatly in a shower of smelly steam. She told his father it was an accident, but he seemed to know better, and he kissed her, and Hermie got a new coat. The great thing about his mother was she was so obvious about the way she went about fooling people that she always got away with it.

He walked down the stairs on tiptoe, carefully avoiding the squeaky stair because he didn't want to get into a political discussion with his mother over where he was going and had he eaten? And he was beautifully careful with the screen door. He was so quiet he could hear the sky.

"Hermie? Is that you?"

"No!"

"Where are you going?"

"To London to see the queen!"

"Be back by noon. Your Uncle Charlie is coming for lunch."

"Bully!" He was by then out of earshot and away from the mundane, shedding his mother's words even before they reached him.

The clear day unfolded before him like pages in a pop-up book. Each house he passed snapped to all freshly painted and pretty. Judy Garland was singing "Over the Rainbow," accompanied by Elmo Tanner, the blind whistler who saw only the beautiful things of life because that's the way it was with blind people if one cared to believe that crap. The lilting harmonica lured him the rest of the way to her house, which stood in the distance on a rim of sand, looking like Camelot. He continued to rehearse as he walked. "The coffee is exquisite, exquisite." "Ah, laughter becomes you." "Nothing is too heavy when love is in the air." "Your voice is like a soft cloud of pink cotton." "Laughter certainly does become you."

Then he was at the house and stopped being silly. He removed the metal hand mirror from his back pocket. It had a hole in it at the top so you could hang it on a nail. But there was no time for that, nor was there a nail or a tree. He held the mirror to his face to check out his appearance and was immediately confronted by nine thousand of his own fingerprints. He wiped the mirror on his pants and looked again. Looking back was an eight-year-old boy with a cowlick on the back of his head like the business end of a worn-down broom. He jammed the mirror back into his pocket and pretended he never looked. It was important to his life that he look mature and handsome, and the mirror hadn't helped. He walked the couple of steps to the porch, opened the screen door, and walked farther. He strongly considered running away because that was, by far, much smarter than going ahead and showing up like a dumb kid. The issue was very much in doubt when her voice came gliding out of every crack in the house. It came as a song of love. "Is that you, Hermie?"

"It is I." He struggled with the thought of bad grammar at a time like that, wondering if it shouldn't have been "me" and not "I." Pronouns had never been his strong point. Especially when they were proper pronouns or possessives or other things along those similar lines.

"Come in. The door's open."

The door was indeed open. She hadn't lied. Fortified by that knowledge, Hermie went in. Again, there was the photograph of the handsome soldier, smiling at Hermie. Or was he laughing? Her voice fluttered out on a butterfly's vapor trail. "I'll be with you in a minute. Why don't you sit down?"

"I certainly will." That sounded wrong. "Shall," he then said. That seemed worse. So he just sat down on the sofa and tried not to sweat, remembering his words to Benjie on that very same subject a hundred years ago at the movie house. Still, he could smell the goddamn Mum coming out of every armpit, and he knew he was using up his protection rapidly. Again he considered running. Maybe, if she hadn't really seen him, she might think it was some other boy who'd run away. And the next time he'd see her on the beach he'd explain to her that his division had been called up. But hadn't she asked, "Is that you, Hermie?" And hadn't he said, "It is I"? And hadn't that been where all the trouble started in the first place? A magnet pulled him to his feet because there was a sudden music in the room.

She was standing there. No, she was walking toward him. No, she was floating, carrying a tray with coffeepot and cups, entering the room like Ali Baba on the magic carpet. He had to blink his eyes to get her feet down to the floor where they belonged and the Mum under his arms was so hot that it sent up sputters of steam through which he could barely make out her incredible face. He was on fire, a five-alarmer. Somebody save the children.

"I think it's cooler than last time." She was, of course, referring to the coffee.

"I hear it's going to rain." He, of course, was referring to the weather.

She dropped it mercifully and set the tray down gently. "Yes," she said. It was the way people said "yes" when they had no idea what you were talking about. "Please sit down." It occurred to him that he had already done that, but if it would make her happy— He sat down again. On his metal mirror. He could feel it bend. If it had snapped, he could have applied for a Purple Heart owing to heavy shrapnel in the ass while carrying out a dangerous assignment. He could tell that the mirror hadn't broken. It was only severely bent. He sat an inch higher than he ever had sat before. She was talking again. "Did you enjoy the film the other night?"

"Yes." Now *he* was doing it. And that was rude. So he went a little further, just to break the ice. "I like John Loder."

"Oh? Which one was John Loder?"

"The other one."

"Oh." That was just like her "yes."

"John Loder's always the other one. Unless when it's Ralph Bellamy. When it's Ralph Bellamy…it's not John Loder." He was being brilliant again. "Anyway, that's how it works. If it isn't one, it's the other. Or else it's Herbert Marshall, who you can tell by his limp. He has a wooden leg. Not many people know that. It's not common knowledge." He knew that she had every right to assume that he was insane. He watched her pour the coffee and waited for her to tell him to get the hell out of her house because he was nuttier than a fucking fruitcake.

"I thought your date was very attractive." She sat down and crossed her legs, and he went out of his mind at the sight of them.

"She was all right." He didn't really care to talk about Aggie when those knees were pointed at his, from not five inches away and gaining.

"Is she a steady girlfriend?"

"Not of mine."

"Oh. Just casual."

"Yes." He wanted to get off the subject of Aggie, once and for all and forever. "Anyway, I don't expect I'll be seeing her again." *Finis*.

"Did you have a fight?" She just wouldn't put it down.

"She doesn't talk. How can we fight?"

"You don't mean she's a…mute?"

"I don't know." And he didn't. He hadn't really heard her speak at all. He began to feel revulsed. He'd been feeling up a deaf mute. No wonder she had no nipple. And what else was wrong with her that he couldn't even begin to guess at?

"Oh," she said. So far she had said two "ohs" and one "yes," and they were all indications that she didn't know what to make of him.

Hermie figured it was time to become charming. He sipped the coffee and let her see that he was thinking about it, gauging the temperature like some kind of fucking expert. "Ummmmm," he said. "The coffee is exquisite."

That got her. She smiled at his poetic grasp of language. "Why, thank you."

"How long have you had it?"

"Actually, I just made it."

"Well, I'll try not to drink too much and you can have it tomorrow."

"That's very thoughtful of you, but—"

"I wouldn't think of it." He hadn't put any sugar or any cream in his coffee, but he still stirred it as though hoping to churn it into butter.

She smiled and sipped her coffee like the Queen of England. And she began to kind of kick her top leg rhythmically. Hermie had heard that women could cross their legs like that, and by moving them rhythmically, they could masturbate. That's why he got a little panicky. If she was masturbating, it was a little too close for comfort. The Mum under his arms was bubbling like a witch's brew. She uncrossed her knees and then put the other one on top. Fantastic. She could masturbate with either foot. Ambidextrous. Of course, she'd pretend she wasn't doing it and would go right on talking as though nothing were happening. "The other boy with you, Hermie—was he a friend?"

For a moment he thought it was her knee that was talking, and he talked back at it. "Yes."

She saw him looking at her knee and grew a bit uneasy and uncrossed her legs and tucked them both modestly beneath her skirt. She was giving her thing a little rest and a little air. If she had had an orgasm, she could sure keep it a secret. "Is he a good friend? Hermie? Hermie?" She even went so far as to snap her fingers under his nose to bring him around.

He looked up because the voice was coming from her mouth. She was some kind of a goddamned ventriloquist. Hermie's own voice sounded to him as though it were coming from around a corner. He looked, but there was no one there. It had been nothing but his own voice saying, "Yes. He's a military acquaintance."

"Ahhh." She was impressed. She liked fighting men. Obviously.

Why else Pete's photograph?

"Yes, he'll be going into the Marines soon. His brother is a full colonel in combat. In the Pacific." Lies, lies.

"Oh, my."

"He comes from a whole family of fighting men." Dentists.

"The two of you seem to have a great deal in common."

"I think so." He was watching how she sipped her coffee. Her lips were moist and had to part to let the coffee in. The way her lips parted and let the coffee in and then pursed up and closed when she had as much as she could take—it was one of the sexiest sights he'd ever seen. Oh, that he were a cup between those lips, and they'd make love in little sips. A poem, by Hermie. Jesus Christ and Lord love a duck.

"I hope it wasn't inconvenient for you to have to come by like this."

"It's okay." I'll come by and heave a sigh, and touch your thigh, and then I'll die. Another poem, same guy. If she didn't stop sucking on that coffee cup, there was no telling how long he could last without grabbing her and screwing her the way John Loder should have screwed Miriam Hopkins. Miriam Hopkins?

She was standing. It made her knees disappear and not a moment too soon. She'd never know how close she'd just come to being forcefully entered, by a guest. She must have thought he was a bit of an oddball because suddenly she was pushing things along. "Hermie, I don't think it'll take too much of your time."

"It's okay. My Uncle Charlie is coming for lunch." That made about as much sense as anything else he'd said so far.

She was walking into the other room, and he had somehow risen and was following her behind. It wigwagged, and music came out of it. Harmonicas and chorales and a couple fiddles. He'd have followed that behind anywhere. Waterloo. Brazil. As it was, he followed it into her bedroom. "It's mostly those boxes." The behind talked. Then it spun away, and her face finished up. "Clothing. They have to go up in the attic." The arm was pointing to a square panel that was set flush into the ceiling.

"And where are these heavy objects?" He was dazed. The two of them were standing less than a foot from her bed, a bed so sweetly covered with a sprightly patterned spread. A fair wind from Java and they'd be on it together. Come in, Java. Do you read me, Java? She seemed very confused, perhaps at something he just said. And she pointed to the ten corrugated cardboard boxes that not even a blind man could miss. "They're right there. Hermie? Are you all right?"

"Ah, I see. Here they are." He was pulling himself together because no one else would.

She smiled and tossed her hair, and a beautiful pink ear peeked out at him. He could have bitten it. "But I'm being very bad, Hermie. Perhaps you'd like to finish your coffee."

"I had enough. You can pour the rest back." The ear was gone, back into the hair. It was playing hide-and-seek with his heart.

"Well—" but she knew not to argue the point. There was a wooden ladder against the wall, and she moved to get it in those long willowy strides of hers. Like a tiger. He wanted to throw himself into the cage and be devoured by her. But he knew that it was out of the question.

"Allow me," he said. And he grabbed the ladder, practically knocking her aside and onto the bed, which wasn't such a bad idea if he had a little more guts. Quickly, like a seasoned ladder opener, he opened the ladder and set it up exactly below the panel in the ceiling.

"How would you like to do it?"

Hermie shook off the double meaning of the question because, in his heart of hearts, he knew that only one meaning had been intended, so why ruin a beautiful friendship? He kept examining the ceiling while saying "Mmmmmmmmmmmm" until his senses returned. Then he climbed the ladder until his head barely touched the panel. He reached up and pressed up on the panel, and it lifted easily and remained balanced in the air on his ten fingers. He flipped it slightly, sliding it to the side and out of the way. Then he climbed a few more rungs and peered over the lip of the opening.

"What's up there?" she called from below.

"Dust."

"May I see?"

"Sure." Hermie climbed down, and she climbed up. In the process she automatically extended her hand to him so that he could support her in her ascent. It was the first time they touched. Her delicate hand went into his, and where he once had knuckles, he now had bells. Her hand was smaller than his, fitting in so easily that there was still room for the other. Surely she, too, had noticed how large a palm he had. Surely she realized that this was no child in the bedroom with her. Not with a palm as big as that. That was some big palm. As far as she knew, it could just as easily have been the palm of Mel Ott or some other big-palmed man. Hermie felt hugely good about the whole thing as he watched her climbing the ladder. Her shapely legs on tiptoe, like curled carvings, tensed just enough to reveal the finely defined calf muscles. More than that, from his fortuitous angle, Hermie could see more. Much, much more. He could see thighs. He had seen her thighs on the beach but never from such a due south vantage point. To really enjoy a swell pair of thighs, a fella had to get into a position where he could look straight up the length of them. It was the angle that counted, and he had an angle on her thighs that could not be improved upon by an earthworm with a telescope. He looked farther and harder, beyond the fabulous thighs. Higher. And he saw—panties. Probably rayon because of the war, but panties just the same. Pink panties with some kind of embroidered design that could drive cryptographers crazy with their hidden meanings. And the buttocks within the panties— The buttocks, Oscy. The ass! That, too, was marvelously tensed. There was never a better, more captivating couple of tensed buttocks in all history. It was a time for Hermie's X-ray vision. He sent up the first few introductory beams, just to see how things were. And damned if the panties didn't begin to melt away, away, away down South in the land of rayon.

"Oh, there's lots of room up here. We should have no trouble."

Hermie straightened up. It was as though she could see what he was up to. Funny place for an eye, eh, Lestrade? Yes, Holmes. His X-ray vision immediately cut out, the plug having been yanked from the socket by her voice. And the panties reappeared on the buttocks above the thighs, and Hermie felt immediately guilty for having indulged in such dirty thoughts about someone he had such high regard for, even though he'd gladly have given his life to climb the ladder behind her and screw her right there, eight feet above the earth. He gazed at the tan limbs so close at hand, barely inches away from his troubled mind, and a wave of loving sentiment swept over him, and he gave expression to his thoughts in a tender whisper to the dear legs. "Laughter becomes you." The legs didn't answer. Perhaps they were too moved to speak.

The woman came down, Venus descending, ass first, and again she placed her hand into his to steady her. She could easily have said, "My, what a big palm." Instead she said, "I guess the best thing would be for me to hand the boxes up to you one at a time, don't you think? Hermie? Hermie?"

"Yes? Yes?" Jack Benny again.

"I'll hand the boxes to you, okay?"

"Okay." He climbed the ladder until he was waist up in the attic, his heart over the edge where, if it burst, she wouldn't be splattered. His hands reached down even though he couldn't see. And soon there was a cardboard box in it. It wasn't heavy. He lifted the box the rest of the way and set it down on the attic floor, careful not to let it make any noise lest she think it was too heavy for him.

As the box came up to him, her voice was in it. "How you doing?"

"Fine." He shoved the box neatly across the attic floor. It was all a simple endeavor, and the boxes kept coming up at him one at a time, sometimes speaking, other times silent. But up there in the attic as he was, an image of her came to him that was both terrifying and awe-inspiring. And the thought almost knocked him, yea verily, from the ladder. The woman was below, out of sight. No one could see what she was doing. No one. She was on her own. There'd have been no sense in her trying to look up Hermie's pants because all she'd have seen was maybe a knee or two. So, being logical, she didn't waste any time on that kind of nonsense. Instead, consumed with a bestial passion and covered with a lid of secrecy, she flittingly caressed his leg, the left one because it was closer to the heart and therefore more sensitive. She caressed it, rubbed it, fluttered her gorgeous lips along the length of it, and, shit-oh-dear, even nipped at it. Even the Band-Aid on that leg came in for a few love bites. Hermie trembled at the thought of her touch, her lips, her mouth, her teeth—sharp, nipping, biting, licking.

"Hermie? You all right?" The voice drifted up at him, concerned, alerted. It also came as a dreadful interruption because he could have sworn she was sucking on his Band-Aid. "Hermie, your legs are trembling. Hermie?"

He snapped out of it. The fantasy left, and the love nipping ceased. And he was just another guy on a ladder with a hard-on, nothing more. His voice came out, hoarse and ragged. "I think the ladder isn't too good."

"Should I hold it?"

She was doing it again. Double meanings. Whatever could she mean? Was he being dense not to follow up? The fantasy returned as swiftly as it had left. This time settling in with greater fervor, more emotion, harder holding. Her hand was stroking his left thigh. He could feel her move in, her warm breath spreading kisses every which way. Should she hold it? He framed his answer, one which would give her every opportunity either to come through or to bug out. "If you like."

If she liked? Lord, did she like. The three buttons on his fly snapped open like the NBC chimes. "There," she said. "I'm holding it. How is it now?"

"Very nice." Very nice? Fantastic would have been more like it. He felt himself all swollen like that bull he had once seen on that farm. Her small fingers couldn't really get around on it. He could envision the expression of surprised pleasure on her face. She wasn't dealing with just a kid. She could do chin-ups on that thing. She could hit a ball out of Ebbets Field and onto Bedford Avenue with it, hold off the Philistines with it, span the Hudson with it, lift the *Normandie*, dig up the Pyramids. She could—

"Should I hold it tighter?" Should she hold it tighter? Should she hold it with two hands would have been a better question. It was taking on such monstrous proportions that if he suddenly turned to either side, he'd have brained her with it. The size of the palm is indicative of the size of the penis. Mathematics, baby. You're learning.

"Hermie? You're really trembling. Hermie?" He didn't care to hear that. He wanted silence. No talking in the balcony. Let's have no more gabbing, folks.

"Hermie, what's wrong?" What's wrong was that she was talking and ruining everything. That's what was wrong.

"Hermie?" Shrink, shrink. Farewell, King Kong. Hello, Eddie Arcaro.

"Hermie, please answer me." The dead don't talk, lady. Save your breath.

"Come down, Hermie. All the boxes are up there, so you can come down. Hermie?" I'm coming down, I'm coming down. Don't nag me. I'm coming down.

He came down, first sliding the panel back into place. He noticed how white her knuckles were from trying to steady the ladder for so long. He probably had been up in that attic for five hours, give or take a year. If he hadn't so dramatically lost his erection, he'd still be up there, unable to squeeze down out of the attic.

She was looking at him very strangely. "Hermie, what was the matter? I thought you were going to fall off."

"I don't think your ladder's very good." A poor workman blames his tools.

"But I was holding it so steadily. And still your legs were shaking."

"Maybe it was my old malaria kicking up." Everything that goes up has to come down.

"What?"

"I said I think those boxes'll be all right." Enough with the fucking proverbs.

She stared at him for another moment, fixing him with those two orbs, fashioned in heaven, to look upon fools. Then she let the subject drop and found her purse. "I think, this time, you must let me pay you."

"I wouldn't think of it."

Just the same she pressed a dollar bill into his pitifully small palm. "I could never have gotten those boxes up there by myself."

He took the dollar bill, and seeing no table nearby, he simply laid it on the bed. No sooner had he done that than he realized that was the way in which a man treated a whore. You just put on the bed whatever you care to pay, and if she doesn't argue, it's a deal and you bang her. But in this case—what an insult! One dollar. One lousy dollar! At least if he had a checking account— He wanted to put his heart alongside the dollar, but it would have been inconvenient.

From the look on her face she was not exactly acquainted with the legend of the money on the bed. She smiled. "Please, Hermie. I have no other way of paying you."

He could think of a couple ways but the words came out of him so gentle and so candid. "It's okay. I like you."

"That's very sweet, Hermie. I like you, too."

"I mean—I don't like many people." If the conversation continued along those lines, Hermie would shortly be proposing marriage. Actually, as he thought about it, how much older than himself could she be? Maybe six, maybe seven years. He could quit school, work in a factory until he was old enough, and then get his commission in the Army. She'd like an officer. Pete was only a sergeant. Better still, in the *Navy* a fighter pilot could be made a full commander before he was even twenty-three years old. If the war lasted much longer, he could come out an admiral and an ace. Then they could pick up the threads of their life where they had left off. A small house near the Academy. With a white picket fence and a cannon on the lawn, and stacked cannonballs, and an American flag. He could teach flying to younger lads. Or he could barnstorm the country, flying under bridges and through tunnels in his jaunty Lindbergh flying cap. He could see her moving in closer. He could smell her, feel her. The sweet plum-ripe lips were puckered and moving in. He steeled himself and got his own lips ready for the mooring. But at the last possible second, she pulled out of her dive and the kiss struck him on the forehead so directly between his eyes that he went temporarily cockeyed and into a deadly spin. But the softness of her lips, the warm wetness of them on his forehead, pulled him out of the spin because he wanted to live, he had so *much* to live for. How he got outside and on the beach would forever be a mystery to him.

He must have left her house via the fourteen stairs to the beach because that's where he was walking, alone, trying to piece it all together so that it might make some sense. He had no idea how long he had been walking like that, glorying in the music of her and in the smell of her, when he saw the shadow coming at him— from out of the sun. The gull. Its silhouette moved swiftly, its wings spread in a devastating gliding dive. He sidestepped, but the blast still caught him, smack on his shirtfront, actually knocking him a few steps back. Four inches farther to the right and the shit would have pierced his heart. Instead, it just broke apart across his chest, a load of gull turd that splattered in the pattern of the filthy rising sun of Japan. It took no more than a few seconds. Then the bird was gone, squawking away in winged triumph. Hermie shook his fist at it. "You fuckin' dumb bird!" But the damage had been done. There was no sense in crying over spilled shit. He rubbed sand on the glob, but it just made things worse, caking up like cement. Whatever that bird had been eating, if it put its mind to it, it could shit a superhighway. What annoyed Hermie more than anything else was that he had always heard that birds couldn't shit in flight, that they had to land first. It was another legend of his youth shot to hell. Lay it alongside Santa Claus and the Easter rabbit. Hermie wondered if it all wasn't part of some kind of weird reincarnation. Maybe it was Johnny Stella come back to get him. Johnny Stella, who had challenged him to a three o'clock fight in the schoolyard, only to suffer a fantastic lucky punch from Hermie that knocked out two of his best teeth. Johnny Stella, who later got killed by a bus while riding his bike across Flatbush Avenue where it intercepted Church. Hermie yelled at the empty sky, for the gull was long since gone. "I

know who you are, Johnny Stella! Try it again, boy, and you'll wish...
you came back as Joe Louis! Ya dumb shit!"

Hermie bumped into Oscy, who looked into the sky at the
nothingness that Hermie had been screaming at. Oscy had a pair
of binoculars around his neck that he lifted and trained on the sky,
which he scoured like a lookout. Seeing nothing, Oscy dropped the
glasses and smiled at Hermie. "You yelling at clouds again, Hermie?"
Benjie was standing alongside Oscy and was also smiling.

Hermie had no patience for the pair of them. "Yeah, I always
yell at clouds. It wards off evil." He tried to walk away. Who needed
their aggravation? Hadn't his heart been hurt enough? Once by love.
Once by shit.

But Oscy was blocking his way, a very dangerous undertaking
in view of Hermie's taut and confused emotional state. "You were
in there a long time, Hermie."

Benjie looked at his Ingersoll. "Twenty minutes." Then he
smiled at Hermie's shirt. "What'd she do—shit on you?"

Hermie was so furious that it didn't matter that he could squash
Benjie's small brain in the huge palm of one of his hands. "Benjie,
you're on borrowed time." Then, without warning, Hermie felt a
long wave of sudden nausea. He got dizzy and had to sit down. His
head was furry, crazy, sick. It was either love or cholera, preferably
the latter, which was curable.

Oscy knelt beside him, very concerned. "Hermie? You sick?"

"I don't know."

"Don't you feel good?" Oscy was nervous. He never saw
Hermie like that before.

Hermie rubbed his temples. "I think I'm nauseous."

"Maybe you better sit down."

Hermie looked up, pissed off. "I *am* sitting down! Jesus
Christ, Oscy!"

Oscy was baffled. "Then maybe you oughta *lie* down."

"Maybe *you* oughta shut *up*." Hermie drew up his knees. That's
what you were supposed to do. Draw up your knees and put your
head down, and magically, the nausea goes away. Of course, should

you *puke* in that position, you're going to be the most unpopular guy in the locker room for a week. He examined his left leg. That strange tingling. "I think— Oscy? I think she bit my leg. See any lipstick down there? My eyesight is failing."

Oscy knelt and examined the suspicious limb. "Just a couple scabs."

Hermie tapped one of the scabs. "I don't remember this one."

Oscy was very definite. "No. You had that one yesterday. And you had that Band-Aid, too. I'm certain."

"How come you're so sure?"

"Because I notice things."

"Scabs and Band-Aids?"

"Yeah. I'm weird, okay?"

"Well—don't you see any new scabs? Or fresh Band-Aids? Take your time."

Oscy examined the leg much more closely, fingering the scab, lifting the edge of it. "No. I don't think they scab up so fast. And this Band-Aid—it's a couple days old."

"How can you tell?"

"Because there's a date stamped on it! Fuck you, Hermie! What the hell am I doing examining your scabs? I'm no intern!"

Hermie's nausea was fading; but he was still a bit light-headed, and his knee still tingled. "Jesus—do you think I have infantile paralysis?"

Oscy was ominous. "Does your neck hurt?"

"My neck? No."

"Then you don't have it. Infantile paralysis starts with a crick in the neck."

"Then what does it mean if your leg tingles?"

"*Adult* paralysis." That was Benjie's invaluable opinion.

Oscy became deadly serious. One of the best ways to become deadly serious in that crowd was to ignore Benjie, which he did. "Try to remember what happened, Hermie? From the beginning." It was Oscy of Scotland Yard. Bulldog Oscy.

"Well," said Hermie, trying to reconstruct it in sequence, "the way it was—we had coffee."

"When did she shit on your shirt?" That was Benjie. He said it and jumped backward, making certain he was out of Hermie's punching range. But he hadn't counted on Oscy, who knocked him on his ass.

"Benjie, we're trying to get to the bottom of this, so shut up."

"Fuck you, Oscy." Benjie stayed where he had fallen. It was not only safer but more comfortable. Also, he could time how long he'd lie there.

Oscy refocused on Hermie. "Go on, Hermie. What else?"

"Well, after the coffee, I put the boxes in the attic, and while I was on the ladder—" Time froze right there as Hermie ran the action through his mind again. The way she opened his pants and played with his prong. The ecstasy and the mad passion of it all. Then, considering who his audience was, he decided to skip all that. "And when I came down—she kissed me." Of that much he was certain. Of the rest, he had no concrete proof. It wouldn't stand up in court. Only in his pants.

"Kissed you?" Oscy's mouth hinged open like a wounded drawbridge.

"Yeah. Here." Hermie pointed between his eyes. "See any lipstick?"

Oscy leaned in, taking Hermie's head in both hands and turning it toward the sun. Another two inches of turn and Oscy could have taken the head home with him as a paperweight. His eyes widened as he looked at the blotch of smudged red between Hermie's eyes. It was unmistakably—"Lipstick." He sniffed at the crimson patch. "Definitely lipstick. Probably strawberry or something in the red family."

Hermie yanked his head free of Oscy's viselike grip. "I like *her* kissing me, Oscy. Not *you!*"

Benjie was leaning in, giving his own personal estimation of the forehead under discussion. "It's a mosquito bite. No—it's blood. She's a fuckin' vampire." He jumped backward again. Out of reach of Hermie *and* Oscy. He smiled. You don't catch Pearl Harbor napping twice.

Oscy stood above Hermie and never looked so pleased. "Hermie, I think you struck gold. I really do."

Hermie wasn't really listening. He was musing at his leg again. "That really looks like a fresh Band-Aid. I'm sure she changed my Band-Aid. Strange." The Band-Aid seemed to emanate a neon glow. It was alive with love. Or with germs with flashlights.

Oscy addressed Benjie in a very official manner. "Benjie—we'll need that book again."

Benjie began to back away slowly, the kind of move that invariably preceded his running for his life. "Yeah? Well, you can just whistle. You drooled all over it the last time. I don't wanna get blamed for any warped pages."

Oscy advanced at the same rate that Benjie retreated. "My field glasses for your dirty book. You'll have a wonderful time identifying enemy aircraft. You can be a hero."

Benjie saw the distance between them narrowing, and his tone became proportionately conciliatory. "Come on, Oscy. Nothing flies over this island but birds."

"Maybe they're enemy birds."

"No go."

No contest. Oscy not only caught Benjie, but in one swift motion, he had the leather strap over Benjie's neck and was slowly twisting it like a tourniquet. "It's a fair swap. What's more, you can have the glasses for *two* days, and I only need the book for one lousy afternoon. What's more, if you don't like my offer, I'm gonna break your nose. So whaddya say?" Benjie was in no condition to argue. He was barely in position even to speak, as his face was turning bloody purple and his eyes were bulging like a bullfrog's. Oscy relaxed the tourniquet slightly, and Benjie fell gasping to his knees, where Oscy proceeded to knight him. "In the name of the United States of America, I award you these field glasses. Good hunting."

"Fuck you, Oscy." It wasn't even a gasp. It was a whisper, under a rock, in the next county.

Oscy smiled and tugged on the strap, and Benjie got to his

feet like a dog tagging on a leash. "Come on, Hermie," Oscy called. "Benjie's been nice enough to offer us his filthy book."

"Fuck you, Oscy—yaaaaaaagh."

Hermie got to his feet and followed his two friends up the beach. But even as he walked, he kept looking down at the Band-Aid which kept glowing. It just didn't look like the kind of Band-Aid he normally used. It had to be a different one, an off brand.

"Fuck you, Oscy." It was far off, away from Hermie. But it was like a radio beam. Blindfolded, he could follow his friends up the beach. It was sixty-three "Fuck you, Oscy's" to Benjie's house.

14

They sat in the grassy-clumped yard behind Benjie's bungalow, just Hermie and Oscy, like expectant fathers. Oscy paced about very anxiously. Hermie just let it all roll off him, pleased that his fate was no longer in his own hands. It was at times like that in Hermie's life that Oscy always proved so helpful. Oscy was a great decision maker. It was Oscy who had determined that they could leap the seven feet that separated the roofs of the two apartment buildings. It was Oscy who had said that they could run blindly out of Jaeger's icy alley and safely belly whop between the moving front and back wheels of the moving Macy's delivery truck. And it was Oscy who had said that Hermie could take Johnny Stella if he'd just run out and throw the first punch for psychological purposes. Hermie looked up into the afternoon sky to see if that same Johnny Stella was still hovering around. He wasn't. Probably off somewhere, eating wet cement for his next shit. Hermie touched his shirtfront. It had hardened to the consistency of linoleum and had wrinkled into a petrified waffle. If his mother couldn't iron out those wrinkles, Hermie could never wear that shirt again except to accordion player rallies. Oscy ceased his pacing. Benjie's back door was opening. Oh...so...slow.

Benjie came out, accomplishing the deed with superhuman stealth. For as everyone knew, beyond every such door there was a mother. Benjie had something with him. An object. It was wrapped within the folds of a green, Indian-patterned bathrobe. And it was tied into knots via the fringed bathrobe sash. Oscy grabbed the bundle and set it onto the ground. He had a difficult time untying the sash because Benjie had utilized every knot he'd learned in Cub Scouts. "Why'd the hell you put in so many knots, you moron!"

"I wanted it secure. I don't know." Benjie was very concerned with what might be coming out the door at him. "Can you hurry up?"

"No, I can't hurry up, you dope. Thanks to you, we might be here all day." Oscy puzzled over the knots, green velvet spaghetti, still alive.

"If my mother—"

"Hermie, do you have a knife?"

Benjie stiffened. "You cut my sash, Oscy, and I call the cops for burglary. That sash is all I have to keep my bathrobe closed."

"What're you hiding, your belly button?" Oscy worked feverishly to unravel the Gordian knots.

"Fuck you, Oscy."

"Oh, shut up." Oscy finally solved the knots and unfolded the robe. Inside was the eugenics book. Oscy removed his sweat shirt and smoothed it out on the grass. The exchange was speedy. The book was moved from bathrobe to sweat shirt within the blink of a bug's eye. Quickly Oscy knotted his sweat shirt's sleeves about the book. Then he picked up the whole bundle and motioned for Hermie to follow him.

Hermie trailed after Oscy, turning only once to look at Benjie, who was sitting on the top step of his back porch, training Oscy's binoculars on them. Hermie then perceived an image of Benjie that he'd take with him to the grave. It was of Benjie, at dawn. On the beach. Searching the skies for enemy birds. And as each bird flew over, Benjie would make a note of it on his pad. "5:15 a.m. A bird... 5:27 a.m. Another bird... 5:41 a.m. Another bird... 5:47 a.m. Another fucking bird... 5:48 a.m. Fuck you, Oscy."

Hermie followed Oscy along the path, watching how delicately Oscy carried the sweat shirt, as though it contained the head of John the Baptist. It had been decided that the abandoned chicken coop was not suitable for the work that had to be done. It was too public a place. Instead, they decided on Hermie's room. The deciding had been decided upon by Oscy. Instinctively Hermie didn't care to do in his room whatever Oscy had in mind. But Oscy had decided that since Hermie stood to be the beneficiary of whatever it was that was going to happen, Hermie also had to assume the greatest risk of discovery.

When they reached the house, Hermie went first because he knew the trail and was best acquainted with the dangers therein. He chose the back door which, like every door on the island, was a squeaky screen door. Yet Hermie manifested a certain mastery over that back door. For one thing, he oiled it periodically to help keep it quiet. The back door, then, was always his exit whenever there were people on the front porch he didn't care to converse with, like his family.

Anyway, with trepidation and on little cat feet, Hermie passed beyond the screen door with Oscy and John the Baptist silently behind. The back flight of stairs had next to be navigated. Hermie went first, silently pointing out to Oscy the one squeaky stair. They passed over it in practiced Cheyenne silence. At the landing they made the turn and carefully trod toward Hermie's room. Slowly, Hermie turned the knob, so well oiled, like the back screen door, that some of the oil trickled into his palm. No matter. No damage. He swung the door open. Silence. Smoothness. No sweat. Much success. Bravo.

"I just cleaned."

Oscy and Hermie exchanged a look. It was the voice of the phantom mother. She was somewhere in the house. In a light bulb somewhere. Or in a picture on a wall. Or in the paint. She of the thousand eyes and thousand ears. She who floated weightlessly throughout her domain like the Ghost of Christmas Past. She who in one chilling phrase could say it all. "I just cleaned." Three little words that simply meant: "I know you're here. Don't get the house dirty. Don't sit on the beds. If that's Oscy with you, don't let him lean his sweat shirt against anything. Don't take anything from the refrigerator because everything in there is catalogued and marked and dinner is in a few hours and if you spoil your appetite with a snack you can just stay in tonight so just don't."

In an act of abject defiance, Hermie slammed the door so hard that Penny Singleton shook. Oscy was looking at the door. "Can you lock it?" Hermie locked the door, but it wasn't enough for Oscy, who pulled over a chair and propped it up under the doorknob. Next, Oscy went to the bed and—

"Don't sit on the bed, Oscy."

"Why not?"

"My mother'll know."

"I wasn't going to sit on it. Jesus." He threw the filthy sweat shirt on the bed and Hermie winced because he knew his mother would eventually pick up the scent. Oscy untied the knot, pulled aside the sleeves, and there was the book, looking for all the world like the first Bible. Oscy picked it up as though it were a live bomb. He looked around for a place to put it.

"There." Hermie was pointing to the small table that served as his desk for the summer.

Oscy placed the book upon the table, like a surgeon, and he told his assistant his requirements. "Paper. Pencil." Hermie nodded. He had them. "Carbon paper." Oscy added, "Otherwise I have to do it twice."

"Do what?"

Oscy didn't answer. He just held his hand out. Hermie shortly filled it with pencil, paper, and the last piece of carbon paper in all the world. The best you could get out of that carbon paper was an echo. Oscy took it and held it to the window. The light poured through. "It'll do." Then Oscy pulled a chair up to the table, stuck the carbon paper between two pieces of white paper, and pencil in hand, he consulted the book's index until he found what he was looking for. "Ah."

Hermie plopped upon his bed and looked up at the ceiling, where the paint was peeling in a pattern that resembled Gene Tierney's luscious overbite. "Just what is it you have in mind, Oscy?"

"Your welfare." Again he said, "Ahhhhhh."

"What ahhhhh?" Hermie asked, dreadfully bored.

"The sexual act, how to perform it. The twelve steps. Simply stated. Pages six sixty-four through six seventy-eight." He smiled at Hermie. "It's here, Hermie. It's all here. Somebody had the good sense to write it down."

Hermie rolled over onto the elbow nearest Oscy. He squinted at Oscy as though trying to make him out in the fog. "What are you talking about, Oscy?"

Oscy had already found the pages he wanted and had begun taking his notes. "You just relax, Hermie. I'll inform you when I need you."

Hermie plopped again onto his back. It was out of his hands, his entire destiny. Oscy had taken over. What a relief to be free of the responsibility. He looked at the women on his walls. June Haver, freshly up, smiled at him through wild blue eyes. What the hell did she have to smile about—she was no Penny Singleton. He picked up the magazine on his night table. *Liberty* magazine. Sometimes it had good things. He thumbed through it, looking at the ads. Goodyear claimed that there were "plenty of miles in your old tires yet if you'll follow this common sense advice now." The USO said it needed "$32,000,000 by Spring." Oldsmobile claimed to be "putting the stings in America's wings." Armour and Company invited Hermie to "meet the best fed fighters in the world. The U.S. Soldier, Sailor and Marine." From time to time Hermie heard Oscy groan or just whistle. Eventually Hermie placed the magazine over his face so that a beautiful girl's mouth fell on his. He dozed off only to awaken at the sound of his breathing fluttering against the buzzing page. He removed the girl's wet face from his and turned once more to see what Oscy was up to. He called reverently to Oscy so as not to disturb him. "Oscy…"

"Shut up, Hermie. I'm almost finished." He mopped his sweaty face with the sweat shirt nearby.

"Just what the hell is it that you're doing?"

"Two copies. One for me. One for you. Keep it with you at all times. Refer to it. Learn it."

"Oscy, excuse me. Learn what?"

"The sexual act in twelve steps. What the hell do you think I'm *doing* here, Hermie? Answering my fan mail?"

"The sexual what?"

Oscy was very patronizing. "Hermie, since you can't go calling on your lady with this book under your arm, I'm condensing it. Point by point. If you stay close to this, you'll do okay."

Hermie swung his legs over the side of his bed. It was beginning to dawn on him, what he had suspected for many, many years. "Oscy, you're crazy."

"Yeah. Like a fox." He never stopped making his scribbly little notes. And he never stopped smiling. "Hermie, you're gonna lay that lady or I'll know the reason why not."

Hermie heard, but he couldn't accept. He even tried to laugh because the idea was so preposterous. "Oscy, I can't lay that lady. Ha-ha-ha."

"If you put your heart in it, you can." He never looked up, just kept writing. Seemingly volumes.

"Oscy, I can't." He heard himself laugh again but knew it wasn't funny.

Oscy stopped writing and looked at Hermie disbelievingly. "Don't you *want* to?"

"Well, *sure* I want to but—ha-ha-ha."

"Then you will. Stick with me." He resumed writing.

Hermie grew immediately thoughtful. Actually, it wasn't such a bad idea. If you could overlook the fact that it was completely impossible, it wasn't a bad idea. As a matter of fact, the more he thought about it, the less completely impossible it became. It would be *nice* to lay her. Very nice. And charming. Nice and charming for her, too, because he'd be very gentle. He'd also know all the right things to do, thanks to Oscy, who was setting it all down on paper, if only the paper didn't combust spontaneously. Watching Oscy like that, knowing that Oscy was devising a foolproof approach, gave Hermie supreme confidence. After all, it wasn't as though she didn't like him. Hadn't she kissed him that very morning? Hadn't she bitten his leg and changed his dressing? Hadn't she ripped open his NBC pants and fondled his gargantuan penis? If all that wasn't an expression of her interest and affection, then there was certainly something rotten in Denmark, what? Hermie kept watching

Oscy. Faithful, unselfish Oscy, so seldom wrong. So inventive and courageous. With Oscy in the wings it was a guaranteed certainty. Hermie not only believed he could lay her, he also believed that it was totally up to him just where and when it would take place. Her place or his? Hers. Only—that photograph of Pete would have to go. Hermie thought of her lying beneath him, her eyes glazed with passion, giving him tit for tat and then some because he was such a gentleman leaning on his elbows like that. He thought of her tawny legs around him, grinding him into her just like in the picture book. He thought of it all, and an image of Sheena of the Jungle swung through his mind, coming in one ear and going out the other. And by the time it went out he realized that he was nothing more than a dirty, frightened little boy with no rights to such evil thoughts or plans. It was all crass. Terribly crass. Not because he didn't want to lay her, but because—"Oscy, I respect her. I don't want to just...lay her." His voice was pitiful and young.

Oscy, without looking up, put his pencil aside like somebody's grandfather. Then he turned and looked up at Hermie as Thomas Edison must have looked at all who doubted him. "Hermie, there's something you don't seem to understand. It's all right to respect a lady. It's fine. And very democratic. Only, she's not gonna respect *you* if you don't try to lay her."

"I find that hard to believe."

"It's true. My brother told me. That's the way ladies are. They want you to *try* even if they don't let you, because, even though they don't *let* you, they *want* you to. Which is why you *have* to."

"I think I understand." But never, never in a thousand years would Hermie understand such warped and misshapen logic. And he began to wonder about Oscy. Oscy. Stupid Oscy. Wasn't he the guy who said they'd never be caught spitting marbles off the balcony railing of the Loew's Kings? They were banned for three weeks. Even missed *King Kong* and *Gunga Din*. And wasn't Oscy wrong when he told Rollo Herzog that rich Wacky Foster wouldn't even notice that his racing bike was stolen? Rollo was arrested. And wasn't it Oscy who said they could steal all the G-man cards in Gelband's store without fear? Gelband beat the shit out of both of them. No, Oscy was not to be listened to if you valued your future life. Listen to Oscy and you could end up in jail or dead or both.

Oscy got up and walked over to Hermie and gave him his copy of the document. "Here, Hermie. If you can count up to twelve, you can get laid. I'm giving you the original and taking this crummy carbon for myself. Greater love hath no man. Start memorizing." Hermie watched Oscy return to his chair and start memorizing.

Hermie looked at the paper in his hand. One page. In numbers one to twelve the sexual act had been written down by Oscy as if it were the Ten Commandments. "Oscy—"

"Shut up, Hermie. I'm memorizing."

"Oscy—"

"Hermie, shut up!"

Hermie kept shut up for as long as he could, studying the paper with the funny words that Oscy had to have misspelled. Then he broke radio silence. "Oscy, this is crazy."

"What?" Oscy was glaring at him.

"Point Three."

"What's crazy about it?" His fingers were thumping the table, just this side of becoming a fist.

"I never even heard of the word."

"It's Latin." Oscy was exasperated. "The original guys were Latins." He resumed his studying. "Jesus."

"I wouldn't even know how to pronounce it."

Oscy slammed his paper down. The paper made no noise. It was his fist that seemed to crack the table. "You don't pronounce it! You just *do* it!"

"Yeah? Well, I don't even know where it *is!*" Hermie didn't like being yelled at, especially by a young imbecile like Oscy. "And what the hell is *this*, in Number *Four?*"

Oscy consulted his list to see what the trouble was. "That's Latin, too!" He looked over at Hermie, kind of appealing to him not to be so dense. "It's *all* in Latin, Hermie. Jesus."

Hermie was beginning to feel just a mite ornery. "Yeah? Well, I may just have to ask her where some of these things *are!*"

Oscy was looking at the ceiling, awaiting divine assistance and speaking with the patience of a fucking saint. "They are all approximately in the same place. Look and ye shall find." He looked at Hermie and tried to smile. "Besides, she's supposed to be helping you."

Hermie was certainly being contrary. "*She* gonna have a copy of these fucking twelve points, too?"

Oscy was still patient. "She won't need them. That's why she'll be helping you."

"I hope so, because I'm gonna need all the help I can get." Seeing it in print like that, so arithmetically laid out, was a drain on Hermie's confidence. He was good in math, but Latin had never been his strong point. All he really knew of Latin was that Gaul was divided into three parts. And the only reason he knew *that* was because he was good in *math*.

Oscy was talking, tapping his paper pedantically. "Point Six, Hermie. Very important."

Hermie looked at his list. Point Six, no matter how Oscy spelled it, was foreplay. "Foreplay," said Hermie, as though the whole thing were as well known as the Declaration of Independence.

"Right," said Oscy. "That word keeps cropping up."

Hermie was feisty. "I still don't know what I'm supposed to do. What do I say—'Hi, lady, how about a little foreplay?'"

"I keep telling you, you don't have to say a word."

"Yeah? Well, Point Two here definitely states that we're supposed to converse."

"Swell, Hermie. Very good. And very observant. But that's Point Two. When you get to Point Six, you'll notice that there's no more talking. Just moaning and sighing. You moan and sigh."

"She'll think I'm sick."

"She'll be moaning and sighing, too."

"Gonna get pretty noisy."

"Turn on the radio."

"What if there's no radio?"

"Then don't turn it on." Oscy hurled himself into a quick lather. "Hermie, God damn you! I am trying to memorize this shit, and you're not letting me!"

That stopped Hermie. It hadn't occurred to him before, but Oscy had made a copy for himself. "What the hell *you* memorizing it for?"

"Miriam."

"Miriam?"

"Yeah. Miriam. Remember Miriam? Well, *I* have rights, too."

"You gonna lay Miriam?"

"You're goddamn right I'm gonna lay Miriam. I happened to overhear a couple lifeguards discussing her, and from what I gather, once she gets started she's really something."

"How do you know it's the same Miriam?"

"It's the same Miriam. Don't try to throw me off."

"Miriam's a pretty common name."

"Yeah, but those *tits* ain't so common. You don't come across *tits* like that every day in the week. They were talking about the *same* Miriam. *My* Miriam."

"Pretty sure of yourself, aren't you?"

"Yeah. I got confidence, Hermie. Too bad *you* don't. If you had confidence, I wouldn't have to lead you around like a pet duck."

"I got plenty of confidence, Oscy. All I need. It just so happens that I'm a little more realistic than you." He was getting very angry. His voice was rising. If the phantom mother was floating around nearby, there could be trouble. But Hermie couldn't stop himself. "And where the hell do you come off calling me a pet duck?"

"Quack-quack."

"I'll tell you something, Oscy. If I follow these twelve points, she might just have a baby. And I can't afford a baby at this stage of my life, so the whole deal is off. Also—fuck you."

Oscy stared at him. Not angry, just nonplussed. "You are so dumb."

"Just watch yourself. You're in *my* house."

"So dumb I can't believe it."

"I may be dumb, but I'm not gonna be a father. Two wrongs don't make a right. So fuck you." Hermie was really spoiling for a fight. He looked around to see what weapons were available. The best thing was a blunt object, the eugenics book.

Oscy showed commendable restraint. He had had, roughly, thirty-eight proper provocations to punch Hermie out, but still he withheld. "You use protection, Hermie. You use a rubber. Ever heard of a rubber? A prophylactic device? A contraceptive?"

Hermie didn't bother to answer because of course he knew what a rubber was. He stood, crumpled up his paper of notes, and let it drop to the floor, an expression of his total lack of interest. The gauntlet had been hurled. The ball was very dramatically rolling around in Oscy's court.

Oscy got up and came over. Hermie's fists were clenched. He knew enough about law to realize that he could kill Oscy and get away with it on the grounds that Oscy had broken and entered. Oscy stood in front of him, just looking at Hermie. He stood there for five hours and thirty-six minutes. Then he bent down and picked up the crumpled piece of paper. Hermie could have easily delivered unto the back of Oscy's neck a fine judo chop. But that would have been a Jap trick, and whatever you thought about Oscy, he was still a bona fide American. Oscy stood up, smiled at Hermie, and walked back to the table where he proceeded to uncrumple the paper and smooth it out. "Lucky for you, Hermie, that this is the original. If it was the carbon, it'd be smudged into oblivion and you'd be shit out of luck."

"Fuck you, Oscy." Hermie was feeling powerful, unbeatable. He wanted to demonstrate his inhuman strength on Oscy's nose, where, once before, he had laid out an example of his pluck and spunk. Whatever it took to provoke Oscy, he'd do it. Like repetition. "Fuck you, Oscy. In spades."

Oscy sighed, not even looking at Hermie, just smoothing out the notes. "A man gets tired of always hearing those words from a so-called friend, Hermie."

"Fuck you, Oscy. You're an idiot. Hear that?"

"I'd expect that from Benjie. Not from you."

"Quack-quack. Go fuck a duck."

Oscy dug deep into his pocket and pulled out his leather wallet, all four corners of which had been bent round. He opened the wallet. "As it just so happens, Hermie, I already have *my* rubber." He wiggled his fingers into the wallet's secret compartment. "When my brother went into service, he willed it to me." And he fished out a small foil-wrapped packet that had seen better days but that was still sealed. "I been carrying it around ever since. It so happens that it's my lucky charm."

Hermie looked at the packet in Oscy's upturned palm. It caught the light and glistened even more than his Band-Aid. It was about as sexy an item as he'd ever laid eyes on. And wrapped in foil like that, it looked like a precious gem. Hermie wanted it. He wanted it more than a Schwinn racer or a new Joe Medwick glove. And he suddenly understood how men could kill just to possess rare and beautiful objects.

Oscy saw the reflection in Hermie's eyes, and he knew he had him. Deliberately he wiggled his palm so that it would catch a few rays of sun and thereby thrust Hermie into a hypnotic state, not a difficult task since Hermie usually walked around half-hypnotized anyway. "It's in here, Hermie. All you need." He was whispering like some kind of Far Eastern Hindu. "Your paper with your instructions—and this. You kiss that lady a couple times, excuse yourself politely, and then return with the contents of this package wrapped around your pecker and you're home. There's no way a woman can resist. It's like catnip." He wiggled the packet a little more. Hermie's eyes dilated like mad. His emotions soared. It was a great test of his Jockey shorts and his poor fly's three buttons. "Whaddya say, Hermie? Whaddya say, eh?"

"How much do you want for it?"

Oscy was shocked. "It's from my brother! It's a fuckin' family heirloom! You have to get your *own*, you stupid shit! You have to *buy* it!"

Hermie's senses were foggy. His head was a little fuzzy. He

spoke dully. "How many food stamps?"

"Food stamps?" Oscy was appalled. "What're you gonna do—*eat* 'em?"

"Aren't they rationed?"

"Why the fuck should they be rationed?"

"I don't know. I would think—don't the soldiers get 'em all?"

"No! They have to leave some for civilians; otherwise there'd be babies plopping out all over the place! Jesus H. Christ, Hermie!"

"But—they're made of rubber and—"

"I don't believe you! I just don't believe you, Hermie! What am I *doing* with you?" He went to the window and wanted to jump out. Instead, he just looked through it until he found that he could control his anger. At which point he turned to face Hermie once more. He smiled wanly. "Hermie, you go to a drugstore and you buy 'em. Okay? Is that too difficult for you to understand? Hmmmmmmmm?"

Hermie was mortified. He had revealed a certain ignorance of the subject. He had been trapped into doing so by Oscy's smooth talk. To cover his inadequacy, he immediately turned contrite. "I'm not gonna risk it. I happen to be underage. Also, for your information, I mean in case you didn't know—*women* shop in drugstores."

"Where d'you *wanna* buy 'em, in a *sporting goods* store?" There was a limit to just how much of Hermie's stupidity Oscy could cope with. That limit had been reached and surpassed more than ten minutes before.

Hermie was losing the debate and rapidly. Besides, that little silver packet was becoming more and more important to his well-being than all the vitamin-fortified cereals in the world. He decided to embark on a little evasive action, a little Damon exerted upon a little Pythias. "If you were really a good friend, Oscy, you'd lend me that."

"What?" Maybe he imagined that Hermie asked that.

"But I'm finding out *you're* not really such a good friend."

"What?"

Hermie became righteously indignant and pretty fucking mad. "Shit, Oscy, do you think I'd *keep* it? I'd return it!"

Oscy could not reply immediately. He staggered as though shot. Then he held his stomach and doubled over and fell onto the bed in a heap, face to the ceiling and gasping. When the seizure subsided, he spoke with a touch of total defeat. "Hermie, I'm beginning to think that maybe you're a homo."

"Swell, Oscy. Thanks a lot." He kicked the bedpost, knowing that the tremor would reach Oscy's head, wishing it would set off a TNT blast in his ass.

Oscy quickly rolled off the bed and attacked Hermie vocally, his hands doing windmills. "Schmuck! A rubber is to be used once and only once! And by only one party! Not even the closest of friends can go halfies on a rubber!"

Hermie took a step toward Oscy. "I don't like you yelling at me. Forewarned is forearmed. Be advised."

Oscy was straining to understand Hermie's resistance, reluctance, and general all-around pigheadedness. "I'm doing this for *you*, Hermie. I'm doing this out of friendship because, though *you* don't know it, I *do*."

"Know what?"

"That your time has come."

"Oh, bullshit."

"It's true. Your time has come. Your *cock* knows it, but your stupid brain has been taking lessons from Benjie."

"Yeah? Well—forget it. Just forget it. Signals off."

"Signals are not off." Oscy said that as though possessing some specially classified top-secret dossier information stuff that Hermie had no knowledge of.

"What do you mean?"

"I mean it's all arranged."

"What is?"

Oscy tried to state it as an unalterable fact that had been chiseled into stone for all time. He wanted Hermie to accept it as being as completely irrevocable as ancient history. "The marshmallow roast. On the beach. Tomorrow night. Me and Miriam." He stopped there for a moment, to make certain that Hermie was following. Which

he was. Then Oscy added the *coup de grace*. "And you and Aggie."
Hermie started to say something, but the voice he heard was still
Oscy's. "Don't try to get out of it because it's all set." He came over
and put an arm about Hermie's shoulder. "It's fate, Hermie, I been
watching you. You been mooning about that lady for God knows
how long. You're ready. But not for *her*. Not yet. I have to sharpen
you up on somebody else. So just this morning, while you were in
there getting kissed, I looked for Miriam on the beach and set it all
up. Miriam said she'd tell Aggie and that it'd be no problem. Okay?
Okay, boy?"

Hermie listened to Oscy's monologue with controlled fury. By
the time he had a chance to speak the fury had turned to something
more resembling desperation. "Aggie? Jesus. I'm not *interested* in
Aggie. I thought, all the time, you were talking about...*her*. You
know—*her?*"

Oscy shrugged helplessly. "Like I said, Hermie, you're not
ready for a main event. You have to start with a preliminary. And
Aggie's all I got." He once again took Hermie's copy of the Twelve
Steps to Stardom and pressed it into Hermie's pocket. "You've got
your instructions. You're on your way."

Hermie was numb. "You're crazy."

"Yes. Crazy. Mad. Mad!" He laughed insanely. "A-ha-ha-ha-ha!"
Then he came out of it. "Hermie, I'm not asking you to get all the
way through Point Twelve because I don't believe in miracles. I'll be
thrilled if you get through Point *Two*. All I want you to do is give
it a try."

"Forget it. I'm not sticking my neck out for *Aggie*. She's a freak.
I don't even know if she can *talk!*"

"She can talk."

"How do *you* know?"

"I asked Miriam. I don't think Miriam would lie. She said that
Aggie definitely had the power of speech."

"You were worried about it, *too*, then, *weren't* you?"

"Let's just say that it occurred to me that she didn't do much
talking. Hermie, please. Believe me. One day, soon, you're gonna

thank me. Meantime, tomorrow night—*I'll* bring the marshmallows. And *you* bring a rubber."

How does one resist a steamroller? With cries and shouts? Does one call a cop or his mother? No. One gets out of the way. But what if the steamroller follows one around, turning when one turns, climbing a tree when one climbs a tree? Hermie went to bed that night with a steamroller named Oscy barreling around in his dreams. And yet, it wasn't all that bad. For after the preliminary there'd be a clean shot at the green-eyed champion. In the middle of deepest night, Hermie switched on his bed lamp and began heavy training by carefully studying his "notes." So what if it was in Latin? By applying himself he could become a fucking whiz in Latin. He might even become a Latin whiz at fucking. *Veni, vidi, vici.* Yaaaaaaaa, Sheena.

15

Hermie and Oscy, the young devils, sauntered up to the drugstore the next morning feeling very *très gai* and serenely confident in their plan, needing only a certain piece of rubberized madness to launch Hermie properly into the warm recesses of all the world's femininity. Oscy wore his usual sweat shirt, for he was to wait outside, having revealed himself to be unwilling to make the difficult purchase since he was already equipped for the night's outing. Hermie, on the other hand, having failed to get Oscy to volunteer for the hazardous condom caper, dressed himself in clothing that might work wonders in making him appear older. He was therefore not merely the only man on Packett Island wearing a tie; he was also wearing the longest tie ever to find its way to the island primarily because it was his father's, and no matter how many double Windsor knots he tied in it, it still came down three inches below his belt buckle. It was also a very loud tie, red and green leaves on a pale-yellow background, a Christmas gift to his father from a color-blind enemy. For those reasons he tucked both tails of the tie into his trousers and pulled his jacket front so close that, unless you had been with Hermie when he got dressed that morning, you had no way of knowing that he was wearing a tie.

It had all been carefully worked out. Oscy took up a position just outside the drugstore, where he casually produced his harmonica and played "Old MacDonald's Farm" in a manner that would curdle all the milk thereon. It may have seemed odd to have Oscy serve as a sentinel when no shoplifting had been planned, but it was a special request from Hermie who feared that The Mother Who Walked the Night might be dropping by, and he didn't want her to catch him buying rubbers, no, sir—ma'am. Hermie took a deep breath that brought air all the way into his toes; then, with a nod to Oscy, he nonchalantly entered the drugstore, a difficult maneuver to perform since the bell on the door announced his presence like Big Ben.

Hermie winced at the clang and began to perspire like a truck horse. But there was no danger of offensive perspiration because he had put such lumps of Mum under his arms that they kept slipping behind him when he walked, making him look as though he were about to perform a racing dive into the Erasmus pool. Unable to control his slithering arms, he plunged both his hands into his pockets, and looking as guilty as they come, he professionally cased the joint.

At the far end of the far counter was the druggist, Mr. Sanders, a crusty New Englander, thin and wiry and craggy and everything you'd expect him to be. On occasion he could even be heard saying "A-yuh" to the lady customer he was attending to. Another lady was just kind of looking around the store, plucking random items from the shelves. Other than those two ladies, Hermie was alone. He moseyed about, kind of checking out the shelves. The Band-Aids caught his eye. He knew a good deal about Band-Aids because, in any given summer, he could consume up to three or four hundred of them.

He noticed the lady at the counter pay Mr. Sanders and leave. The bell on the door chimed her exit, and as the door swung open, the sound of Oscy's miserable harmonica trailed in. It meant that Oscy was still at his post. Good man, that Oscy. The door shut. The bell rang. The harmonica was stifled in the middle of a chord they'd never find again.

Hermie moved over to the toothpaste section. A placard there announced that empty tubes should not be discarded. The other lady, the silent stroller, was still on the premises, showing no inclination to leave. It unnerved Hermie to have her around. Especially since Mr. Sanders was walking toward him and saying, "Can I help you?"

"Help *her*. She was here first." Hermie pointed to the strolling lady, who just smiled and continued to be a strolling lady. Maybe she was some kind of guard. Hermie made a mental note to tell Oscy that there was a Pinkerton woman on the premises and that the drugstore therefore was not a good place to attempt any kind of shoplifting in. Mr. Sanders returned to the far counter and hurled himself into inventory. Druggists did that a lot, took inventory. It was a way of life.

Hermie ambled along, aimlessly whistling "Jingle Bells" to keep cool. He edged his way gradually toward the door, where the irritating tones of the harmonica grew louder, sounding like a strangling chicken. Hermie opened the door. The bell chimed, and Mr. Sanders looked up to see Hermie leave without buying anything.

Oscy stopped strangling the chicken when he noticed Hermie standing alongside him, taking the sea air in big inhalations and casually inquiring, "Everything all right out here?"

"Yeah," said Oscy, wondering what the hell was going on.

"Good," said Hermie. And he studied the sky. He always made people out of clouds when he had the time. And up there was either Dick Haymes or Maria Montez or Carmen Miran—

"Did you get 'em?" Oscy knew a stall when confronted with one.

"No. Not yet."

"Well, get 'em."

"There's a lady in there."

"Oh." Oscy seemed to understand. The bell chimed as the door opened, and the strolling lady came out, on her way home. The door shut behind her, and the bell went off again only not so loud because it was inside where Hermie was supposed to be. "That her?" asked Oscy.

"Yeah."

"Any others inside?"

"Maybe. They could be bending down."

Oscy shoved him. "Go on, Hermie. For Chrissakes."

Hermie reentered the drugstore, the bell blasting in his ear, telling him there was no way back, especially since Mr. Sanders, more than just curious, was striding toward him. "Yes?"

"It's me"—Hermie smiled—"same guy as before. Just stepped outside for a little air." He kept talking like a fool. "Nice air out there. A lot of very nice sea air. This whole island has nice air. Yes, sir."

Mr. Sanders grew apprehensive at the jabbering little fool with his clothes all drawn in tight on such a warm morning. "Just what is it you're looking for? Maybe I can help you." Only he didn't look as if he wanted to help. He looked more as if he were going to make a citizen's arrest.

"Oh, I'll know when I find it." Fat chance. Rubbers were kept under lock and key. And in a back room. Or a cellar. Or a vault. Or a cave that there was no access to at high tide.

"Perhaps if you'll tell me—"

Hermie had to come up with something—and, soon. "Ah, I just remembered."

"A-yuh?" And he waited to hear Hermie's request. Except it didn't look as if he were planning on waiting too long, so Hermie took a flier.

"A strawberry ice-cream cone."

There was something suspicious about that boy, thought Mr. Sanders. One thing was for certain: he was not to be left alone, out of sight. "All right," he said. "Come with me." He went behind the fountain counter, making certain that Hermie was following close by. Hermie slid up onto one of the stools, and Mr. Sanders confronted him across the marble counter. "One dip or two?" He had the ice-cream scoop ready. It looked like a microphone. Hermie wished the old son of a bitch would stop pressing him and just sing.

"Better make it a double." He tried to avoid the eyes of the weather-beaten old Yankee. With guys like that around, no wonder the British ended up with all their fucking tea in Boston Harbor.

Mr. Sanders constructed the double dip and pushed it across at Hermie. "Okay. That'll be twelve cents." Ming the Merciless. Killer Kane. The whole bunch of 'em rolled into one. Hermie had picked for himself some adversary. He wanted to bolt for the door and get out of there, but there was too much involved. It was still far off, but there was a championship at stake. He decided that the bull had to be taken by the goddamn horns. So he leaned across the counter, looking at the Yankee via his reflection in the marble countertop and said, "There a—there's something else I need."

The countertop answered, upside down. "A-yuh?" It came as a menacing growl. Sylvana, the evil scientist, had spoken, and Hermie backed off, gutless, and said, "Sprinkles."

The Yankee thrust the cone into the chrome bowl of chocolate sprinkles. Then he handed it right across to Hermie, who silently figured that he could ask for nuts and a cherry and still be within his rights. "Anything else?" snapped the druggist.

Once more into the fray, another summoning of courage, one last crack at the moon as he balanced the ice cream in his tiny hand. "I hate to bother, but—" He took a lick at the cone. Good. Strawberry. Not surprising since strawberry had been what he asked for. Still, it was a fine-caliber strawberry, rich with little chunks and tasty seeds.

"Speak up, boy!" That was a bark. A definite bark from behind clenched teeth. Not easily done.

"How about a napkin?" Hermie was surprised at how readily he could turn tail. It was a gift. But he was fast running out of deceptive tactics.

The paper napkin came flying at him; good thing it wasn't a manhole cover. "Anything else?" That was sarcasm.

"How about some rubbers?" That was quick. Hermie wasn't even sure he'd said it. Maybe it was Oscy standing behind him. Or Edgar Bergen. Or Tokyo Rose.

"Pardon?" The Yankee had a surprised look on his face. The son of a bitch was off-balance. Hermie knew he had the opening he needed. He waded in like Henry Armstrong. Hit the son of a bitch again. But with poise and carriage. Shit, it had to have some poise and carriage or else where was he? "I understand you carry them."

"Carry what?" Aha. Evasive action from the other side.

"Come on. You know what." What poise. What fucking carriage. He took another lick at his ice cream. What strawberry.

"Do you mean contraceptives?"

"Right." The old bastard caught on fast.

"You want to *buy* some?"

"Right."

"What for?"

What for? The guy had to be some kind of fuddy-duddy nincompoop. Hermie delivered a half-smile, as if he and the old codger were school chums. "Come on, you know what for." He buried his face in the ice cream because the heat of his hand was causing the strawberry shit to run down his wrist. The trick was to not look at his opponent.

The Yankee took a moment to assess the situation. Then he walked down to the far end of the marble counter and over into the drug section, the place where the hot stuff was dispensed. Kotex. Pills. Rubbers. He signaled for Hermie to come over. Hermie slid off his stool, feeling like a gangster about to pick up some protection money. He shuffled over, in no particular hurry. All was moving well. Oscy was posted outside. And *he* was about to make his purchase. The Yankee looked squarely at him but with an expressionless face. "What brand?"

What brand? That was news to Hermie. "Brand?"

"Brand and style." Mr. Sanders was sure playing it cool.

Hermie wondered if the old fart wasn't just toying with him. A diplomatic response was called for. "Oh—the usual." That should do it. Now another lick of the ice cream.

The druggist's hands disappeared from the counter. Then they reappeared. They disappeared and reappeared two, three, four times. And soon Hermie was looking at a collection of different-sized and different-colored little packages that his mother could make one helluvan afghan out of. There were enough rubbers there for the entire Second Marines. "There's a number to choose from, you know." The old man said that flatly, as if everyone in the world knew it.

Hermie was unsettled. For a moment he thought he felt his mother looking over his shoulder. He looked, but she was gone. She could do that. He looked back at the druggist. "Do you have to flash 'em around?"

There was still no expression on Mr. Sanders' face. "Which is your usual?" Hermie was standing square at the Maginot Line. In front of him was a collection of dandy little packages, all neatly sealed and wrapped and alive with raw sex. Behind him was his callow youth. He had just been asked to make his selection from the Crown Jewels of England. With so little experience in those matters, he decided to go with his favorite color. "The blue ones." He began to wonder if the color on the outside of each package was matched by the color of the rubber within. The last thing he wanted to do was frighten Aggie by confronting her with a huge blue pecker. But then, red might even be worse, not to mention green. And plaid could send a young girl screaming off into the night. He wished he'd gone with the flesh-colored package, but it was too late. The dye, as it were, had been cast. And the heat of his hand was beginning to do away with his ice cream as though a disintegrator gun were working on it. A few drops of melted strawberry plopped onto his sneakers. All of him was melting.

Mr. Sanders pushed the blue packages toward Hermie as if he were betting chips in a poker game. "How many would you like?"

Another question to boggle the mind. How many? Oh, well. Take a shot at it. "Oh, three dozen."

The druggist almost smiled, but not quite. He was playing Hermie like a trout, in a shallow stream, in a net. "Planning a big night?"

"Just the usual." It had gotten him *this* far, so why not try it again?

The druggist shoveled all the other packages under the counter and pulled out a whole carton of blue ones. Blue was obviously a big seller around those parts. The druggist counted out a seemingly endless number of them, and Hermie wondered how many Marines would have to go without because of his horny selfishness. "That'll be twelve dollars."

Twelve dollars to lay Aggie seemed pretty steep. Maybe he was being cheated. Those old Yankee traders just loved to take the city slickers. Hermie figured he'd better offer up a little resistance, or else he'd be sweeping out that drugstore for the rest of the summer, just to pay back the fucking money. "Twelve dollars?" God, his voice sounded tiny.

"And twelve cents. For the ice cream."

"I see. How much for just a dozen?"

"Four dollars."

"And how many for a dollar?"

"Three."

"I'll take two."

"They come three to a package."

"Can I owe you for the ice cream?"

Mr. Sanders became very stern. Yet he also became quite fatherly. "All right now, son, fun is fun, but how old *are* you?"

"Sixteen."

"How old?"

"Sixteen. We're inclined to be small in my family."

The druggist studied Hermie, watching him squirm and letting him. Watching the ice cream running down Hermie's wrist. Tapping the package of rubbers. "What are you going to do with these?"

"They're for my brother. He's older. But he's not much taller." He was running off at the mouth again. "None of us are very tall. There's even a couple midgets in the family." He figured he'd better cut that stuff out because he was hanging himself pretty neatly. He licked the ice cream in a spiral motion because the damn stuff was quickly leaving town.

"Why can't your brother come in and get them for himself? Too small to reach the counter?" Mr. Sanders laughed at his own dumb-assed Yankee witticism.

"He's been a little under the weather." Hermie was flying blind, but he still hadn't been thrown out. Also, he sensed that the druggist was kind of enjoying himself.

"Then what does he need them for?" asked the druggist.

"He says they make him feel better." Hermie was playing the stupid little kid. It seemed to be getting results.

"Is he going to eat them?" The old son of a bitch was really knocking himself out with all that high comedy. Meanwhile, Hermie

142

wondered where he'd heard that question before?

"I don't know what he's going to do with them. He never tells me." Hermie figured that stupid ignorance was the best approach, especially since all else had failed.

The old man was really beaming. Two teeth were missing. Two were gold. The rest were brown. Except one, which was a fang. "Do you know what these are used for?"

"They're for servicemen, that's all I know. My brother's a Ranger. One of the smallest Rangers they have, but he still uses a lot of them." Hermie tried to look like Benjie. If he could look like Benjie, he could get away with the whole thing.

"Care to take a *guess* what they're for?"

"Well, I know what *I'd* use 'em for."

"Oh?" That stopped him.

"Yeah. I'd fill 'em with water and throw 'em off a roof." He had heard that a lot of kids did that. From a six-story building they could make quite a splat. "I think maybe the Rangers fill 'em with nitro and throw 'em at enemy tanks. My brother told me that. I think he can curve 'em." Hermie knew he had the dumbest look on his face imaginable. He had succeeded in looking like Benjie. Wait till he tried it on Oscy.

Mr. Sanders had to smile at the dumb kid. "Well, I just wanted to make sure you knew what they were for."

Hermie was getting so good at playing dumb, he couldn't resist taking it a bit further. With wide eyes he said, "Is that what they're really for? I thought maybe my brother was kidding me."

Mr. Sanders was finding a plain brown bag. "Well, different people fill 'em with different things." He chuckled. He had always figured he was a jocular type; now he knew for sure. He couldn't wait to tell the gang around the fucking cracker barrel about the dumb Brooklyn kid and the rubbers. That would be a real thigh slapper, yessiree bob.

"Be pretty wild thrown out of a B-17 at twenty thousand feet, wouldn't it?" Hermie wanted the snaggle-toothed old ferret to have a lot of real yoks around the rhubarb. Yessir-ee-rube.

The old man smiled. "Technically, son, I shouldn't be selling these to minors, but seein' as how they're for someone in service, well, I'll close my eyes to it." He rang up the cash register. "Let's call it a dollar even, okay?"

"A-yuh." Hermie handed him the dollar, which, as it turned out, was all he had; only originally he had expected some change. Still, he was glad to be done with it and lucky at that to have outcrafted the wily old druggist. And so, with the rubbers in one hand and the fast-fading ice cream cone in the other, he walked toward the door as a magnificent advertisement for adolescence. Ice cream and rubbers, there was a song in there somewhere, best sung by Bobby Breen.

Just as he reached the door, it opened and the bell tinkled, and of all people, Aggie walked in. Oscy was still at his post, blaring dissonant harmonic warnings, but Hermie had been too deep in battle to hear the blare. The door closed, and Oscy was out of it again. Aggie smiled at Hermie. Also, she spoke. That was new for her. "Hi, Hermie."

"Hi, Aggie." He clutched tightly at his bag of blue rubbers. No sense in her seeing them so early in their relationship. He put away the last vestiges of his leaky ice cream by chomping on the empty cone.

"I had a very nice time at the movie the other night."

"I did, too."

"We never really had a chance to really discuss the film, did we?"

"I guess not. How's the old arm?" He thought he'd better ask. At least to let her know that he knew it was an arm all along.

"It's fine, thank you."

"I do that a lot. I don't like to offend so, I just…squeeze an arm. Lets a girl know I like her and she doesn't have to panic that I'm getting fresh."

"Sure. Arms are all right." She shrugged. What the hell else could she say to such sexual theorizing?

"Yeah. Nothing wrong with arms." He was running out of sparkling chatter. "Well—there you go." He smiled like a drip.

"It was very nice of you to ask me to the marshmallow roast

tonight. I'm looking forward to it."

"Me, too." He could smell the rubber burning in the paper bag. In a minute there'd be smoke, then the fire department, then his arrest. And old man Sanders could go to the hoosegow *with* him. Hermie smiled. "Well, Oscy's outside. He's bringing the marshmallows."

"And what are *you* bringing?"

"So long."

He went out through the chiming doorway, sweeping past Oscy, who fell immediately in step with him, slapping his harmonica against his palm and getting a load of spit there in a hurry. Which he then wiped on his sweat shirt, often referred to as the city dump. "Did you get 'em?"

"Yeah. They're blue." He rattled the bag as if to demonstrate the color to Oscy.

"Blue?"

"Yeah. I'm pretty sure."

"Blue's okay." What the hell did *Oscy* know? "They in the bag?"

"Yeah." He rattled the bag again. For emphasis.

"How many'd you get?"

"They come three to a pack, you know."

"I know." The hell he did. He looked very excited. "How many packages did you get?"

"I figured I'd hold it down to one." Big shot.

"Yeah." Idiot.

"Aggie's in the drugstore."

"I know."

"Think *she's* getting some, too?"

"I don't think women use 'em. It's the man's job."

"Seems we have to do everything."

"How do you think you feel, Hermie?"

"Okay."

"Think you're up to it?"

"I think so. You?"

"Sure." Oscy played his harmonica again, and the two boys went down to the grocery store to buy a couple hundred marshmallows.

16

The rest of the day Hermie spent in heavy training. The Twelve
Fabulous Steps he thoroughly committed to memory. He could
even recite them aloud better than he could handle the Pledge of
Allegiance. Still, he figured he'd better bring the "notes" along just
in case his mind went blank. In the privacy of his room he did
push-ups to get his muscles in tone. He did fifty push-ups without
effort and could have done a lot more except he kept seeing Aggie
lying beneath him with her eyes closed and she was counting his
push-ups. It was hardly a romantic conversation. Nobody wanted to
screw a girl who was saying, "Forty-six, forty-seven, forty-eight..."
He studied the movie stars on his walls, trying to convince himself
that Aggie had the same basic equipment they had. But that was
like saying a bluebird was a P-47 because they both had wings. He
figured, if things got rough and if it was dark enough, he'd pretend
that Aggie was Penny Singleton, no law against that. But Aggie
had dark hair, and that was quite an imposition on his imagination
because Penny Singleton was so blond and flaxen. So instead of
Penny Singleton, for Aggie he selected Dorothy Lamour, who,
though a lot better-looking, in the right light and counting push-
ups, might just pass. Hermie was getting himself all a-twitter with
stupid fantasies like that, which was the last thing he wanted. Also,
it occurred to him that if he was going to imagine that Aggie was
Dorothy Lamour, Aggie might just retaliate by imagining that *he* was
Freddie Bartholomew, and the thought of Freddie Bartholomew
screwing Dorothy Lamour seemed somehow outlandish. He
could, of course, make a deal with Aggie whereby she could be any
woman she liked and Hermie could be any man he liked, subject to

both their approvals. Hermie figured he'd go with James Cagney, not because there was a resemblance, but because they were both kind of cocky. He wondered who Aggie'd pick. Any number of beauties were available. Like Joan Bennett. Hermie hoped that Aggie wouldn't pick Joan Bennett. It wasn't that he didn't *like* Joan Bennett, not at all. It was just that Joan Bennett looked so much like Hedy Lamarr, and Hedy Lamarr, Hermie had heard, though John Loder probably hadn't, was Austrian born and very likely a Nazi. And Hermie'd be goddamned if he'd screw a Nazi while his cousin Ronald was up in Kiska getting his nuts shot up. Hermie quickly divorced himself from all that kind of thinking because it was getting him so confused between politics and sex that, if he didn't watch himself, he could easily end up screwing Conrad Veidt, who was not only a real German but much more charming than Hermie, as witness his portrayal of the sub commander in *U-Boat 29*. Hermie switched on the radio, and goddammit if the Songbird of the fucking South wasn't singing "God Bless America." He didn't listen long for fear that he wouldn't be able to get Kate Smith off his mind and that as a result, instead of Aggie or Dorothy Lamour or Conrad Veidt, he'd end up with Kate Smith, which would be like screwing a building and what if she wanted to get on top, as so many women, he had heard, liked to do? They wouldn't find his remains until low tide. Why couldn't Penny Singleton sing "God Bless America"? He looked at her photograph which he had so neatly autographed. "To Hermie, with devastating affection and great yearning, Penny 'Sexpot' Singleton." "All my love, forever, Pete." And the woman's face was swimming in space before his eyes, smiling that everlasting smile of hers. *She* was the one he wanted. Why was he getting himself all involved with *Aggie*? Why couldn't he make love to the woman he most desired instead of a dumb substitute? Why? Why did his mother decide to have chicken for dinner that night? Didn't the condemned man have a right to have steak before he went to the wall? And could the condemned arrange to keep his blindfold on while screwing Aggie? And did his sister have to stand in the hallway and keep screaming that he was using

17

It got to be 11 p.m. without any help from any of them. The fire was a fine one, crackling in the heady summer night. It had been magnificently constructed by Hermie, who, in a former life, had undoubtedly been a great outdoorsman as well as the first man to write "shit" on a cave wall because that, more or less, was just about the way he felt. The rushing sound of the breaking surf came as intermittent whispers that leaned in and then laughed out. And a few generous sprinklings of stars made the whole scene too painful for an unwilling Romeo to cope with. Hermie had consumed by then, oh, perhaps thirty toasted marshmallows, and he felt like a candy bar. Oscy and Miriam had split off over an hour before, giggling as they dragged their blanket off into the darkness to do only God knew what. That, of course, had left Hermie with Aggie, the Sphinx. She was wearing a loose sweater, obviously a hand-me-down from Kate Smith. Also, it had sleeves. Unmistakable sleeves from shoulders to wrists. She had taken careful pains to guard against any navigational errors Hermie's wandering hand might make. And she had also avoided any open flesh if, in truth, Hermie really got his kicks from squeezing arms. All that Hermie's hand would have to contend with was a boat-neck opening around the neck of the sweater that was so large that an elephant could get in. Or, if it so desired, his hand could come up under the sweater from below, via an unelastic waistband that couldn't keep out a dinosaur. Hermie knew that, somewhere within the loose-fitting garment, two breasts hung silently like meat on a hook. And, very likely, they were complete—nipples and everything. As for any action below the belt, Hermie, a realist, hadn't planned on it, not really. In spite of his learning the Twelve Hot Steps, he pragmatically knew the odds against his going beyond bare boobs. Aggie was wearing dungarees as was everyone else that summer. As for her belt, it looked rather formidable. For all Hermie knew, it had a lock on it. And a seal. And an alarm. Hermie was fairly certain that Aggie would let him have some boob, but that would be as far as he'd be allowed to go. Very few young men on the island ever got beyond boob, even though, if you listened to their stories, they were getting laid more often than the ancient horny Romans. Still, Hermie knew that the complete man should make at least a half-assed attempt at some action below the belt. So he didn't close the book on it. He'd see how things went. He'd play it by ear.

"It's a very nice fire." That was Aggie. She was on his blanket, making conversation. It was good to hear her voice because it meant she wasn't dead. Once or twice it occurred to him that she might well be dead and that it would be tricky getting her corpse home without looking as if he'd screwed her to death.

"I can throw on more wood if you like." He had been throwing on wood as if he were stoking the *Yankee Clipper*. The fire was so hot they could have roasted a boar on it.

"It's a bit chilly," said Aggie, as she kind of hugged herself. Never again would Hermie get so strong an invitation to move in. He looked over at her. Even in the firelight he could see the hot passion building in her eyes. And as he watched he saw that her legs, they kind of moved. And her knees, which but a moment ago were touching each other, were now a few inches apart and spreading rapidly. Her whole body, which had been sitting upright when last he looked, was slowly bending backward, more and more until—plunk—she was lying flat on her back, looking at the sky, one knee bent for the sake of being demure, but the rest of her afire with Latin desire. She was his. All his. All he had to do was lean over and get it. So he leaned over and hovered above her, one arm supporting him on each side of her, suspended in his world-famous push-up position—and she slowly lowered her bent knee until there was nothing between them except for what he could muster. No words were necessary, but they came out anyway. Out of Hermie. And he'd never know why. "Tough to find good firewood on a beach."

She looked up at him. "Oh?" Women were always saying "oh" to him. What the hell did it mean? Her arms were motionless at her side, and her breasts were aimed at his nose. Had they been loaded with ammo, he'd have been caught in a deadly crossfire. A guy could get crosseyed trying to figure out which of the pert pistols to look at.

"Yeah," he said. "Actually, this stuff I'm burning is somebody's fence." His arms were beginning to tremble. Also his toes because he was balanced on them, too. He was in the air above her on ten little fingers and ten tiny toes.

"Really?" She squirmed. Her other knee, having been fully rested, came up slowly to measure the distance between their two bodies. It gently nudged Hermie in the one place he was beginning to overhang in.

"Can I toast you another tasty marshmallow?" It was him again, only because of the foreign pressure on his body, it came out a couple octaves higher than Lily Pons.

She took a while to answer. And all the while she kept pushing her knee a little higher and therefore a little deeper into his nearest extremities. She was trying to tell him something, but Hermie kept pulling up and back. He'd shortly be off the ground. "Don't you think," she said, wiggling her knee in an incredible corkscrew motion, "that we've had enough marshmallows?"

"You can never have enough of a good tasty marshmallow." And he pushed himself off with all his remaining strength, his body withdrawing from her curious knee and arriving miraculously in a sitting position back at the marshmallows. He was sweating like a fiend. Also, he was scared shitless. He hadn't counted on that kind of reaction from himself. Fright. Personal terror. Sexual panic. Nor had there been anything in the Twelve Dopey Points to cover such a situation. All he knew was that he couldn't face her because he was obviously only half a man. What the hell was wrong with him? What weird disease had done him in? How could he be set on fire by that dumb girl and be unable to do anything about it, in spite of the fact that she was so spread out behind him that he could have walked right up her insides while wearing a full set of shoulder pads?

But Aggie knew a few things, if not by feminine instinct then by the latest report from her knee which had just checked in. There was nothing wrong with Hermie or his anatomy. He was just nervous. And she had gone just about as far as she dared, manifesting an almost brazen feminine interest in the process. Also, if the truth were known, had Hermie responded in an aggressive manner, she'd have quickly pushed him off and run away screaming "Rape." And so it came as a momentary relief to her to know that she was in no danger of having her morals tested. Therefore, she felt very good about things and decided to not be too forward, but just forward enough to let Hermie know that she liked him and that, if he could regroup his forces, a couple goodies still awaited him. A couple squeezes. A couple handfuls. But that's all. "It certainly is calm tonight." She looked up at the sky. "Does that mean it'll rain tomorrow?"

Hermie was very gratified to discover that she was neither angry nor insulting. "I think the night's too clear. All those stars, you know."

"Yes, you're right. You know a lot about weather, don't you?"

"Well, I know when it's *raining*." He hadn't intended that to be funny, but since she laughed so convincingly, he figured he'd better do likewise. So he laughed and toasted another marshmallow and embellished his last comment. "There are certain kinds of clouds. Nimbus. That means rain. That's meteorology, which we have to learn in preflight because it helps you fly better when you know if it's going to rain, or snow for that matter."

"Yes," she said. She could say "yes" and she could say "oh," and Hermie figured it was just a way in which women filled in the gaps when they were getting hot.

Hermie turned to her and offered her the twig with the marshmallow dangling on it. "Here you are."

She sat up because it had come at her so suddenly. And she

opened her mouth and took in the whole marshmallow, slowly pulling her head back so that only the naked twig remained. And Hermie got so excited; only he didn't know why. She rolled the marshmallow around inside her mouth, and Hermie finally could see the resemblance. She tried to say something, but her mouth was too full.

Hermie looked down at his hand, the tricky one. It was moving. It had been involuntarily launched, and it was moving out. He looked over at Aggie, and she was flat on her back again, unable to speak because her face was so stuffed. He felt his body slide toward her, and he watched his hand move about her waist and disappear beneath her loose sweater. The hand was cold, and the flat belly was warm, and the girl went "eeek." And the hand, frightened, withdrew and hid itself in Hermie's pocket. Hermie's mouth tried to retrieve at least a part of the awkward and dreadful moment. "How'd you like the tasty marshmallow?"

Aggie couldn't speak because her mouth was too full. And she couldn't hear too well because of the pounding in her temples. So she picked herself up on her elbows and smiled. She was perhaps one of the world's greatest smilers. She was a rare bird indeed. The warm-bellied, quick-smiling eeker. Find *that* in your John James Audubon.

Hermie retired to the fire feeling strangely good. He had made a move. He had demonstrated beyond the shadow of a doubt that he was not a homo. But more than that, *she* had been the one to call it quits. All this was fine with him because he was shaking like a flivver, and had she allowed him to go further, he might have just passed out at the encountering of a navel, especially if it was an outsie, which was the most uncommon of all navels. He toasted and ate four more marshmallows before Aggie spoke. Aggie knew that the situation had died aborning. She had no illusions of Hermie's trying again. She had said "eek," and that was the end of it. There was nothing left to do but inquire about the other people in the world. She did so with remorse and a certain coldness. "Shouldn't we save a few marshmallows for Miriam and Oscy?"

Hermie looked off into the night like a pointer. "We may never see them again."

"They seem to be getting along very well." That may have been a sarcastic dig. Hermie couldn't tell.

"Yes. They're very friendly." It pained Hermie to realize that the rest of him was not as masculinely aggressive as his hand. He knew that, in spite of her "eek," Aggie had wanted him to get funny with her. He knew that the "eek" was merely a reaction to the sudden temperature differential. Shit, any warm belly would go "eek" if suddenly a cold hand slid across it. He cursed himself for not making certain that his hand was warm before sending it off on Objective: Tit. If nothing else, he had learned that you never go for a warm tit with a cold paw. Unless, of course, you wanted to be rebuffed. And he thought about *that* for a little while. Maybe, subconsciously, he had deliberately sent out a cold hand because he knew it would make her go "eek" and that that would be the end of it and he could withdraw from combat in the crummy belief that there was nothing wrong with him. He began to feel more and more like a homo. Why did he always take such pains with his hair? Why were some of his shirts so loud that his father thought they were his sister's? Why could Aggie look so good to him one minute and so repulsive the next? Why had he allowed Oscy to claim big-boobed Miriam without at least a small discussion on the matter? How close had he himself come to running away that night at the movie house? He plucked the petals of his mind. Homo. Not a homo. Homo. Not a homo.

There was a noise not too far away but coming closer. A huffing and a puffing. A padding on the sand, almost imperceptible to the naked ear but not to the son of the greatest pair of ears on earth, the Listening Mother. Hermie peered into the darkness, squinting so tightly that his teeth appeared between his pulled-up lips.

Out of the darkness, trotting, came Oscy. His shirttail flapping in his wake like a midnight witch, his belt askew and smacking his belly like a shutter in a heavy wind. And as he ran, he kept trying to button his fly lest his pants fall down and trip him. He stopped about ten yards short of the fire, his vision somewhat impaired by the sudden sharp light, and he looked around like a blind man. "Pssssst? Hermie?"

Hermie, ever the gentleman, asked of Aggie, "Would you excuse me for a moment, please?"

Aggie said, "Sure," but she didn't know what to make of it.

Hermie was gallant. "Thank you." He stood, smiled at her as though thanking her for the dance, and then walked over to where Oscy stood, studying his notes and holding up his pants. "Hi, Oscy." Talk about your disinterested calm.

Oscy was harassed. He didn't even look at Hermie. He just stuck out his hand, "Lemmee see your notes. My lousy carbon copy is smudged from sweat. Come on, come on. Fork over!" Hermie dug out his copy of the document, which he had folded and stuffed into his key pocket. Oscy grabbed it and unfolded it impatiently. Then he held it to the light and studied it closely. "Yeah. Just as I thought."

"What number you up to?"

"Six."

"Six? Six is foreplay!" Hermie was knocked out. "You up to six?"

"Yeah. But that crazy Miriam—she's up to *nine*."

Hermie took a backward step, a gesture of stunned awe. "You're kidding?"

"I'm not kidding. She's ruining my timing." He was studying the notes with scholarly concentration. "Uh-huh. Uh-huh. Uh-huh. Jesus Christ." Then he thrust the paper back at Hermie. "How you doing with Aggie?"

"Well, I—"

"No time for gabbing, Hermie." And he turned and ran back into the night, tugging up his pants as he went, looking like the last man in a potato sack race.

Hermie wandered back to Aggie, who had heard nothing but who wasn't exactly blind. "That was Oscy," she said. She was a regular Mr. Keen.

Hermie sat down on the blanket, pushing his notes back into

his pocket. "Feel like another marshmallow?"

"What's that paper?"

"This?"

"Yes."

"Oh. It's a map." He stuffed it in before he had a chance to fold it properly. It lumped up in his pocket like a golf ball.

"Buried treasure?" Aggie asked. What a simpleton she was turning out to be.

"Yeah," said Hermie. "Buried treasure." And *he* was beginning to think it was, too.

"Well, can I see it?"

"Why don't you just have another marshmallow?"

"Oh, I—" That was about all she had a chance to say before the burned-to-a-crisp marshmallow came thrusting at her. It fell apart in her fingers, but she still managed to smile. Hermie was getting pretty goddamned sick of all her smiling. And he was beginning to wonder what he ever saw in her in the first place.

He ate a couple more marshmallows, some of them raw just for a change of pace. He figured he'd probably get the gout, but it didn't much matter. It was as good a way of dying as any. He ignored Aggie, not rudely, but just by busying himself. He picked up debris and things and kept feeding it all to the fire until the flames were climbing so high they could guide in the whole Luftwaffe. Among other things that his fire feeding proved: Coke bottles don't burn, and the best you can get from seaweed is smoke. Hermie knew that he'd screwed up completely and that it was *Miriam* he should be with. Miriam was some hot blond potato. Aggie was more like a nun. He tried to figure out some deal he could offer Oscy so that they could switch girls on the next marshmallow roast, which, by the by, would be without marshmallows or else without Hermie. But what the hell could he give Oscy besides Aggie to sweeten the offer? The answer was nothing. He looked over at Aggie, and there she was, at it again, flat on her back with that one stupid knee in the sky, wiggling it around as if it were some kind of compass. That Aggie could fall on her back at a moment's notice. It was as if there were a hinge on her ass. In her loose-fitting clothes she looked like a pile of laundry. He wished he could just go over and screw her without all the polite chitchat. It was the polite chitchat that was driving him up the wall. "Point Two: Converse." Well, fuck Point Two. Oscy was up to foreplay, and Miriam was God knows where. Boy, did he ever want a crack at Miriam. But Oscy had her. Oscy was also running toward the fire again. He arrived and then stood there, disheveled, looking as though he'd gone ten rounds with a Mixmaster, mopping his hair into place with one hand, holding up his sagging pants with the other. "Hermie? Hermie?"

Hermie addressed Aggie with poise and carriage. "Would you excuse me again?"

The hinge on Aggie's ass sprung her into a sitting position. She wasn't sure she liked the way Oscy looked, but still she said, "Yes."

"You're very kind," said Hermie, and he went to join Oscy at the fire. "Say, Oscy—"

"Gimmee a rubber." Oscy had his hand outstretched.

"What?"

"A rubber, a rubber! Come on, Hermie!" He sounded desperate.

"But what happened to your heirloom?"

"It was spoiled. They don't keep. Hermie, for Chrissakes—" He shoved Hermie hard. Hermie then pulled the blue foil package from his pocket. Oscy was in some kind of a hurry. "Open it! Will ya open it!"

Hermie broke the foil. Up till then it had been his hope that when the seal was broken, it would be on his own behalf, but those days were over. Three individually hand-rolled little rubbers met his eye, like newborn kittens, thirty-three and a third cents apiece. Oscy's hand shot in and pulled one from the litter. Then he was running away with it. Hermie, quite put out, called angrily after the hysterical runner, "Don't you even say thank you!"

The voice that came back at him was Miriam's. "Thank you, Hermie." It was followed by distant laughter, Oscy and Miriam.

Hermie was really steaming. He folded up the foil and stuck it back in his pocket. He returned to Aggie. Her hinge had her still sitting upright. He tried not to look at her because he hated her so much for giving him such a hard time, whereas her blond friend Miriam was out there in the night, screwing Oscy's brains out.

"Why did Miriam say thank you?" Aggie asked that like the imbecile she really was.

"Because she's a lady!"

"I see."

Hermie snapped at her like a mongoose. "See what!" Jesus, did he ever hate her for thinking her tits were so special that a guy had to beg her for a squeeze. Who the hell did she think she was, Carole Landis?

She seemed surprised at his question. "See what?"

Hermie was a small fire. For the first time he noticed the blemishes on her adolescent face and the few crooked teeth in her half-open mouth. What the hell was he doing with a girl with crooked teeth? He had enough crooked teeth of his own to look at without gazing at hers. "You said you saw! What did you see?"

"Well, actually—nothing."

"Then don't say you see when you don't see, okay?"

"Okay. Gee." She wondered what she'd done to get him so angry.

"Have a marshmallow, folks!" He pushed a marshmallow right at her, and she opened her mouth just in time not to wear it on her nose. Hermie watched the marshmallow blobbing around in her mouth. It wasn't nearly as exciting as the other time. What the hell was so exciting about watching a girl with blemishes eating a marshmallow, anyway? He must have been out of his mind.

He decided to let her sit there and think things over. He also decided not to feed the fire. Fuck it. Let it go out and all mankind with it. Who was he feeding it for anyway, Oscy? Oscy was the son of a bitch who took his girl, his rubber, and his self-respect. Aggie? Her miserable tits were obviously so cold she could boil 'em in oil and still never get a sizzle out of them. So what the hell was he doing trying to keep *Aggie* warm? Besides, he'd built that fire so well that it could burn a year and still have enough left to cook Joan of Arc. He took a quick look at Aggie. Her hinge had sprung, and she was frozen in an upright position. For the first time, she didn't bother to smile. The hell with her. She'd used up enough smiles to keep Laurel and Hardy in business forever. It was obvious that their relationship was ending. Tomorrow they'd be just friends, which was a lot more than they'd been yesterday. He could forget her just like that. And if, in future years, he ever *did* remember her or recall her to mind, it would be as a deaf-muted, crooked-toothed, acne-skinned, nippleless girl.

Huffing noises drew Hermie's attention to the direction whence Oscy had arrived two times already. This was the third. Only he wasn't in such fine fettle anymore. He drew up to the fire and stood there, waiting to die. He tried to call Hermie, but all that came out was a wheeze. "Huuuuuuh. Huhhhhhh."

Hermie looked at Aggie once again to enlist her permission to be excused. But before the request could even be verbalized, Aggie merely waved at him, motioning that it was all right for him to go. And judging by the kind of wave she whipped out, it was also all right for Hermie never to return.

Hermie got the message and went over to Oscy, fully geared to punch him out for his thoughtlessness, selfishness, and cheapness. But by the time he reached his forlorn companion another emotion had consumed him, kind of pity and nostalgia and encouragement, so that all he could say to Oscy was, "Need a rubber?"

"I need a breather." Oscy truly looked as though he hadn't quite made it under the Macy's truck. His breathing was impaired, returning to regularity only ever so slowly. But say what you wanted about Oscy, he was no quitter, which was why he added, "I also need another rubber."

Automatically, Hermie dug out his package of rubbers and opened it. Oscy took one of the rubbers, and Hermie said, "That's sixty-six cents, Oscy." Oscy couldn't comprehend, so Hermie explained. "Two rubbers, sixty-six cents. I'm not running a charity, you know."

Oscy was so dulled he could only nod and say, "S'okay." Then he seemed to sag. His knees kind of splayed out sideways, as though a heavy object were resting on his shoulders, like maybe the world.

Hermie got scared. "Oscy? Jesus, you okay?"

Oscy pulled himself up straight. "Huh?"

"You okay?"

"Oh, sure. I guess I must've—dozed off."

"Dozed off! How the hell can you doze off?"

"I'm awfully tired, Hermie." And he shook his head to gather his few remaining senses.

"Did you get to Point Twelve?"

Oscy's voice was so small as to sound as though it were coming out from behind loose grains of sand. But it was also proud, infinitely proud. "Twelve? Hermie…we are so far past Twelve—"

A gong went off in Hermie's head. It struck twelve. "But—Twelve is as far as the book goes. What's after Twelve?" Bong, bong, bong, bong…

Oscy looked at Hermie through dancing eyes. Even though he was tired and probably mortally wounded, those pale-blue eyes had true twinkles in them. "Thirteen." And then, with a nice wave of the fresh rubber in his hand, he walked away. Then he stopped and turned and said, "Fourteen." Then he resumed walking only to stop and turn again. "Fifteen. Hermie, you have no idea." He walked on, being gradually eaten up by the night, all except his voice which seemed to come from a faraway megaphone. "Sixteen. Seventeen." His voice grew smaller and smaller. "Eighteen." And he was gone, just like that, counted out. But talk about your long counts. Bong, bong, bong, bong…

Hermie stood there aghast and akimbo. Oscy not only had crossed over, but had also burned all the bridges leading back. Oscy was off into manhood, a walking whorehouse. Oh, sure, Oscy was known to kid a guy from time to time, but never Hermie. And never about anything so serious. No, Oscy had undoubtedly screwed Miriam to a fare-thee-well and then some. And the son of a bitch was going back for more. What stamina. Play *that* on your *Colgate Sports Newsreel*, Bill Stern.

Aggie was standing alongside him. Upright. She hadn't forgotten how to stand. "I think Miriam and I should be getting home."

"Huh?" Hermie took a moment to evaluate the situation. Yes. He would best be serving Oscy by getting Aggie the hell off the beach. "Oh. Sure. Come on. I'll take you home." He took her arm, the one he had once squeezed so tenderly. It meant nothing to him. It was just a thing to grab onto, a way to get her out of the way so that Oscy could enjoy his screwing without any interruptions from tourists or curiosity seekers.

Aggie shook free, calmly determined. "I think I'd better get Miriam."

"Aggie, I don't think so." But she was already in motion, passing Hermie and on her way to where Oscy was last seen. Hermie followed like a dopey puppy. "Listen. Listen, Aggie? I'll take you home. Aggie?"

Aggie wasn't buying. Nor was she stopping for anyone. She even accelerated. Her eyes began to fill with tears, and her hair flew about. She was vulnerable and scared and kind of pretty, running like that. Hermie trotted alongside her, inadequately, as if he were asking for her autograph. The moon, unnoticeable when they sat by the fire, was providing Aggie with some very dramatic lighting. Even in her big, loose sweater she looked quite lovable. And her breasts, the little darlings, damned if they didn't have some bounce to 'em. Hermie reached out and took her wrist and wrenched her to a stop. She wheeled at him, looked at him, pulled her hand free, and started to say something. "Hermie, this—" That's all she could crank out before taking off again. And Hermie stood there, riveted to the sand, flat-footed and fifteen. He watched her as she reached the trysting place and pulled up short. He watched the back of her as she suddenly went rigid, and he knew pretty damned well that she had found Oscy and Miriam.

Hermie found himself walking toward the spot, his feet like snow plows, his ass full of lead. By the time he arrived there Aggie was leaving. She passed him as though she were a ball that had bounced off a wall without losing a smidgeon of velocity. "Say, Aggie—" He stopped talking because he saw the incredulous look on her face as she swept by. The phrase was "She looked as though she'd just seen a ghost." But even that could not fully depict Aggie's clobbered countenance. Hermie had never seen a look like that, except maybe once or twice on his mother's face when the radio said that a plane had crashed, like the one with Carole Lombard on it because Hermie's father was supposed to have been on that same plane. His father never again phoned ahead to say what plane he'd be on. He'd always phone from LaGuardia when he arrived, and then the whole family only worried that he might get killed in the taxi drive home. Anyway, Hermie watched her go. It was the last he ever saw of Aggie, the very last. Pretty girl running.

Hermie found his breath coming in spastic bursts as he walked ahead to see what Aggie had seen. He knew what he'd see. It would be no surprise. It wasn't. And he stopped five feet short of the blanket, driven by curiosity, consumed with disbelief, sinking with despair.

Oscy was on top of Miriam, in her. His pants were down and lassoed around his ankles. His loose belt buckle smacked rhythmically at the blanket. And he hadn't even bothered to take off his lousy sweat shirt. Miriam's legs were all around him, the toes of her bare feet clawing at the moon, her blond head stuck over Oscy's grinding shoulder, her eyes closed, her teeth bared, her arms clamped around Oscy's back but inside his sweat shirt. The whole thing looked like a wind-up toy with a couple of parts missing, causing erratic misses in its smooth operation. It all filtered into Hermie's brain like a series of dirty photographs, grainy and cheap. The back of the man's head, the blurred face of the woman impaled on the unseen lance, dancing on it, hurting from it, loving it. The moon kept slipping in and out, giving the action the look of penny pictures that cranked at Coney Island. It was Point Twelve. Definitely Point Twelve. Point Twelve with bells on. Point Twelve covered by the throb of the hammering surf, steaming on a damp blanket. Point Twelve featuring the crafty despoiler of Claire Trevor aflame in his goddamn sweat shirt. Oscy, the boob-grabber, drilling for oil, stabbing at the center of the earth, firing himself into the bobbing blond marshmallow that lay two thighs to the wind. Hermie turned and got out of there.

yearning to fight a shark, to drag it to shore by its tail and have his picture taken beside it as it hung headdown on the hoist, largest shark ever captured by man in those or any other waters. He wanted to spot a landing party of Nazis, maybe thirty men in all, sneaking up on America only to encounter the heroic young man who beat them back into the sea in a manner to be worked out later. He wanted to do something. Anything. Because he felt his life slipping away. All around him there were people who were involved, in things, in events, in life. They were fighting wars, and making movies, and getting laid, and being successful, and writing news dispatches from far-off places. Yet he was doing nothing. All he was doing was eating marshmallows and squeezing arms and watching close friends get laid. He didn't want to see or even talk to Oscy because he knew he was no longer in a league with Oscy. Oscy had crossed over. Oscy, at fifteen, had gotten laid. In Hermie's neighborhood, most of the guys waited until they were *married* to get laid. And many of *them* were so nervous that they usually didn't get laid until the second or third night. One guy, he'd heard, took a month to get laid and then it was with the *maid* because his wife couldn't wait for him to get it up, so she skipped out. Hermie knew that he could have done with Aggie exactly what Oscy did with Miriam. He had had the same opportunity, the same night, the same beach, the same notes, and three rubbers to Oscy's one. Why then hadn't he done it? To keep saying that Aggie was unattractive was a crock. She was just as attractive as, if not more so than, Miriam, except maybe she had a few pounds fewer tits. The thing he had to face up to was his own masculinity—or lack of it. No putting it off any longer. Aggie had been camped on her back the better part of the evening. He could have had her even with *two* cold hands and with an *icicle* for a pecker. That "eek" of Aggie's was nothing. It might even have been some kind of *love* noise that women make. He had Aggie, on her back, making love noises in the night—and he'd bugged out. Oscy had screwed Miriam all the way to China, but he, Hermie, had to take his erection home with him. And he, Hermie, had to lie on his back all night because the damned thing had a memory like an elephant. It remembered Miriam as she was and Aggie as she should have been. It was like a third eye in his forehead that saw only sex and, as such, gave him no rest. He lay down with it at night, and he woke up with it in the morning. He left the house with it and was walking down the beach with it. It was taking over his life because it wouldn't go away. It hung around like a mine-sapping device, like a water diviner. And no doubt, when the summer was over, and he'd returned to school, it would ruin all chances of his making the basketball team since he'd foul out of every game within the first five minutes, hacking down opposing players and from two yards away, unless they were sensational hurdlers. Nor would the bloody thing do him much good in biology either since he'd be studying human life next to Winifred McAllister, whom he *always* ended up next to, and whose watery blue eyes and pert bobby socks had been driving him half out of his mind since the day he first passed within the hallowed Gothic arch of Erasmus Hall.

He tried to think of something else to take his mind off it and perhaps cause it to return to its rightful size. He thought of other things, cabbages and kings, batting averages and song lyrics. Lunch. Boats. Cars. Sea gulls. He looked into the sky to see if his old nemesis was planning some more saturation bombing. Nothing was in the sky, but someone was on the horizon. The woman. Swell. Just what he needed, some more torture. She was sitting on a high dune near her house. *Her* house. He was walking down the beach toward *her* house. Why? Why had he done that? His heart donned wings, and the answer flapped in his mind, simple and basic. She. The woman. Her. Her was the reason he couldn't screw Aggie. Her was the one who was the captor of his heart. Not Aggie. Not Miriam. Not Winifred McAllister. Not Conrad Veidt. But her. Small wonder he had found Aggie so repulsive. His heart and his mind had been elsewhere all along. What was all that stuff about preliminaries? Sometimes a kid comes along who is so good, so quick, that he gets a crack at the title right off campus. How many times had John Garfield done that very thing? Maybe not exactly off campus, but certainly right out of the poolroom.

Hermie looked at her, all huddled up in a sweater a little too large, probably Pete's, writing, probably a letter, probably to Pete. Hermie walked toward her but via an oblique angle that found him climbing to the top of the dune well before it reached her house. He then proceeded along the dune's crest and came around behind her turned back, arriving there just as the sun broke through. The sun, the sun! A fucking omen.

She was startled to see the sun break out so sharply all about her and to find herself mantled within a giant shadow. She swiveled her pretty head and looked up at the imposing figure of Hermie. And it pleased him to see her so taken by surprise. Her mouth was open in a searching smile as she tried to make him out. And the adult, full-grown male in Hermie, told him that he had the advantage of her. He fiddled with the buttons of his OPACS club sweater, the one that once had his name embroidered over the left-hand pocket. It had started out as "Hermie" in script. When they ordered the sweaters, the OPACS voted that "Hermie" was what would go on Hermie's sweater because that's what his name was. He had stumped for "Herm" because it was more mature and he figured he'd have the sweater for a couple years, so why be hung with a name out of his childhood like "Hermie"? Oscy supported him vocally, and Benjie abstained, but still the sons of bitches voted for "Hermie" over his pocket. It wasn't too long after the sweaters had arrived that Hermie began to unravel the "e" and then the "i" in the avowed hope of stopping the process and holding at "Herm." But the whole piece of script was in one chunk, and once he'd pulled out the end, the rest of it couldn't be deterred from unraveling. He was "Herm" for only one week in spite of the chewing gum he applied to the running wound. He was "Her" for three days which was pretty embarrassing. He was "He" for another three days. He was "H" for a day and a half and not even his mother and her nimble thimble could stop the lousy embroidery from unraveling. After the "H" went, he was nothing for a week before the club fined him sixty-cent damages, ten cents for each letter, because that's what it had cost. He told the club to go fuck itself and was fined another dime. They settled out of court when autumn came because it was Hermie's football. In the spring they reinstituted charges against him, but Hermie's uncle, the Philadelphia lawyer, invoked some kind of statute of limitations and he got Hermie off with only a severe reprimand if he promised under oath never to go against the will of the OPACS again. Hermie told them to go fuck themselves and was fined a quarter. He paid because the Philadelphia lawyer was out of town, but he never again wore the sweater except when no OPACS were around, except for Oscy and Benjie. Because they had supported him in his legal battles, he would, from time to time, wear his nameless sweater in their presence, especially since neither of them was too happy with the names over his own pocket. Benjie had opted for "Ben," and Oscy had campaigned for "Spike." They lost. Anyway, all that was far away and behind Hermie as he knelt down behind her, on one dangerous knee, a little to one side. "Hi," he said. Shit, did he ever sound masculine.

She looked up at the heroic silhouette while shielding her eyes with one of her delectable, Lux-beautiful hands. "Hermie?"

"Right." He had hoped she might have figured he was Pete because there *was* a resemblance. No matter. He would keep the sun behind him as long as he could, to keep her off-balance. Just another of the little tricks he was picking up. He was learning.

"Could you come around front, Hermie? It's so bright."

Keeping his voice so low that he could have sung "Old Man River," Hermie spoke. "Think I was someone else?"

"Oh, I knew it was you." The glare was still bothering her. "Hermie? Could you come around front? Please?"

"Sure." Her wish was his command. Besides, she was off-balance enough. No sense in blinding her. He came around and sat beside her but was still on higher ground. He enjoyed his height advantage. And the higher he was, the lower his voice. "How've you been?"

"Do you have a cold?"

"No." Enough of that shit. He went back to his normal voice. "Have you been all right these days?"

"Oh, yes. Fine." That smile. That face. The eyes. The hair. Fuck off, Aggie. "And *you?*"

"Oh, fair to middlin'." He wasn't exactly certain what that meant, but he figured *she'd* know.

She brushed that wisp of hair back from her eyes, but the sea breeze kept throwing it back. It was a losing fight, but she was so intent on seeing the tall guy she was conversing with that she kept fighting the breeze regardless of the outcome. "It's a lovely morning, isn't it?"

"Yes." He wanted to expand on his answer but couldn't find the additional words. He blamed the dull subject matter for his inability to be more clever. And then it hit him. He had said "yes" just as she used to. It meant that he had an advantage. Good. The wheel had come around full cycle, full fathom five, so to speak. He turned his head to the sea, giving her a chance to see his profile. He, of course, had never seen it, but he'd been told that it was a fine profile. Then he remembered that it had been his mother who told him that, so he stopped the profile bit and faced her again.

"Should be a very nice day." She was continuing that line of conversation. Maybe she was getting at something. Maybe he should take the hint and follow along.

"Yes. I watched the sun come up. It's an experience." He said that with feeling. And he noticed how she looked at him, as though a poet had just spoken. So he went further. "Seeing the sun come up like that...is certainly an experience." It sounded familiar even to him.

She was all one glowing smile. Even in that dumb oversized sweater she was rapturously exciting. And those long, cool legs in the flattering shorts, stretching toward the ocean in graceful angles and dips—he had to change his position or be strangled by his own bathing suit. "Do you do that often, Hermie?"

"Do what?" he said, thinking she had referred to his movement to rescue his genitals.

"Watch the sunrise?"

"Oh, yes. Well—no." It was getting a bit sticky, that subject, so he switched over to something he knew more about. "How are those boxes we put away? Any trouble?"

"Oh, no trouble. They're still up there." She said it with pride, intending for Hermie to take it as a compliment, which he did.

"I think they'll be all right." He wasn't really aware of it, but he was brushing some grains of sand from his Band-Aid so that the flashing neon could be seen.

She leaned in and noticed. "Did you hurt yourself?"

He was taken a bit by surprise and pulled back. "Oh—that."

She was looking right at it. Could she see it glowing? Would she kiss it again? Would the animal chained within her come gnashing out again? "I noticed it the other day."

You bet your sweet ass you noticed it. You *put* it there. "It's not serious."

"Shouldn't you change that Band-Aid?"

It was time. Time to get at it. Time to stop beating about the Band-Aid. "I'm thinking of keeping it on as long as possible." Was that enough to the point, oh, blessed loved one?

She seemed to back off. "Oh."

"Is that okay with you?"

"I guess so." Could she have forgotten so soon?

He'd help her. "I don't do this often."

"I see."

He'd help her some more. "It's a special Band-Aid."

"Is it medicated?"

"It's enchanted." Could Hemingway have paid greater homage to a Band-Aid? Could Edwin Arlington Robinson? Could Edgar Guest? Could Nick Kenny?

"Oh." She turned back to her writing.

Hermie had to admit to himself that the Band-Aid bit hadn't gone over so well. Perhaps she had just plain forgotten that she herself had put the Band-Aid there to cover the fang marks she made with her bloodsucking. Maybe she plastered Band-Aids on guys all over the island. Maybe every guy who came to her house— plumbers, electricians, burglars—maybe they all got in on a little of her sex-crazed bloodsucking. Maybe you could tell how many times a guy had been to her house by the number of Band-Aids on him, like swastikas on the fuselages of RAF Spitfires. Maybe she was some kind of Band-Aid fiend. Maybe she flew around at midnight sucking on guys' legs. Maybe he'd better drop the whole thing because, very likely, all of it was only vicious rumors. "Writing a letter?" he said. Brilliant. That was like telling her that he just happened to notice that she was breathing.

She smiled without looking up. "Yes." She was getting used to the way he talked. Might as well, he wasn't going away.

"I'd ask you to the movies, but it's the same picture. Like to see it again?" He surprised himself by resorting to so direct an approach. But he immediately felt good. It was manly to be forthright about asking for a date. How often he had heard his sister after a telephone conversation with some jerk, complaining to his mother that the guy never got to the point which was why she had no respect for him.

"Oh, I don't think so."

"I don't blame you. Once you know the ending, it kills the thrill. There'll be a new picture playing soon. Maybe you'd like to see it."

"Well, I really don't go to too many movies." Maybe she'd heard that he was a sex-crazed arm squeezer.

"It's a good one. I saw the posters. *H. M. Pulham Esquire*. Robert Young, Hedy Lamarr, and Ruth Hussey. I put Ruth Hussey in the same class as John Loder. She's pretty, but she never seems to do too well."

She kept writing, just nodding to let him know that she had heard but that she wasn't really all that interested.

He wasn't sure where the courage came from, but it arrived and he spoke. "I'd be pleased to take you." She looked up and smiled. She was another of the world's great smilers. People with false teeth smiled a lot, but he was pretty sure all of hers were real. "*H. M. Pulham Esquire*. I think it's Paramount."

She finished up her letter. Skinny V-mail tissue. She licked it shut, and when her darting tongue flicked the glue to life, he felt it right in the groin. "Oh, Hermie, I don't think so. But thank you. It's very sweet of you to ask me."

He was losing ground. He figured he'd drop back to old reliable. "Do you have any more heavy objects at home that need moving?"

"None that occur to me." She was paying more attention to the goddamn envelope than to him.

He was beginning to feel silly. "Well, if you think of any, feel free."

She stood. "Thank you, Hermie. You're very thoughtful."

He stood, too. Good, he was definitely taller. It gave him new courage. And he'd need it for the next thing he was going to say. "Will you be at home tonight?"

"Pardon?" She stiffened, and the smile she flashed was slightly lunatic.

Once again he had her off-balance. Therefore, move in. But with delicacy and aplomb. "I thought I might drop by. I have to be in that neighborhood." Some neighborhood. Hers was the only house for half a mile.

"Oh. Well—feel free to drop by." The breeze was busier when she was standing, and she had to keep pushing the hair from her face. Hermie would have liked to have done it for her. He'd like to have put his fingers through her hair. It had to be a sensational feeling. Like satin.

"I'm not saying I'll be there for *sure*, so don't count on it." He said that to cover himself, in case it turned out that he'd prove chicken and not show up. He had chickened out with Aggie; he might chicken out with *her*. Who knew? He was capable of definitely not showing up, and he was aware of it and didn't want to cause her any inconvenience if she went and prepared things. With a lover already in service, what gorgeous woman needed a shitty kid not showing up after she'd gone to the trouble of Cheezits and coffee?

"Goodness, it's getting late. I have to run this letter down to the post office."

"I'll run it down for you." Bullshit. He'd burn it. But first he'd read it and see how she really felt about Pete. Maybe it would turn out to be a "Dear John" letter. If it did, Hermie would be at her house for damned sure. He might even move in. All was fair in love and war, so fuck you, Pete.

She must have read his mind. "No. No, thanks. It's very tricky postage. Overseas and all that. Well—" She turned to go back up to her house. "Bye, Hermie."

He watched her walk away, and it hit him like a howitzer. He didn't know her name! What the hell was that! He was hung up on a woman, and he didn't even know her name! He didn't even know her initials! If nothing else, it was discourteous never to have even asked. No wonder she wanted to get away from him. Imagine a gentleman wanting to screw a lady and never even taking a moment out to ask her her name. Worse, what if her name turned out to be Frenesie or Tallulah or something so equally idiotic that he'd never be able to say aloud, "I love you, LaZonga." He called to her. "Hello?"

She stopped on the first of the fourteen steps and faced him. And in her too big sweater she looked like the Little Match Girl. "Excuse me," Hermie said, "but I don't even know your name." He waited four hundred years for her answer to make its way through the air.

"Dorothy."

"I had a cat named Dorothy... Got hit by a truck."

Dorothy smiled. Dorothy. She had a name, and it was beautiful. Beautiful Dorothy. And she waved and smiled and climbed the fourteen steps like a Ziegfeld Girl and at the top of the stairs she turned again and smiled again. "Dorothy on the Porch," by Rembrandt. She went into the house. "Dorothy Going Through the Door," by Da Vinci. "Dorothy Out of Sight," by Michelangelo. "Door," by Salva Door Dali. Yuk.

Hermie let himself walk down toward the ocean, feeling as high as a tidal wave, give or take a couple cowlicks. "Dorothy in My Heart," by Rubens. He looked at the house again, up there on the high dune. "Dorothy in Her House," by the sea. "Dorothy, I'll See You Tonight," by God. "Dorothy, Break Out the Cheezits," by Nabisco.

Hermie on the Beach.
Hermie in the Ocean, Swimming.
Hermie in Love, Damned Near Drowning.
Shazam.
Hi-Ho, Silver.
Yaaaaaaa, Sheena!

Hermie, on the beach drying. For about fifteen minutes. He was one of those fast driers, though his bathing suit took a little longer, especially the supporter, which could remain wet until September if you didn't watch it. In another fifteen minutes he was in town, sitting at the counter in Margie's Pie Place. He was having a kind of breakfast, orange juice, apple pie, coffee, peach pie, coffee, a cruller, and water. The only other customers that early were fishermen, who, having completed their dawn labors, had come in for some breakfast cheer. They had brought into port such things as cockles and mussels, alive, alive-o, and they had a tendency to give the place a fishy smell, though Margie never complained. There were three salt-crusted fishermen, fresh off a Fletcher's Castoria calendar, all sitting at the far end of the place, stuffing their craws with bacon and eggs and toast and endless amounts of coffee. Their voices were gruff, and Hermie knew that though no one in the world ever truly said, "Yo-ho-ho and a bottle of rum," those three fishermen were capable of saying things like "Jib the boom and mizzen the mains'l and fire a shot across their scow, me hearties!"

Hermie sipped his coffee, feeling very good and very belonging. He watched Margie from over the rim of his cup and through the steam that made it look as though her quaint ass were burning. Margie was about thirty, maybe fifty, but she was neat and firm, and in her white starched dress the swells and curves of her body were avast and what is the name of your ship? Nor were her legs exactly covered with barnacles. They were fine. Margie, you could tell, was a sailor's wife. She was supposed to have a husband in the Navy somewhere because he used to pilot one of the ferries before the war, so what the hell would he be doing in the Army? With his new awareness of the sensuality of women, Hermie knew that no normal woman could go too long without a proper screwing for old times' sake. And that was true of Margie, too, because on that crummy island she had a lot of time to sit around and think and do nothing but listen to foghorns. Hermie shifted his gaze to the three fishermen, and he determined that not a one of them was under eighty-six. Therefore, if Margie was suddenly called upon to favor a man right then and there with some hot sex, by all that was logical, Hermie had to be the first choice. Hermie was aware of the sexy way he was beginning to look at things and people. Whatever mystery women once held for him had gone up in a puff of Oscy. Miriam was a woman, and she screwed. Aggie was a woman, and she'd be hurting that morning because Hermie hadn't blasted her quarter deck with his six-incher. Dorothy? Dorothy was something else. Dorothy was the Dark Lady in Shakespeare's sonnets in English class. Yes, Dorothy had a need for sex, just like Miriam and Aggie, but it was different. With Dorothy it was romantic and adorable. And where Miriam and Aggie would just lay it on the line for the first guy to come by and ply them with marshmallows, Dorothy kept it locked up and primed for the day a noble prince would come by and ask for it in a nice way like "Hello, there, my lady. I have traveled far this night and my steed is tired and can go no further. So what ho you and I rejoin to the inn for a few moments of reverie in your chambers, where I will regale you with authentic ballads on my ukulele…"

"Will that be all?"

Margie was looking at him as she mopped up the counter with her dish rag. His eyes met hers. Yesterday he'd have been the first to quit, the first to back off. But that was yesterday, and today was today. He kept looking at Margie, and damned if she didn't look away first, and with a funny look of embarrassment and defeat on her face. A surge of power shot right through Hermie's pecker, extending his self-esteem and forcing him to raise his knees, which then proceeded to bump up against the underside of the counter, which hurt.

Margie made a few circles with the dish rag on the counter and then returned to try again. "Want anything else?"

Yeah, baby. I want something else. I want *you*. Right on the counter, thanks for cleaning it. I want you to lie down and spread out and don't give me any nonsense. And when I'm through, baby, I'll tip my hat and clink a doubloon on the counter and go out and fuck my way through all of Port Royal, leaving wenches lying on benches, their skirts over their heads, their muffled voices calling for more grog.

Margie tried again. "More coffee?" She was smiling at him, which could mean many things. How long had her husband been at sea for Margie to be so in need of sex? The top button of her blouse was unbuttoned, and her good-sized chest was all coiled up inside like a crouched tiger. If he leaned over and pressed her belly button, her charming boobs would shoot out at him and go right past his head, one to starboard and one to port, and Hermie'd be amidships, somewhere in the boiler room, sending up more steam until the old hull was headed for Portsmouth Harbor at a pace that would make Lloyds of London jump with joy and sing sea chanties. Hermie's knees were pressed so hard and high against the counter that if he didn't lower the pressure soon, he'd be bent like Lionel Barrymore for the rest of his life. So he slid off the stool and straightened up ever so slowly. "What do I owe you?" He said that like a sailor who'd just finished off a whore.

Margie closed her eyes and added up the tally. For all he imagined of her, he figured he owed her a good hundred dollars. So when she said eighty-five cents, the whole bubble burst, and there was immediately more room in his supporter. He dug out the four quarters from the waterlogged pocket of his bathing suit, and he plunked them onto the counter. One of them rolled off, so he had to pick it up which killed some of the mood. He didn't wait for any change. It was all for her, for doing such a good job on him. He left Margie's Pie Place, swearing to return when the proprietress was alone, at which point he'd give her such a hearty banging that she'd pay *him* and beg him to open an account with her which she would never send out bills on. He scoffed at the thought of her appeals and walked out with less room in his supporter than ever.

Foremost in his mind was the avoiding of Oscy and Benjie because, as he had always known it would one day happen, he had grown far too mature for them. Sure Oscy had gotten laid. But *anyone* could lay Miriam. The trick was not to dirty one's self with unworthy women. That's why he had turned down screwing Aggie. Screwing Aggie would have been a step backward. Screwing *Margie*, on the marble countertop, though more of an accomplishment and a little on the chilly side, would not have been much better. A guy's first lay should be a love lay. Dorothy. Dorothy would be a love lay. Love lay beautiful Dorothy. Oh, he knew the difficulties he'd encounter in pulling off a love lay with Dorothy, but somehow he knew that it was ordained to happen. That it was fate and kismet. Also a lot of luck. Anyway, he wanted to be alone all day, and since the island was so small and a guy with a towering erection so noticeable, he took the ferry to the mainland.

He sat up front, in the prow so to speak, letting the cool spray play on his jaggedly heroic features. He watched the gulls flitting about but had little fear that Johnny Stella was among them because, as everyone knew, even when he was alive, Johnny Stella and water were incompatible. Johnny Stella had a sweat shirt that made Oscy's sweat shirt smell like Loretta Young's kimono.

There were no women aboard who interested him, unless he cared to lavish a few imaginations on the chunky girl who bore a far off resemblance to Eugene Pallette. An he didn't care for that, not after having invested fifty cents in a round trip so that he could get away from all the things that were bothering him.

When the ferry docked at the mainland, however, there *was* a girl who sparked his creativity. A tall, thin job, with straw-colored hair brushed into a neat pageboy. She was flat in the boobs, but fine of fanny, and for her, Hermie selected the telephone booth just near the ticket window. He had her standing against the glass door and he was giving it to her real good, sticking quarters into her mouth while he was on the phone telling his mother that he was having a nice time and would she please give his regards to Oscy who was probably jerking off into a bottle of warm water, which he once tried doing in the basement of 31 Ocean Parkway, much to the amusement of the entire membership of the OPACS, each of whom had put up a nickel a man to see Oscy do it. Oscy didn't quite do it, though the water flew. Vociferously he claimed he had done it, but a careful examination of the water by impartial observers proved that Oscy was a liar. He then asked for two cents apiece from the members because of A for effort, but he was turned down on that, though, in all fairness, the membership allowed him a penny a man against the original nickel for the next time Oscy would attempt the watery feat. Oscy never attempted it again and was lucky to even get his pecker out of the bottle because either it was too small or Oscy was King Kong. As a matter of actual fact, it was touch and go for quite some time, with the president of the OPACS, newly elected for the usual two-week term, about to smash the bottle with his trusty gavel when Oscy, through a superhuman effort, plus some honest-to-goodness fright, managed to pull free from the bottle with such suction that it sounded as if a bomb went off and with such force that Oscy flew backward, his bare ass bouncing off the hot furnace and flying drops of water hissing on the steaming metal like people hooting at the villain in a Frankenstein movie. Anyway, with his penny a man, Oscy bought himself the latest edition of *Wings* comic book, which was full of hot nurses and leggy aviatrixes, and nobody saw Oscy for a week because he was such a slow reader. Hermie's fantasy ended quickly when a tall man with a chin right out of Andy Gump entered the phone booth. Hermie just didn't find him attractive enough to plunk as much as one imaginary quarter into his tiny mouth even if the man had one.

Hermie hung around the ferry pier until lunch-time, watching the ferries lazily come and go, picking up and depositing people, among them a lady or two that Hermie wouldn't have minded sharing a diving bell with. He had just enough money for lunch, which consisted of a shrimp salad sandwich, two Cokes, a dish of banana ice cream, and, while he was waiting, a basket of oysterettes, each of which he broke open and ate in hopes of discovering a pearl but without any luck.

Around 4 P.M. he decided to make the return trip to Packett Island. There was no one aboard to spark his imagination except maybe one woman, but she spent the crossing in the ladies' room and who needed that? When the Island became visible on the horizon, all that Hermie could think of was Dorothy. He was drawing closer to Dorothy. Coming home to Dorothy. Home from Bataan. Home from Corregidor, one of the few men to escape the fiendish Jap trap. The band would be there playing "The Monkey Wrapped His Tail Around the Flagpole," and he'd be carried off the boat on a stretcher by an honor guard, and women would cry and men would cheer. Medals would be pinned on his blanket, and wooden-legged veterans of World War I would salute and fall over. His stretcher would be left on Dorothy's porch like *Our Gal Sunday*, and Dorothy would minister to him all night until the fever broke. Around midnight his eyes would flutter and he'd call her name and she'd sob with joy. There'd be no love-making because of his weakened condition, but after a few days of sitting in his wheelchair in the sun-drenched garden, he'd begin to feel better and she'd tell him she was going to have a baby, and Hermie made a point of remembering to take with him his last remaining rubber when calling on Dorothy that evening.

He got off the ferry in a roundabout way just in case Oscy and Benjie, the Idiot Twins, might be hanging around. He walked into the ferryhouse, into the men's room, and out the window. It was a bit out of the way but worth the effort because, if they *were* around, he had very definitely given them the shake. About 5 p.m. he entered his house via the back door and stayed in his room until just before dinner when his mother took him aside and grilled him. He never really remembered what he told her except that he had eaten healthy meals, and that seemed to satisfy her. It occurred to him that he could do anything he wanted and never upset his mother as long as he ate well. He could be a killer and a rapist and a forger, but as long as he weighed five hundred pounds, he'd always be Mama's little boy.

For dinner his mother had conjured up spaghetti, which was fine with Hermie because it gave him very little time for conversation. He was chastised from time to time for slurping, and his sister remarked twice that he had the manners of a filthy slob, but as long as he kept eating, he had his mother for an ally, and his sister finally left the table, enraged that, for a brother, God had given her Peter Pig. His father read the paper all through dinner, unusual for him because he relished good manners. But Rommel was still giving Africa fits, and his father, an expert on war with his pinochle-playing friends, was upset that the British Eighth Army couldn't handle the wily Desert Fox. Anyway, when Hermie finally left the table, it was without having said a thing other than "Pass the salt" and "How'd the Giants do?"—neither of which got any results.

He tried to catch forty winks of shut-eye because he wanted to be well rested for his call on Dorothy. But it was impossible for him to sleep, and so, at approximately 7 p.m., he went into the shower until 8 p.m. If his sister, the pig lady, was knocking the door down, he had no way of knowing it because the water was on full force. In the shower he sang a medley of hit war songs. "He Wears a Pair of Silver Wings," "When the Lights Go On All Over the World," and "Right in Der Fuehrer's Face." He was no Sinatra, but neither was he Hildegarde, which would have been no mean trick.

When he left the bathroom, his sister was waiting outside like for a bus. She didn't say a word when he breezed past her. She didn't say a word for maybe thirty seconds, at which point the Voice of Horror filtered out of the bathroom with its usual observation. "There's no hot water!" They could put that on his sister's tombstone: "There's No Hot Water." The thought came to Hermie, just briefly, that maybe his sister was screwing around on that island just as he was. But he put the thought out of his mind because it was too ghastly. Although, on second thought, if he wanted to be fair about it, his sister had a good chest and legs a little like Lynn Bari, who was supposed to have the best gams in filmdom. Anyway, because there was a war on, anything could happen. Including his sister getting laid. But with who? He gave it the five seconds of thought it was worth and then dropped it completely as being something his *mother* could worry about when she wasn't cooking.

Hermie dressed in his finest garments. A blue shirt, very, very neat and open at the collar so that his embryonic Adam's apple was excitingly exposed. His white duck trousers, pure as the driven snow, were a Davega special intended for proms and unworn by human legs. Saddle shoes, brown and white, with a little white polish on the brown and a little brown on the white because who the hell could handle that kind of horseshit? And his socks. Socks were proper. He hadn't worn socks the whole summer, but he knew that socks were correct for the situation. The socks he had chosen were hysterically argyle, knitted by his sister for some college man who was getting drafted. Only she gave them to Hermie because they had imperfections in them, like little pieces of wool that stuck out like worms. At first he thought he had the socks on inside out, but the inside was even worse. His sister was not one of the world's better knitters. Anyway, Hermie decided to take a chance, and he snipped the scraggly ends off and prayed to God the socks wouldn't come apart like the lousy embroidery on his OPACS sweater. He put them on, and they were resplendent. Red, white, and gray, the flag of Madagascar very likely. He brushed his hair until it stopped fighting him, and miraculously, the first part he made needed no improving on. He took that to be another omen in his favor. He felt so good that he didn't hear the croaking harmonica outside. Life was falling marvelously in place for him. He was shedding the agonizing skin of youth, and an irresistible fellow was emerging, smiling at him in the mirror. And when he left his room, it was with the knowledge that when he returned he'd be a man. He was, from head to toe, a walking erection that radiated sex and confidence and maturity. He disdained bringing along his notes because that suddenly seemed ugly. But in his pocket he placed the last of his red-hot rubbers because, as the Coast Guard so aptly put it, *Semper Paratus*.

He took the back way out, stepping through the doorway like David Niven, smooth and confident. Oscy was standing there. Oscy, magnificently depressed, and Hermie would have swapped him even up for the goddamn sea gull because, if nothing else, the sea gull never insisted on playing a harmonica. The sea gull got rid of its shit in other ways. As for Oscy, he was blowing the shit right through the partitions in his harmonica. "Three Blind Mice," as played by the maestro, was smelling up the sweetness of the special world that Hermie had taken two hours to construct. Upon seeing Hermie, Oscy stopped playing and smacked the harmonica against his palm. Another load of spit dropped out only to find itself soon sucked into Oscy's sweat shirt. That sweat shirt was fast becoming America's secret weapon. They could drop it on Berlin and the Germans would surrender. Hermie acknowledged Oscy's presence with a little nod and a sharp right-angle turn. But Oscy moved deftly in the way, blocking Hermie's passage to paradise. "It's all over," Oscy said, and for a minute, Hermie thought that Oscy's father had died because for years he'd been plagued with a deviated septum.

"What's all over?"

"Me and Miriam."

Hermie didn't really care to hear, but Oscy looked so weird. "What happened?"

"I'm embarrassed to tell you."

"Then don't." Hermie was not going to put up with any mystery stories, so he stepped around Oscy and got going.

Oscy caught up with him and walked alongside. "Hermie, you won't believe it."

"After last night I'll believe anything." Hermie just wanted to get away. Oscy, only fifteen years old, was sure as hell going to rob him of his new maturity.

"It's not what you think."

"Oscy, I'm in kind of a hurry."

Oscy nodded; he'd get right to the point. "We had a little argument this afternoon because I grabbed her boobs on the beach and got sand on them or something. Then, when I went to her house to apologize—" He took a dramatic pause and then completed his thoughts. "She's got appendicitis. They took her to the mainland. I just hope, for her sake, they don't cut up her boobs."

"I don't think the scar goes that far." He wasn't interested but he *was* curious about why he hadn't seen Miriam since he *had* seen every ferry that docked at the mainland that day.

"She said she was breaking our date and the next thing I knew—appendicitis. She sure goes to extremes. They loaded her on the speedboat on a stretcher."

The speedboat—that explained why Hermie hadn't seen Miriam getting off the ferry. No matter, he had feigned rapt interest just about as long as he could. He accelerated and said, "Well, maybe it's all for the better."

Oscy's arm caught him and spun him to a halt. "All for the better! How the hell can you say such a dumb thing!" Oscy was really mad. His blue pupils turned red in their white settings. He was in great danger of being saluted.

But Hermie was mad, too. He didn't care to linger. He pulled his arm free. "Because I'm not really interested!" He figured that his own eyes were red, white, and brown. Not worthy of a salute, but maybe Oscy'd get the message.

"Bullshit! You're interested! You took yourself some long look at us! We knew you were looking!" They were nose to nose and getting dangerously close to open warfare.

"I only caught a glimpse." Hermie stepped back, ready to put up his dukes. There was no uncertainty in his voice. "Shut up, Oscy. I'm not interested in the dirty details."

Oscy seemed very surprised. His voice softened. "You mean— you don't want me to tell you?"

"Yeah. That's what I mean. Exactly. I don't wanna hear about it."

Oscy remained stunned. A smile tried to happen on his face, and his shoulders hunched, and his hands opened and went a little sideways. "But—I was gonna tell you everything."

"Don't." Hermie walked away. Fuck you, Oscy. Those were the words with which history would mark this era. "The Fuck You Oscy Age." 1938 through 1942. Especially Packett Island. And especially that street. It was "Fuck You Oscy Street," right on the corner of "Fuck You Oscy Boulevard."

Oscy fell in step again. He walked alongside Hermie with his hand reaching out from time to time to paw at Hermie's shoulder, to spin him around, to make him face him. "One day you're gonna wanna hear about it, hotshot, and I won't tell you."

"Good." Hermie kept shrugging off Oscy's hand. He was like a gyroscope inexorably on course, no matter what. He kept walking down the street.

"Something's wrong with you, Hermie. You're not normal."

"Good." He shook off another of Oscy's grabbings, and he was getting pretty damned tired of it. He felt his arms tightening, and he knew his fists were clenched and that it wouldn't take much to push him to the point of no return.

Oscy had to have sensed Hermie's unwavering attitude. He walked alongside him a bit farther before switching subjects. "You look all dolled up."

"Good." It was also good that Oscy had seen fit to stop pawing at his new blue shirt.

"Do I know that shirt?" He was trying to be friendly.

"It's new."

"It's very nice. You go for blue, don't you?" A sneaky smile appeared on his crummy ugly face.

Hermie knew that Oscy was referring to the color of his pack of rubbers. He also knew that if Oscy kept up that kind of crap, he'd pull out that last surviving rubber and slap it over Oscy's head and hold it there till the son of a bitch stopped breathing. Then he'd leave him there, on the street, like a shot-down blimp, the world's biggest hard-on.

"Going to *her* house?"

Those were certainly fighting words. Hermie wasn't afraid to fight; it was just that he hated the thought of getting mussed up. He didn't think it was nice to go a-courting like a street fighter. "Fuck you, Oscy." Oscy could take that any way he wished. He could take it as a challenge or as an offhand remark or as a weather report. It was strictly up to him. Hermie would not fire the first punch.

Oscy let the moment go by, choosing instead to keep needling

Hermie, which he did with that wide steeplechase smile of his. "Have your instructions handy, lover?"

Hermie was not the kind of guy not to know when he was getting the needle. But he chose to rise above the infantilism of it all. "It's not going to be that kind of evening. But you wouldn't understand because you're...crass."

"Crass?" Oscy had to laugh. "What the hell is crass?"

Hermie was surprised to see all his patience vanish, just like that. He stopped, turned on Oscy, and grabbed his slimy sweat shirt, crumpling the chest of it in one fist while cocking his other fist right under the nose he had so well bloodied a few days ago. "Oscy, you better leave me alone or you're gonna feel this!" His fist felt like one big lump of steel. One wrong word from Oscy, one random smile, and Hermie'd ram that steel fist flush into Oscy's mush, and his nose would come out on the other side and would bleed down his neck and wet his ass and trickle down the backs of his knees and form a red pool in his fucking sneakers, and he could go squish-squish-squish all the way home.

Oscy was hardly a statesman, but neither was he a coward. He looked at Hermie's fist, the one crumpling his moss-coated sweat shirt. "Remove your fucking hand, Hermie." The threat of death was strongly implied in Oscy's words to Hermie's hand.

Hermie held fast. He wanted to hit Oscy. All he needed was one false move. "Remove your big mouth."

Oscy looked into Hermie's face and saw no laughter there. He knew he could take the measure of Hermie every time. And he was particularly ready *that* time to do so. What he couldn't understand was Hermie's apparent desire to be killed. Talking to Oscy like that amounted to suicide, so why was Hermie doing it? Bigger men than Hermie had been properly decked by Oscy, yet Hermie really seemed to want it. Which was why Oscy, a true sadist, withheld, at least for the moment. "What the hell you so mad about, Hermie?"

Hermie shouted so that the whole island could hear. "I don't know!" And he didn't. Oscy was his best friend. Oscy had had a terrible crisis with Miriam. Oscy was interested only in Hermie's welfare. Oscy could also beat the crap out of Hermie. All those thoughts ripped through Hermie's mind but in no particular order. And when they all added up to nothing, Hermie released Oscy's Wheatena-covered sweat shirt and walked away saying "aaaaaaaaaah."

Oscy watched him go and didn't follow. He just called out another taunt. "Got your rubbers?" Hermie kept walking. "You know what, Hermie? I'm sorry I ever tried to help you!"

Hermie stopped, wheeled, and shouted back, "That makes two of us!"

"I gave up my binoculars to get you educated, you fuckin' ingrate!" They were separated by some twenty feet, facing each other like the first stage of a gunfight.

"Tough!" Hermie would hold his ground. He'd make his stand. He'd had enough. If Oscy came up to him, he'd pop him a good one, clean clothes or no clean clothes. Fuck you, blue shirt.

Oscy stayed where he was. "The word's gettin' out on you, Hermie! You're a homo!"

"Come over *here* and say that, you big tub of shit!"

Oscy looked at Hermie and kept looking. If it was anyone else but Hermie, he'd have sailed into him and very likely killed him for that kind of talk. But it was Hermie. And Hermie was sensitive and poetic and pretty crazy. Oscy said "aaaaaaaah" and waved his arm at Hermie in total disgust. Then he walked away in the opposite direction, stopping only to yell, "Homo!" Then he *really* walked away. Truly.

Hermie watched Oscy grow smaller and smaller, then gradually disappear in the waning light, kicking stones and tossing twigs, but never turning. And even after Oscy lost himself around a corner, Hermie held his position because Oscy was the kind of man who could return at a moment's notice and with a regiment of men.

When he could no longer feel the blood in his clenched fists, both of which were grimly cocked in Marquess of Queensberry fashion and of no real use against a killer like Oscy, Hermie relaxed. He unwound his fingers. He stretched them and felt the blood returning via the ten usual routes. And then, taking a few deep breaths, so deep that if anyone fell into them, it was sure they'd never reach bottom, Hermie turned his back on the entire abridged confrontation. And he walked again in his original direction. For the moment, with the casting out of Oscy from his life, he had broken all ties with his youth, severed all vestiges of the inanities of his former life. Ahead lay Dorothy, and you could take that thought any way you like. He knew how preposterous an idea it was, Dorothy falling for him. But he was living in America, and America was a place of dreams, settled by men who nurtured dreams, defended by men who depended on dreams. And so onward he walked, and each step of the way his confidence grew like Topsy, and then he saw the house on the dune, silhouetted against the gray-purple sky, and he stopped because he knew how scared he was. He indulged again in dreams of America because they had always sustained him in times of self-doubt. He thought of the disaster at Pearl Harbor that no one had a right to expect America to recover from. He remembered his father's reaction when he asked him, "What's Pearl Harbor?" His father had smiled grimly and said, "It's a place the Japs are going to be more sorry about than us." He remembered President Roosevelt's voice and the way men flocked to enlist and the way the women hurried to man the riveting machines. He thought of all the brave people who had answered their country's call, and he knew that he was of that stock, that breed. He also knew that none of it was working and that he was a half a minute away from running home and hiding under the bed, so he'd better try thinking about something else. He tried a number of things. Like how good he was in art, especially cartooning. And how much he missed his Uncle Harry, who died at twenty-seven of leukemia. He thought about all the girls he had been in love with in his life and how helpless he'd been to do anything about it and how this was the first time that he'd ever behaved in a manner that was even halfway grown-up. And he knew that if he turned back after all the desire and all the preparation, if he called it quits and went back to his room and kissed Penny Singleton, he'd be nothing but a shell of a man for the next thirty years of his life and little more than a tombstone after that, a tombstone that would read: "Here Lies Nothing at All. Don't Fall In." And so he went forward and that pleased him because it meant there was still hope for him, not necessarily as a great lover but as a man.

One thing was bothering him, though. The rubber in his pocket. It worried him. He wasn't sure how to go about the necessary operation of slipping into it. The little package hadn't come with instructions as Rinso did. All that was on the package—and in very small letters, like whispers—were claims of how thin the rubbers were and how sensitive and highly recommended by doctors who, apparently, took off a lot of time to try them out. There were no names of satisfied customers on the packages. Nobody in Cleveland, Ohio, whom you could call up and ask, "Did you really say this?" Nobody even in Altoona, PA, whom you could do an FBI check on to see if he really existed. Hermie removed the rubber from his pocket, tossing away the tattered remains of the blue package. He examined the rubber, and it didn't look all that exciting. As a matter of fact, it looked kind of dumb all rolled up like a yellow worm and held in place by something that looked like a tiny cigar band. It looked dirty. It seemed like a dirty thing to do, to excuse yourself and then come back wearing the thing like it was a lollipop wrapper. It also wasn't foolproof. Sometimes they broke. Oscy once told him how the jokers who made them sometimes used to put pinholes in them just for kicks. Hermie'd sure hate to get one with a hole in it, a dud, so to speak, maybe even signed by the name of the factory worker with a message on it like "Surprise! You've been fucked!" Hermie'd sure hate to end up with a baby that his mother would want to send to the pound or that his father would want to just put in a burlap bag and drop off the pier. And there was *another* thing to consider. Using it on Dorothy, correction, *in* Dorothy, first flashing it in her presence, could only indicate to her that he had planned on screwing her long before he came a-calling and very long before the foreplay had even begun. And that was bound to take some of the magic out of it for the both of them. A woman like Dorothy wants her screwing to be unplanned and accidental. She wants it to be a spontaneous act of love. Yet how the hell can it be spontaneous if the guy arrives at her door all suited up? Which brought up *another* question. Should he put it on *before* he got to the house and therefore eliminate a lot of embarrassment? After all, if the damned things were really so thin and transparent and if it were a dark evening, which it was getting to look as if it would be, maybe she'd never even know he had it on. Also, to help things along, he'd be getting her drunk. Hermie began to think that that theory had merit, real merit. And so he slowly slid off the cigar band, and the rubber opened in his palm like a tiny flower, moving around like a bug taking shape in the new world. He studied it. It was about the size of a quarter, give or take a dime, and he had to admit that it felt smooth and strangely exciting. He wasn't sure, however, just how he was supposed to get it on. To do *anything* with it, he would, of course, have to learn more about it. And so he began to unroll it, pushing his finger gently into it and rolling down the sides of it the way you'd do in putting on a pair of gloves. His finger got pretty damned excited and carried away with passion, and before Hermie could stop it, it had unrolled the whole rubber. Hermie's heart stopped when he looked at the rubber unfurled. His heart stopped because he knew he'd gotten the wrong size. The rubber he was looking at was meant for Primo Camera, and Hermie was more of a Tom Thumb. He held it by its ring, at its open end, and he let the rest of it dangle in the breeze like a small windsock. It was no longer yellow. It was transparent. Damned if he couldn't see practically right through it, even in the lousy light. It was true, a guy could wear a rubber and a girl didn't even have to know he had it, like a glass eye. So the question was answered. Yes, you put it on beforehand and nobody need be the wiser, provided you can fill the damned thing and that it didn't gather up at the bottom of your pole like a bellows. Hermie unbuttoned his white ducks and groped around for himself; only he wasn't getting any cooperation. His once-enormous shaft not only was not in the mood, but might even be not in his shorts. When he finally found it hiding in a corner under a pocket flap and brought it out into the lovely evening air, it was such a pitiful thing that Hermie almost wanted to cry. And you'd cry, too, if you were a 28 short and some salesman was trying to get you into a 46 extra-large. Hermie stiffened his shoulders, which was about all he could get stiff under those conditions. And he held the rubber in front of his pecker the way you'd hold a twig in front of a dog just before you tossed it and yelled "Fetch." But the dog wasn't buying; it just sulked some more. Hermie looked at the rubber; it appeared so large that he knew if he put it on his pecker, most of it would hang over the side like Santa Claus' stocking cap. He put the theory to the test and proved himself to be correct, except there was no pompon at the end of it. Hermie removed the rubber before the crickets could laugh at him. It had felt sensational, he had to admit, and maybe, with a little help, he might just be able to fill up the goddamn thing with maybe just a little slack. But a new thought sprang into his mind, and it troubled him. He had been carrying that rubber around in his pocket; he had sat on it, strained it, exposed it to so much dirt that maybe it was no longer sanitary. And how could he, in good conscience, stick so unsanitary a thing into sweet Dorothy? The whole idea revulsed him, and he grew annoyed with himself for having broken the hermetically sealed package just so's Oscy could screw Miriam, who, as it turned out, was probably already alive with appendicitis germs and God knows what other filthy diseases. Hermie looked at the germ-ridden membrane in his hand and at the way his fingers recoiled and kind of let it drop to the ground as though it had already been used by Tony Galento. He knelt down beside it, knowing that there was no chance in the world that he could ever make use of it, especially since it had just been dropped in the sand. Had he not dropped it, yes, there might have been a chance but now—forget it. Reverently Hermie dug a little hole in the gritty turf and nudged the rubber into it with his shoe. Then he covered it with sand, and covered with sand it would remain, for years and years, like the Time Capsule at the World's Fair. He turned his head to the sky, inhaled a lot of good clean air, and immediately accepted two rather irrefutable facts. First, he could no longer lay Dorothy because if he did so without wearing protection, she ran the risk of having a baby. Not immediately, but soon enough.

And second, by getting rid of that particular germ-crawling device, he had nobly eliminated all chance of Dorothy's becoming contaminated by the filthy thing. Conclusion? He had unselfishly arranged that there be no screwing of Dorothy that night. Following the acceptance of the two facts and the one conclusion, there came a summation, but in two separate waves. The first wave was one of sadness, for he was being denied Dorothy's sacred insides. The second wave was rather remarkable in that it was one of boundless joy, owing to the fact that an inhuman obligation had been removed from his shoulders, a huge obstacle taken from his path, a choking lump wrenched from his stomach. And the truth of it all, and he knew it, and he wanted to die because of it, except he also wanted to live—the truth of it all was that by not trying to get laid, he was not risking humiliating failure. It was as the prophets had once stated, "Never put off until tomorrow what you can put off until next week." Fear had overcome desire, and self-deception had proved stronger than both. And so when he advanced on her house, it was with elation at the prospect of a nice social call, a man calling on a lady of a summer's evening, a laugh or two over a lemonade, a few jokes, a couple of songs around the pianola…and the icy fright that had gripped his heart all day relaxed its hold, and he walked blithely down the road, absolved of all the responsibilities of both man and boy…floating somewhere within the confusion between.

But something was very definitely out of whack. Something about that house. For one thing, it was dimly lit. Maybe one or two lights were on, but if they were, it was in the back. And then it was quiet, oddly quiet. Not that Hermie had expected Ben Bernie and all the lads to be playing on the front porch, but she might at least have had the radio on, or even the Victrola, some kind of music, Xavier Cugat or even a hymn. And as he drew closer, he would have settled for Kate Smith because it all was so desperately quiet. He could sense the foreboding, feel the foreshadowing. Quietly he passed beyond the screen door, and he heard his own footsteps thumping across the slightly sagging porch. It was four steps to the door that led into the living room. The door was open, but Hermie, ever one for protocol, knocked on the door frame just the same. There was some light in the room but no response to his knocking. "Hello?" The sound of his voice stopped everything; his walking, his breathing, his heartbeat, even the summer bugs shut up and laid low. Again, no answer. He knocked again and called again. "Hello?" Nothing.

He stepped into the tidy living room, immediately becoming aware that it wasn't as cheery and as chipper as he had remembered it. "Hello?" No answer, no sound, not a blessed thing. Except for an odd rhythmic scratching. *Sker-ratchety, sker-ratchety.*

He stood dead center in the room and looked around, pleased that he could be so calm in so strange and unexpected a situation. On a table there stood a bottle of some kind of scotch whisky, half-empty. Beside it was a glass, completely empty. And beside that there was an ashtray, totally full, cluttered with half-smoked cigarettes that had been crushed out and abandoned. "Dorothy? It's Hermie. Hermie from the beach." No answer.

He continued to look around. There was the framed photograph of smiling Pete, beaming out at Hermie, the pipe still clenched between the strong, straight teeth. And the writing: "All my love, forever, Pete." Hermie took a few steps farther into the room and the sound grew louder. *Sker-ratchety, sker-ratchety, sker-ratchety.* It could have been a cricket but not likely because crickets didn't drink or smoke. Ha-ha.

It was the portable phonograph, its lid swung back in an open position as in an alligator yawn, its arm moving back and forth like an admonishing finger saying "no…no…no." The record on the turntable kept rotating. It had finished, but the phonograph arm hadn't been removed and returned to its starting position. Hence the *sker-ratchety, sker-ratchety, sker-ratchety.* Hermie lifted the phonograph arm and placed it gently back upon its receptacle, letting the record continue to spin because it wasn't hurting anything. He studied the label of the spinning record but couldn't make it out and was only getting himself dizzy. The room was now deadly quiet, too quiet. Hermie tried to whistle "Pistol Packing Mama," but his mouth was too dry.

The dull yellow of the telegram caught his eye. It was behind the bottle and had been cruelly crumpled and then painfully smoothed out. "We regret to inform you that your husband…"

The cold message sank sickeningly into Hermie's mind like rain on a sponge. There was a sound behind him, a door opening. He turned.

Dorothy was in the room. She smiled at him, a smile of recognition. But her eyes were damp and red, and she wore a look of lonely vulnerability. So much so that Hermie wanted to take her to his arms and cup her cheek in his hand, as his mother used to do with him whenever he came home crying over something that was too much for him. Slowly, regularly, she kept running a brush through her hair, a small gesture of femininity, something to hang onto, to do, to stay sane. "Hello, Hermie."

"Hi."

"I don't look very nice, do I?" She moved past him, tragically beautiful. Little Girl Lost in a fluffy pink robe.

"I think you do."

"Oh, I think I don't." She smiled at him again, a searchlight in the dark. A moment of endless silence drifted by, during which she brushed her hair to a princess luster. Then she was over at the phonograph, placing the needle back at the beginning of the still-spinning record. The voice was a woman's, and for a moment, because her back was turned to him, Hermie thought it was Dorothy singing. The song was soft and torchy, conjuring up every vision Hermie had ever had of those sad ladies singing, of love gone by or lost, accompanied only by the aging male piano player whose fingers idled the ivories while a cigarette dangled dry on his lips and while a shot of booze sat waiting for him on top of his piano. And, from time to time, a silent but understanding waiter would pass by and keep the booze glass full. Real. Unreal. Real. Unreal.

> Last night I started out happy,
> Last night my heart was so gay,
> Last night I found myself dancing

In my favorite cabaret.
You were completely forgotten,
Just an affair of the past,
Then suddenly something happened to me,
And I found my heart
Beating, oh, so fast.

It was their song. Dorothy's and Pete's. And if Dorothy was beyond crying, Hermie had not yet arrived at that point, and his vision turned blurry because he was looking at her from somewhere in the rain. He watched her lay the hairbrush aside and begin to sway back and forth, over and again, as if the song were a measure of the distance between love and death and she the calculator of the impossible separation.

I saw you last night and got that old feeling,
When you came in sight I got that old feeling...

She moved away from the phonograph and began to straighten out the small disorders within the room. She picked up the glass and the ashtray.

The moment that you danced by I felt a thrill
And when you caught my eye my heart stood still...

She smiled again as she passed him on little pink scuffs that made no noise. He watched her go through the doorless opening and into the kitchen.

Once again I seemed to feel that old yearning,
And I knew the spark of love was still burning...

Hermie gravitated toward the kitchen, watching her at the sink as she let the water run over the ashtray. A display of vacuous female activity that was in defiance of the truth. It was a thing that women did so that men could never know their minds.

There'll be no new romance for me,
It's foolish to start,

> For that old feeling
> Is still in my heart.

She continued to wash the ashtray, running her fingers over it. It was never meant to be that clean. The piano player took the next few bars, allowing his own miseries to gain expression. Somehow it was Hermie's turn and he spoke over the piano. "I'm sorry."

She turned to him, her flowing hair preceding her wan smile. Then she turned back to the sink and continued to wash the ashtray. She turned off the water just as the vocalist returned to the song.

> Once again I seemed to feel that old yearning,
> And I knew the spark of love was still burning...

Dorothy faced Hermie. She was standing with her back against the sink, supported by her hands, only the thumbs of which were visible over the enamel edge. She looked at Hermie and bravely shook her head as if to say, "Well—easy come, easy go." When she walked toward him, it was just to touch someone who was alive and caring. And when the little pink scuffs arrived at the stalwart saddle shoes, Hermie could see that he was taller than she was. He knew that there were tears on his face, but he also knew that he needn't be ashamed, for even the best of men were known to cry. She reached up to his face, catching one of his tears on the point of her finger, and it ran to her because she was then the rightful owner of all the tears on earth. She captured another and another, letting the salty little things trickle across her nail and drop off the side like men overboard. All the tears thus gone, she moved to place her head within the hollow of his shoulder, just to rest, just to be with. Instinctively, Hermie put his hand to her cheek and pressed her closer to him, his other arm slipping about the small of her back, where he could feel the soft crying and hold the gently racking figure.

> There'll be no new romance for me,
> It's foolish to start,
> For that old feeling
> Is still in my heart.

The piano played and the voice sang sadly, and without knowing quite how or just why, Hermie found that he and Dorothy were moving, easily, dancing. But shouldn't the record have been played out? Had she managed to escape his arms long enough to start it over, leaving only a faint echo of herself in his grasp? Could she really have done that without his knowing it?

Last night I started out happy,
Last night my heart was so gay…

Or had they done it together, dancing past the phonograph just as the record was spinning out and starting it anew?

Last night I found myself dancing
In my favorite cabaret…

Or had he done it completely by himself, reaching over without her being aware of it and placing the needle back at the beginning because he wanted to hold her forever and ever?

You were completely forgotten,
Just an affair of the past…

And were those his feet down there, saddle shoes in the night, pretending to know what they were doing? And was it Dorothy he held, truly Dorothy, clinging to him as though he were Pete come home, smiling even as the tears escaped from under her lovely lashes?

Then suddenly something happened to me,
And I found my heart
Beating, oh, so fast.

The lyric threaded up into air and took physical form, hanging down into the room like barrage balloons over Britain, NIGHT. OLD. SIGHT. FEELING. He danced her between them, steering her in and out of them, trying to keep them from touching her, from hurting her more than they already had. They hung there wickedly, swiveling left and right on gnashing steel cables, DANCE. THRILL. CAUGHT. STILL. Hermie and Dorothy weaved between them, baseless shadows, weightless silhouettes unhindered by floor, by wall, by time. Slowly her face turned up to look into his. She studied him seriously, running her fingers over his features like a blind woman, trying to place him, to recall him. A moment—and quickly she cocked her face a half turn sideways, never removing her eyes from his, and an impish smile of recognition told him not to try to fool her, for she knew who he was. A child's laugh followed, and she tossed her hair like a wet puppy. And the hanging words took to the wind, and a new music inhabited the room, a Dorothy music, all sunny and bright. And her arms, unembarrassed, stretched toward him, and her face came up at his, and the kiss that happened caused the room to circle the people. Colors shifted in and out like slides on a microscope, and there was a small game of Touch and Whisper in which she disappeared from his arms only to reappear behind him, her hands over his eyes with guess who, darling, and welcome home. Words took shape in Hermie's mouth, protest words, not even words—sounds. But they flew away, unformed, unsaid random vowels barely strung.

Another room yet familiar, with no boundaries and little dimension. Just things, to mark well, to remember. A lamp on a small table. A clock. A vase with fresh flowers. A comb, a book, a letter. The sprightly patterned bedspread lifting and turning down. Little framed paintings on the walls, flowers, always flowers. The fluffy pink robe floating then settling gracefully across the back of the chair. The new blue shirt likewise on the bedpost, followed and covered by the white duck trousers. Pink scuffs on the floor, saddle shoes beside them turned pigeon-toed, an argyle sock tucked neatly into each one. Now an embroidered pillow buoying up the dear face, the lovely hair in a spreading compass rose. Dorothy looking up and smiling, speaking private words, reminding him of things and times that were not his. Dorothy eyes open, Dorothy eyes closed. Dorothy with urgings and promises. Dorothy beneath him, tender arms turned steel, warm legs drawing him down, beyond the velvet tangle, beyond thought, beyond stopping, beyond his own voice saying, "No right, no right"...for it was summer and first time and he loved her so. Dorothy. I love you, Dorothy.

All he could really hear easily was the clock. But if he strained hard enough, he could hear the phonograph needle scratching in the next room. He lay still beside her, afraid to move. Both of them were on their backs, with their own thoughts. Even in the poor light he could make out the panel in the ceiling. For fully ten minutes he half expected it to slide open so that Oscy could appear and scream down at him, "Hubba-hubba, did you use a rubber?" He of course had not used the rubber. The rubber was down the road, buried without ceremony but now possessing one frightened mourner. He hoped she wouldn't become pregnant because that would be just too cruel. The worst of it was he couldn't think of anything to say to her. Like a coward, he had allowed it to happen. He could have stopped it. He could have brought her to her senses. He could have slapped her or thrown cold water on her face. Instead, he had done nothing. And in addition to that, he was now *doing* nothing. He was just waiting for the ceiling panel to slide open so that Pete could drop down on him and slit his throat with a bayonet. But Pete was dead, so there'd be no leaping out of the attic for Pete, no more of anything. Hermie glanced over at her, trying not to let her see any movement on his part, hoping that maybe she'd think he was dead, wishing that he was.

It was puzzling the way she lay there, under the sheet, just as though she were on the beach, her face to the sky, her fine nose at just the right angle. Whatever was in her mind he didn't even try to guess at. He just hoped that she wouldn't feel terrible. He wouldn't have cared if she had turned on him and called him everything in the book, just as long as she wouldn't feel awful and guilty and rotten.

He thought about saying a few comforting words, telling her that he had been in situations like that before because men were dying pretty regularly and—He let the thought drop right there.

He then thought of offering her marriage. At least, if he told her how much he loved her, maybe she wouldn't feel so bad or soiled or taken advantage of. But no words were forthcoming from his giant brain and so he continued just to lie there, praying for an unseasonable monsoon or some other kind of instant but relatively painless death because he, too, wasn't feeling all that deserving of much more anguish.

He thought of telling her that maybe it was a mistake, that maybe Pete *wasn't* dead, that maybe it was somebody else. The Army often got things fucked up like that. But he knew that the odds were against that being the case. Besides, what had that to do with the fact that he had just finished making love to a war widow who had helplessly allowed it to happen because she was in no emotional condition to stop it? No matter how he juggled the situation around in his mind, no matter how he twisted it or interpreted it or lied about it, he knew that in the long run, he was going to be worse off than she. She'd make it in life because she'd one day realize what and how it had happened. *He'd* be in trouble because it was his first time, which meant he'd remember it forever because that's the way the legend goes. Plus he'd always remember that in a situation of crisis, his true character had come to the fore, revealing him to be more interested in sex than in compassion. He knew that for all time, he would be indelibly stamped as a shit, and a fuck, and a prick, and a…bounder.

She got up. Perhaps he had been thinking too loud. That worried him. He watched her put on the robe as though he weren't even in the room with her. His heart jumped. So many incredible things had happened that it was just possible—maybe he'd turned into the Shadow. And maybe she didn't see him at all and figured that she'd just had this terrific hot dream. While her back was still turned, he lifted the sheet and quickly looked to see if he was still there. He was. Most of him.

She left the bedroom and walked into the living room, disdaining the little pink scuffs that remained embarrassedly beneath the bed. He wished that she'd have put them on because August nights could get chilly, and this night, though special in so many ways, was no exception when it came to cold floors. He realized that he was feeling responsible, but how else could he live with himself?

He could see the back of her in the living room. She was just standing there. Her hair was a little mussed, but that was to be expected since she'd just gone a few rounds with the Fiend of East Nineteenth Street. Then she disappeared from his view, moving to the side of the room he couldn't see. Shortly after that, the sound of the scratchy phonograph needle ceased, probably for all time. Then she reappeared, only farther up in the room where she found her cigarettes and lit one up. She was maybe thirty feet away, but her voice traveled well, and even though she wasn't facing him, he could hear her clearly say, "Hermie, I think you'd better go home."

At least she wasn't mad. He eased himself out of bed and began to dress. He didn't want to move too fast because that would make him look like a guy who couldn't wait to get out of there. Nor did he want to move too slowly because that would be disrespectful of her wishes. So he moved kind of medium. He was surprised to find the front of his blue shirt damp. Then he remembered the tears that had happened there, and he grew weak because of his inability to really do something to help her feel not so awful. He slipped easily into the loud argyle socks because they glowed in the dark and were the first things he saw. The laces of his saddle shoes were still tied. He probably had just kicked the shoes off without untying the laces. Sure must've been in some kind of hurry. To get into his white ducks, he had to remove his shoes and put them on again afterward. He was not being smooth. He walked into the living room, stopping only to take a deep breath because, surely, the matter bore discussion and he wanted his throat to be in shape. But when he got there, she was gone. Through the doorway he could see her, out on the porch, the orange dot of her cigarette moving gently in the darkness. It was the side of the porch that overlooked the ocean, and he wondered if she wasn't scanning the sea, looking for the boat that Pete might be sailing home.

Hermie took another deep breath and went out onto the porch, wondering if when he got there, she might be somewhere else, like halfway down the beach. But she was there, proud and straight and thoughtful and calm and looking a shade taller than he. He wanted to say something, anything, but she saved him the trouble by speaking first, her voice almost a whisper. "Good night, Hermie."

He wanted to go, and fast. Yet to leave her like that—Then he realized that it was the way she wanted it. And more important than that, he knew at the very core of him, it was the way it had to be. He heard himself say "Good night" and felt better because it strongly implied that he understood everything, which he did and he didn't.

So he left the house via the beach side, descending the magical fourteen steps without falling on his ass, for which he was grateful because he was striving so hard for poise and carriage. When he reached the sand, he removed his stupid shoes and socks, and while he did that, he looked back. He saw the orange dot, nothing more. He walked, carrying his shoes and juggling a few other feelings that might take him a while to figure out. One thing was for sure. He had gotten laid. He had gotten laid with the woman he loved. He had gotten laid, first time, and it had been with the one woman on earth he most wanted. Was that not a delightful and wondrous thing? Then how come he felt so lousy?

20

The mist was so thick the next morning that maybe it wasn't even dawn. How long he had been sitting on that beach would never be known. For sure it had been hours. And for sure he had never gone home, because nobody hung around on a beach in white ducks and saddle shoes unless he had lost his yacht. His mother, by then, had probably called out the Coast Guard, and the dredging for his body would be well under way. The funeral if he were truly dead, would be Tuesday. And it would be a big day for his aunts Clara and Dora because they were the greatest criers ever to come over from the Bronx. A few gulls called to one another on winds that rode eight o'clock in the morning. That's what Hermie figured the time to be. Eight o'clock. It also could've been nine. There was no way of knowing, nor did he give much of a shit about it. He watched the waves creep out of the ocean and grope along the sand. He watched them wriggle up as far as they could and then retire grudgingly back into the sea. He found it all very remarkable and worthy of an entire copy of *National Geographic*, provided you were a fish.

A figure was walking out of the mist, and Hermie watched it draw closer. It could have been anyone, but it happened to be Oscy because it was playing the harmonica as though it were an enemy. Oscy sat down next to him for the longest time, smacking the harmonica against his palm so often that not only spit came out, but rust and a couple sand fleas as well. Eventually Oscy spoke. He made it sound very unimportant. "Miriam pulled through."

Hermie said nothing, and Oscy was respectful of his mood. He played the harmonica again, bleating out some frightening sounds that better belonged in a jungle. He played and spoke intermittently, like a comedian accompanying himself. "I saw her mother this morning. They froze her appendix. I'm very relieved about it, but she's through for the summer. Won't be back on the island again. My first lay—gone with the wind." He played a version of "Taps" that would have offended Benedict Arnold. Then he spoke again, never looking at Hermie, who could easily have been a sand castle. "Seen Benjie anywhere? The rat still has my glasses." When no answer was forthcoming, Oscy played a few bars of "Farmer in the Dell" and then resumed his monologue, with about as much sensitivity as he'd ever manifested in his entire life. "Hermie, you shouldn't feel so bad no matter *what* happened. And you don't have to tell me. But—if you *want* to tell me, you can. But you don't *have* to—unless you *want* to."

Hermie said nothing, and so Oscy just looked up at the sky, unto which he delivered another of his searing bits of philosophy. "Sometimes life is a big pain in the ass." He remained silent, not even resorting to his harmonica. Then, in an effort to resurrect Hermie, he said, "I thought maybe we'd attack the Coast Guard station today. Give 'em a scare." So ended Oscy's speechifying, and he turned again to his nauseating mouth organ. London Bridge was shortly falling down. And it would have if it had been able to hear Oscy.

Meaning no disrespect but not much caring how Oscy took it, Hermie got up and walked away. Oscy made no move to follow. He knew it was a very private time for Hermie. Besides, after London Bridge there was "Red River Valley," followed by "Oh, Susannah," followed by "Camptown Races," the last few sickening notes of which Hermie never heard because he was mercifully out of earshot. First chance he'd get, Hermie would send Oscy an anonymous note suggesting that he abandon the harmonica, or else he'd wake up one morning to find it shoved up his ass where it could rust in peace.

Dorothy's house stood lonely and fog-shrouded where Hermie had left it. Maybe Dorothy was up by then, making her famous coffee. The one conclusion that Hermie had come to as a result of his all-night meditations was that he couldn't let it all end like that. He had to talk to her, to mend their fences, to discuss their relationship, and perhaps to figure out her next move. Because she had seemed so self-possessed when he left her, Hermie had pretty much convinced himself that she was all right. But somewhere during Oscy's speech, it occurred to Hermie that perhaps the opposite was the case. Perhaps she had gone back to drinking. Perhaps she had spent the whole night crying, missing Pete, despising herself for going to bed with that dumb kid. Perhaps she had committed suicide. They did that thing in India a lot, even though it was illegal. The wife throws herself on her husband's funeral fire. Anyway, by the time Hermie was halfway up the fourteen steps, he had convinced himself that he'd find Dorothy lying dead on the floor, her wrists slashed, and nothing but a note to remind the world that she had passed by.

The first thing that struck him was the lack of life about the house, as if all life had been turned off, the plug pulled out on everything. For instance, the few pieces of porch furniture had been pulled out of weather's way and pressed against the shingled walls of the house. The little wagon was there, too, turned upside down so as not to catch any rain or snow that the months ahead would bring. It was all very ninth inning, very final. The screen door leading onto the porch was unlatched, and Hermie stepped through and beyond it. The front door, the one to the house, was closed. Also, the two windows that faced out on the porch had the shades drawn. There was an envelope tacked to the front door, one word on it: "Hermie." That was him. He read his name for ten seconds while also knocking on the door. No answer. He tried the door. Locked. He removed the tack from the envelope and peeked through one of the windows because there was still a half inch of visibility between the bottom of the shade and the window ledge. He couldn't see much, except for the fact that the house was pretty empty and that Pete's photograph no longer sat smilingly on the mantel because those days were over. The other window had a similar half inch to look through and a similar view beyond. Nobody was home.

Hermie looked at the envelope in his hand and was in no particular hurry to open it. He leaned back against the door and allowed himself to slide slowly to the porch floor, where he arrived in a sitting position. As he opened the envelope, he looked out to the ocean. It was very large. A very large ocean indeed. One of the largest in the world. He had never quite looked at it that way before.

He removed the piece of writing paper from the envelope. He stalled around, even sniffing the paper to see if there was any perfume there. But he couldn't really tell because of the sudden overpowering salty sea air that seemed to be wiping over everything, wiping everything away. Eventually, because it had been so ordained, he read the words set down in so fine a style and with so sweet a hand:

> DEAR HERMIE,
>
> I must go home now. I'm sure you'll understand. There's much that I have to do. I will not try to explain what happened last night because I know that, in time, you will find a proper way in which to remember it...

The man was standing on the beach, and it all rushed back at him, swift and clear, as he looked up at the house on the high dune. It hadn't changed that much over the years. A new roof, a couple of paint jobs along the way. Not much more. There were a few razor-sharp memories in there, too, but the years had planed them down to an acceptable smoothness so that the once rough edges no longer cut as they used to. He never saw Dorothy again. Nor did he ever learn what became of her. Nor did he ever ask anyone. Nor did even the loosest-mouthed island gossips volunteer a word. Dorothy was gone. New people bought the house.

As for the letter, he still had it, in a drawer somewhere. And from time to time, whenever the world had punched him around too much, he'd stop whatever it was he was doing and he'd reread the brave words and replay the lovely voice.

> What I *will* do is remember *you*, and I will pray that you be spared all senseless tragedies. I wish you good things, Hermie, only good things.
>
> Always,
> DOROTHY

The man turned away from the house and moved back in the direction from which he had come, the sand of all those years ago coming over his toes, morning cool and early damp. And he pondered the one small truth that Hermie had taken so many years to get straight in his head. Life is made up of small comings and goings, and for everything a man takes with him, there is something he must leave behind. Not an altogether brilliant concept, but a comforting one, very comforting. For so many of the people who had touched his life were no longer alive, except in his mind, where he could be with them again whenever they chose to occur to him. His mother, so protective and loving. His father, so hardworking and unfortunately anonymous. And Oscy. Crazy heroic Oscy, killed in Korea on Hermie's twenty-fourth birthday, and they hung his Silver Star on his brother, the dentist. The fog was hunching in again, but the voices cut through clearly, giving new credence to the old theory that sound was always alive and always moving in perpetual concentric circles and that, depending upon where you stood and how receptive you were, you might just hear words of another time spoken again.

Hey, Hermie!
Come on, Hermie! Jesus!
Hermie! Hey, Hermieeeeeeeeeee

And then they were there, right in front of him, milling about like three nutty jumping beans. Oscy, Hermie, and Benjie, slamming at one another viciously. Running, dodging, shouting. In the fog, then in the clear, passing so close by that he could reach out and touch them. But he didn't try, because he knew they weren't there.

He watched Hermie evade a bone-crushing block and then stop to look up at the house on the dune, to fill his mind with it, to memorize it for that day when he might care to recall it once more. And then Hermie was gone, Oscy and Benjie with him, somewhere in the fog, inhabiting days long over, laughing invisibly, but never ever gone.

The man walked on. He had things to do and this whole

moment had been a self-indulgent sidetrack. But even as he walked, old visions kicked up a fuss in his mind, and odd recollections came spinning out. In the summer of '42 they raided the Coast Guard station four times. They saw five movies and had nine days of rain. Benjie broke his watch, Oscy gave up the harmonica, and in a very special way, Hermie was lost forever.

When he got back to his Mercedes, a single sea gull was flapping and squawking in the sky, and a big blast of shit was already beginning to harden on the car's windshield. Someone had remembered him after all, and he cried all the way home.

MORE FROM HERMAN RAUCHER

MAYNARD'S HOUSE

Austin Fletcher, a disturbed young Vietnam War vet, is willed a small house deep in the woods of northern Maine. He comes to own it by the generosity of a brother-in-arms—a fellow soldier and confidante, Maynard Whittier, killed in action by a wayward mortar shell. The rugged landscape of Maine is an intoxicating blend of claustrophobic interiors and endless frozen wastelands. Little by little, the mysterious force in the house asserts itself until Austin isn't exactly sure what is in his mind and what is real. And just when our hero's had enough and is ready to quit the place, a blizzard arrives and the real haunting begins.

A GLIMPSE OF TIGER

Tiger is a nineteen-year-old runaway who comes to the big city to start anew. There she meets Luther, a quirky con artist with charm to burn. Together they pull small scams and petty crimes on the populace of New York in the 1970s, making their money and falling in love. But a con artist is a con artist seven days a week, and soon Tiger finds herself wondering if Luther will ever be able to settle down and start building a life with her.

This mesmerizing, surprising novel explores two unforgettable people as they live and love in Manhattan—and enchants readers with a romance impossible to forget.

THERE SHOULD HAVE BEEN CASTLES

Ben is the writer who can't seem to make it; Ginnie is the dancer who can't seem to miss. In 1951 they are two scared kids in love–determined to hold onto each other no matter what. Together the world is theirs for the asking.

In the exhilarating landscape of 1950's show biz, from the neon glamour of the New York stage to the starry glitter of Hollywood, they have love and success—pure, intense, and perfect. It should go on forever, fueled by enough romance and glamour for all the record books and fairytales that ever were. But can their love prevail or will it all come tumbling down due to an unexpected twist neither of them could have foreseen?